The Coming of Evil

El Murid threw his arms up and cried, "The Power of the Lord is upon me! The Spirit of God moves me! Witness, you idolaters, you wallowers in sin and weak faith! The hours of the enemies of the Lord are numbered! There is but one God, and I am His Disciple! Follow me, or burn in Hell forever!"

He hurled his right fist at the earth. The stone in his amulet blazed furiously.

A lightning bolt flung down from a sky that had not seen a cloud in months. It blasted a ragged scar across the gardens of the Shrine. Singed petals fluttered through the air.

Thunder rolled across the blue. Women screamed. Men clutched their ears. Six more bolts hurtled down like the swift stabbing of a short spear. The lovely flowerbeds were ripped and burned.

In silence El Murid stalked from the grounds, his strides long and purposeful. At that moment he was no child, no man, but a force as terrible as a cyclone. . . .

Books by Glen Cook

The Swordbearer
The Fire in His Hands

Published by TIMESCAPE BOOKS

THE FIRE IN HIS HANDS

GLEN COOK

A TIMESCAPE BOOK
PUBLISHED BY POCKET BOOKS NEW YORK

This novel is a work of fiction. Names, characters, places and incidents are either the product of the author's imagination or are used fictitiously. Any resemblance to actual events or locales or persons, living or dead, is entirely coincidental.

Another *Original* publication of TIMESCAPE BOOKS

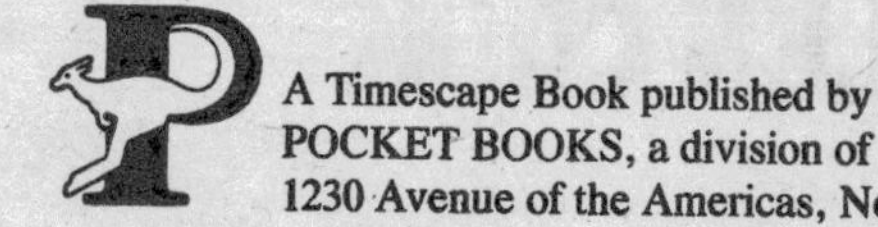
A Timescape Book published by
POCKET BOOKS, a division of Simon & Schuster, Inc.
1230 Avenue of the Americas, New York, N.Y. 10020

ISBN: 0-671-45907-4

First Timescape Books printing January, 1984

10 9 8 7 6 5 4 3 2 1

Printed in the U.S.A.

This one is for Jenny Menkinnen, librarian, whose tireless efforts kept me in skiffy fixes throughout my boyhood years. Maybe it's your fault.

Chapter One

Making of a Messiah

The caravan crept across a stony wadi and meandered upward into the hills. The camels boredly tramped out their graceless steps, defining the milemarks of their lives. Twelve tired beasts and six weary men made up the small, exhausted caravan.

They were nearing the end of their route. After a rest at El Aquila they would recross the Sahel for more salt.

Nine watchers awaited them.

The camels now carried the sweet dates, emeralds of Jebal al Alf Dhulquarneni, and imperial relics coveted by the traders of Hellin Daimiel. The traders would purchase them with salt recovered from the distant western sea.

An elderly merchant named Sidi al Rhami mastered the caravan. He was captain of a family enterprise. His companions were brothers and cousins and sons. His youngest boy, Micah, just twelve, was making his first transit of the family route.

The watchers didn't care who they were.

Their captain assigned victims. His men stirred uncomfortably in the shimmering heat. The sun's full might blasted down upon them. It was the hottest day in the hottest summer in living memory.

The camels plodded into the deathtrap defile.

The bandits leapt from the rocks. They howled like jackals.

Micah fell instantly, his skull cracked. His ears moaned with the force of the blow. He hardly had time to realize what was happening.

Everywhere the caravan had traveled men had remarked

that it was a summer of evil. Never had the sun been so blistering, nor the oases so dry.

It was a summer of evil indeed when men sank to robbing salt merchants. Ancient law and custom decreed them free even of the predations of tax collectors, those bandits legitimized by stealing for the king.

Micah recovered consciousness several hours later. He immediately wished that he had died too. The pain he could endure. He was a child of Hammad al Nakir. The children of the Desert of Death hardened in a fiery furnace.

Plain impotence brought the death wish upon him.

He could not intimidate the vultures. He was too weak. He sat and wept while they and the jackals tore the flesh of his kinsmen and squabbled over delicacies.

Nine men and a camel had perished. The boy was a damned poor bet. His vision doubled and his ears rang whenever he moved. Sometimes he thought he heard voices calling. He ignored everything and stubbornly stumbled toward El Aquila in exhausting little odysseys of a hundred yards.

He kept passing out.

The fifth or sixth time he wakened in a low cave that stank of fox. Pain lanced from temple to temple. He had suffered headaches all his life, but never one as unremitting as this. He moaned. It became a plaintive whine.

"Ah. You're awake. Good. Here. Drink this."

Something that might have been a small, very old man crouched in a deep shadow. A wrinkled hand proffered a tin cup. Its bottom was barely wet with some dark, fragrant liquid.

Micah drained it. Oblivion returned.

Yet he heard a distant voice droning endlessly of faith, God, and the manifest destiny of the children of Hammad al Nakir.

The angel nurtured him for weeks. And droned unceasing litanies of jihad. Sometimes, on moonless nights, he took Micah aboard his winged horse and showed him the wide earth. Argon. Itaskia. Hellin Daimiel. Gog-Ahlan, the fallen. Dunno Scuttari. Necremnos. Throyes. Freyland. Hammad al Nakir itself, the Lesser Kingdoms, and so much more. And the angel repeatedly told him that these lands must again bend the knee to God, as they had done in the day of

Empire. God, the eternal, was patient. God was just. God was understanding. And God was distressed by the backsliding of his Chosen. They were no longer bearing the Truth to the nations.

The angel would answer no questions. He merely castigated the children of Hammad al Nakir for having allowed the minions of the Dark One to blunt their will to carry the Truth.

Four centuries before the birth of Micah al Rhami there was a city, Ilkazar, which established dominion over all the west. But its kings were cruel, and too often swayed by the whims of sorcerers interested only in advancing themselves.

An ancient prophecy haunted the wizards of Ilkazar. It declared that the Empire's doom would find it through the agency of a woman. So those grim necromancers persecuted women of Power without mercy.

In the reign of Vilis, the final Emperor, a woman named Smyrena was burned.

She left a son. He persecutors overlooked the child.

That son migrated to Shinsan. He studied with the Tervola and Princes Thaumaturge of the Dread Empire. And then he returned, embittered with the bile of vengeance.

He was a mighty wizard now. He rallied the Empire's foes to his standard. The war was the cruelest that earth remembered. The wizards of Ilkazar were mighty too. The Empire's captains and soldiers were faithful, hardened men. Sorceries stalked the endless nights and devoured nations entire.

The heart of the Empire, then, was rich and fertile. The war left the land a vast, stony plain. The beds of great rivers became channels of lifeless sand. The land earned the name Hammad al Nakir, Desert of Death. The descendants of kings became petty hetmen of tattered bands which perpetrated bloody little butcheries upon one another over mudhole excuses for oases.

One family, the Quesani, established a nominal suzerainty over the desert, bringing an uneasy, oft broken peace. Semi-pacified, the tribes began raising small settlements and refurbishing old shrines.

They were a religious people, the Children of Hammad al Nakir. Only faith that their trials were the will of God gave them the endurance to weather the desert and the savagery of their cousins. Only an unshakable conviction that God would someday relent and restore them to their rightful place among the nations kept them battling.

But the religion of their Imperial forebears was sedentary, a faith for farmers and city dwellers. The theological hierarchies did not fall with the temporal. As generations passed and the Lord did not relent, common folk drifted ever farther from a priesthood unable to shed historical inertia, unable to adapt dogma to the circumstances of a people gone wholly nomadic and grown accustomed to weighing everything in the balance scale of death.

The summer had been the hardest since those immediately following the Fall. Autumn promised no relief. Oases were drying up. Order had begun to evade the grasp of Crown and priesthood. Chaos threatened as desperate men resorted to raid and counterraid and younger priests split with their elders over the meaning of the drought. Undisciplined anger stalked the barren hills and dunes. Dissatisfaction lurked in every shadow.

The land was harkening for the whisper of a new wind. One old man heard a sound. His response would damn and saint him.

Ridyah Imam al Assad's best days were far behind him. He was nearly blind now, after more than fifty years in the priesthood. There was little he could do to serve the Lord any longer. Now the Lord's own must care for him.

Nevertheless, they had given him a sword and set him to guard this slope. He had neither the strength nor the will to employ the weapon. If one of the el Habib came this way, to steal water from the springs and cisterns of Al Ghabha, he would do nothing. He had his weak sight to plead before his superiors.

The old man was true to his faith. He believed that he was but one brother in the Land of Peace and that such good fortune as came his way should be shared with those whom the Lord had called him to guide.

The Al Ghabha Shrine had water. El Aquila had none. He did not understand why his superiors were willing to bare steel to maintain that unnatural balance.

El Aquila lay to his left, a mile away. The squalid village

was the headquarters of the el Habib tribe. The Shrine and the monastery where al Assad lived rose two hundred yards behind him. The monastery was the retirement home of the priests of the western desert.

The source of the noise lay somewhere down the rocky slope he was supposed to guard.

Al Assad tottered forward, trusting his ears far more than his cataracted eyes. The sound reached him again. It sounded like the muttering of a man dying on the rack.

He found the boy lying in the shadow of a boulder.

His "Who are you?" and "Do you need help?" elicited no response. He knelt. With his fingers more than his eyes he determined that he had found a victim of the desert.

He shuddered as he felt cracked, scabby, sunburned skin. "A child," he murmured. "And not of El Aquila."

Little remained of the youth. The sun had baked most of the life out of him, desiccating his spirit as well as his body.

"Come, my son. Rise up. You're safe now. You've come to Al Ghabha."

The youth did not respond. Al Assad tried to pull him to his feet. The boy neither helped nor hindered him. The imam could do nothing with him. His will to live had departed. His only response was a muttered incoherency which sounded surprisingly like, "I have walked with the Angel of the Lord. I have seen the ramparts of Paradise." He then lapsed into complete unconsciousness. Al Assad could not rouse him again.

The old man made the long and painful journey back to the monastery, pausing each fifty yards to offer the Lord a prayer that his life be spared till he had carried word of the child's need to his abbot.

His heart had begun skipping beats again. He knew that it would not be long before Death took him into Her arms.

Al Assad no longer feared the Dark Lady. Indeed, his aches and blindness made him look forward to the pain-ease he would find in Her embrace. But he begged an indulgence, that he be allowed to perform this one final righteous deed.

The Lord had laid a charge upon him, and upon the Shrine, by guiding this victim of the desert to him and Shrine land.

Death heard and stayed Her hand. Perhaps She foresaw richer harvests later.

The abbot did not believe him at first, and castigated him for having abandoned his post. "It's an el Habib trick. They're out there stealing water right now." But al Assad convinced the man. And that left the abbot no happier. "The last thing we need is more mouths."

" 'Have you bread and your brother naught to eat? Have you water and your brother naught to drink? Then I say this unto you . . .' "

"Spare me the quotations, Brother Ridyah. He'll be cared for." The abbot shook his head. He got little thrills of anticipation when he thought of the Dark Lady claiming al Assad. The old man was one too sincere pain in the neck. "See. They're bringing him in now."

The brothers dropped the litter before the abbot, who examined the tormented child. He could not conceal his revulsion. "This is Micah, the son of the salt merchant al Rhami." He was awed.

"But it's been a month since the el Habib found their caravan!" one brother protested. "Nobody could survive the desert that long."

"He spoke of being tended by an angel," al Assad said. "He spoke of seeing the ramparts of Paradise."

The abbot frowned at him.

"The old man is right," one of the brothers said. "He started talking on the way up. About seeing the golden banners on the towers of Paradise. He said that an angel had showed him the wide earth. He says he has been told by the Lord to bring the Chosen back to the Truth."

A shadow crossed the abbot's face. That kind of talk distressed him.

"Maybe he did see an angel," someone suggested.

"Don't be silly," the abbot countered.

"He's alive," al Assad reminded him. "Against all the odds."

"He's been with the bandits."

"The bandits fled across the Sahel. The el Habib tracked them."

"Someone else, then."

"An angel. You don't believe in angels, Brother?"

"Of course I do," the abbot replied hastily. "I just don't think they reveal themselves to salt merchants' sons. It's the desert madness talking through him. He'll forget it when he recovers." The abbot looked around. He was not pleased. The whole Shrine was gathering over the boy, and in too many faces there was a desire to believe. "Achmed. Bring me Mustaf el Habib. No. Wait. Ridyah, you found the boy. You go to the village."

"But why?"

A technicality had occurred to the abbot. It looked like the perfect exit from the difficulties the boy was generating.

"We can't nurse him here. He hasn't been consecrated. And he would have to be well before we could do that."

Al Assad glowered at his superior. Then, with anger to banish his aches and weariness, he set off for the village of El Aquila.

The hetman of the el Habib tribe was no more excited than the abbot. "So you found a kid in the desert? What do you want me to do about it? He's not my problem."

"The unfortunate are all our problems," al Assad replied. "The abbot would speak with you of this one."

The abbot opened with a similar remark in response to a similar statement. He quoted some scripture. Mustaf countered with the quote al Assad had used earlier. The abbot kept his temper with difficulty.

"He's not consecrated."

"Consecrate him. That's your job."

"We can't do that till he recovers his faculties."

"He's nothing to me. And you're even less."

There were hard feelings. It had been but two days since Mustaf had petitioned the abbot for permission to draw water from the Shrine's spring. The abbot had denied him.

Al Assad, cunningly, had brought the chieftain up by way of the Shrine's gardens, where lush flowerbeds in careful arrangements glorified God. Mustaf was in no mood to be charitable.

The abbot was in the jaws of a merciless trap. The laws of good works were the high laws of the Shrine. He dared not abrogate them before his brothers. Not if he wished to retain his post. But neither was he ready to allow this boy to mutter his heretical insanities where they could upset the thinking of his charges.

"My friend, we had hard words over a matter we discussed recently. Perhaps I reached my decision a bit hastily."

Mustaf smiled a predatory smile. "Perhaps."

"Two score barrels of water?" the abbot suggested.

Mustaf started toward the doorway.

Al Assad shook his head sadly. They were going to dicker like merchants while a boy lay dying. He departed in disgust, taking himself to his cell.

Within the hour he surrendered to the embrace of the Dark Lady.

Micah wakened suddenly, rational, intuiting that a long time had passed. His last clear memory was of walking beside his father as their caravan began the last league to El Aquila. Shouts . . . a blow . . . pain . . . reminiscences of madness. There had been an ambush. Where was he now? Why wasn't he dead? An angel . . . There had been an angel.

Snatches returned. He had been returned to life, to become a missionary to the Chosen. A disciple.

He rose from his pallet. His legs betrayed him immediately. He lay panting for several minutes before finding the strength to crawl to a flapway.

The el Habib had confined him to a tent. They had quarantined him. His words had made Mustaf tremble. The chieftain could sense the blood and pain beyond such mad perspectives.

Micah yanked the flap.

The afternoon sun slapped his face. He threw an arm across his eyes and cried out. That devil orb was trying to murder him again.

"You idiot!" a voice snarled as someone pushed him back inside. "You want to blind yourself?"

The hands that guided him to his pallet became tender. The afterimages faded. He discovered his companion to be a girl.

She was about his own age. She wore no veil.

He shrank away. What was this? Some temptation of the Evil One? Her father would kill him. . . .

"What happened, Meryem? I heard him yell." A youth of about sixteen slipped inside. Micah retreated in earnest.

Then he remembered who and what he was. The hand of the Lord had touched him. He was the Disciple. No one could question his righteousness.

"Our foundling got himself an eyeful of sun." The girl touched Micah's shoulder. He flinched away.

"Back off, Meryem. Save the games for when he can handle them." To Micah he said, "She's father's favorite. The last born. He spoils her. She gets away with murder. Meryem. Please? The veil?"

"Where am I?" Micah asked.

"El Aquila," the youth replied. "In a tent behind the hut of Mustaf abd-Racim ibn Farid el Habib. The Al Ghabha priests found you. You were almost dead. They turned you over to my father. I'm Nassef. The brat is my sister Meryem." He sat down cross-legged facing Micah. "We're supposed to take care of you."

He did not sound enthusiastic.

"You were too much bother for them," the girl said. "That's why they gave you to Father." She sounded bitter.

"What?"

"Our oasis is drying up. The one at the Shrine is still wet, but the abbot won't share his water rights. The holy gardens flourish while the el Habib thirst."

Neither mentioned their sire's pragmatic deal.

"Did you really see an angel?" Meryem asked.

"Yes. I did. He bore me up among the stars and showed me the lands of the earth. He came to me in the hour of my despair and gave me two priceless gifts: my life, and the Truth. And he bade me take the Truth to the Chosen, that they might be freed of the bondage of the past and in turn carry the Word to the infidel."

Nassef flashed a sarcastic look in his sister's direction. Micah saw it plainly.

"You too shall know the Truth, friend Nassef. You shall see the flowering of the Kingdom of Peace. The Lord has returned me to the living with the mission of creating his Kingdom on earth."

In ages to come there would be countless bitter words spilled over El Murid's returned-to-life remarks. Did he mean a symbolic rebirth, or a literal return from the dead? He would never clarify himself.

Nassef closed his eyes. He was four years older than this naive boy. Those years were an unbridgeable gulf of experience.

He did have the manners to refrain from laughing. "Open

the flap a crack, Meryem. Let the sun in little by little, till he can face it."

She did so, and said, "We should bring him something to eat. He hasn't had any solid food yet."

"Nothing heavy. His stomach isn't ready." Nassef had seen victims of the desert before.

"Help me bring it."

"All right. Rest easy, foundling. We'll be right back. Think up an appetite." He followed his sister from the tent.

Meryem paused twenty feet away. Softly, she asked, "He really believes it, doesn't he?"

"About the angel? He's crazy."

"I believe it, too, Nassef. In a way. Because I want to. What he says . . . I think a lot of people want to hear that kind of thing. I think the abbot sent him down here because he was afraid to listen. And that's why Father won't have him in the house."

"Meryem—"

"What if a lot of people start listening and believing, Nassef?"

Nassef paused thoughtfully. "It's something to think about, isn't it?"

"Yes. Come on. Let's get him something."

El Murid, who was still very much the boy Micah al Rhami, lay staring at the tent above him. He let the leak of sunshine tease his eyes. A compulsion to be on his way, to begin preaching, rose within him. He fought it down. He knew he had to recover completely before he began his ministry.

But he was so impatient!

He knew the wayward habits of the Chosen, now that the angel had opened his eyes. It was imperative that he bring them the Truth as soon as possible. Every life the Dark Lady harvested now meant one more soul lost to the Evil One.

He would begin with El Aquila and Al Ghabha. When these people had been saved he would send them to minister to their neighbors. He himself would travel among the tribes and villages along his father's caravan route. If he could find some way to bring them salt . . .

"Here we are," Meryem announced. There was a musical note in her voice Micah found strange in one so young.

"Soup again, but this time I brought some bread. You can soak it. Sit up. You'll have to feed yourself this time. Don't eat too fast. You'll make yourself sick. Not too much, either."

"You're kind, Meryem."

"No. Nassef is right. I'm a brat."

"The Lord loves you even so." He began talking softly, persuasively, between bites. Meryem listened in apparent rapture.

He spoke for the first time in the shade of the palms surrounding the el Habib oasis. Little but mud remained of that once reliable waterhole, and that had begun to dry and crack. He made of the oasis a parable paralleling the drying up of the waters of faith in the Lord.

His audience was small. He sat with them as a teacher with students, reasoning with them and instructing them in the faith. Some were men four times his age. They were amazed by his knowledge and clarity of thought.

They threw fine points of dogma into his path like surprise pitfalls, baiting him. He shattered their arguments like a barbarian horde destroying lightly defended cities.

He had been more carefully schooled than he knew.

He made no converts. He had not expected to do so. He wanted to start them gossiping behind his back, unwittingly creating a climate for the sort of speeches that *would* win converts.

The older men went away afraid. They sensed in his words the first spark of a flame that could consume the Children of Hammad al Nakir.

Afterward, El Murid visited Mustaf. "My father's caravan? What became of it?" he asked the chieftain. Mustaf was taken aback, for he did it as an equal, not a child to an elder.

"Ambushed. All wiped out. It was a sad hour in the history of Hammad al Nakir. That I should have lived to see the day wherein men turned upon a salt caravan!"

There was something a little evasive in the way Mustaf had spoken. His eyes had become shifty.

"I have heard that the men of el Habib found the caravan. I have heard that they pursued the bandits."

"This is true. The bandits crossed the Sahel to the country of the western infidel."

Mustaf had become nervous. Micah thought he knew why. The hetman was essentially honorable. He had sent his own people to extract justice for the al Rhami family. But there was a little of the brigand in all the Children of Hammad al Nakir. "Yet there is a camel outside which answers to the name Big Jamal. And another which responds to Cactus. Could it be sheer coincidence that these beasts bear names identical to those of camels which belonged to my father? Is it coincidence that they bear identical markings?"

Mustaf said nothing for nearly a minute. Coals of anger burned briefly in his eyes. No man was pleased to be called to account by a child.

"You are observant, son of al Rhami," he finally replied. "It is true. They were your father's animals. When news came of what had happened, we saddled our best horses and rode swift and hard upon the trail. A crime so hideous could not go unpunished. Though your father's people were not of the el Habib, they were of the Chosen. They were saltmen. The laws shielding them are older than the Empire."

"And there was booty to be had."

"And there was booty, though your father was not a wealthy man. His entire fortune could scarcely repay the cost we paid in horses and lives."

Micah smiled. Mustaf had revealed his bargaining strategy. "You avenged my family?"

"Though our pursuit carried beyond the Sahel. We caught them before the very palisades of the heathen traders. Only two passed the infidels' gates. We were gentlemen. We did not burn their wooden walls. We did not slay the men and enslave the women. We treated with their council of factors, who knew your family of old. We presented our proofs. They took council, then delivered the bandits into our mercy. We were not merciful. They took many days dying, as an example to others who would break laws older than the desert. Perhaps the vultures still pick their bones."

"For that I must thank you, Mustaf. What of my patrimony?"

"We treated with the factors. Perhaps they cheated us. We were but ignorant devils of the sands. Perhaps not. We bore scimitars still stained with the blood of those who had wronged us."

"I doubt that they cheated, Mustaf. It's not their way. And, as you say, they would have been frightened."

"There is a small amount in gold and silver. And the camels did not interest them."

"What were your losses?"

"One man. And my son Nassef was wounded. That boy! You should have seen him! He was a lion! My pride knows no bounds. That such a son should have sprung from my loins! A lion of the desert, my Nassef. He will be a mighty warrior. If he outlives youth's impetuosity. He slew three of them himself." The chieftain glowed in his pride.

"And horses? You mentioned horses."

"Three. Three of our best. We rode hard and swift. And there was a messenger, that we sent to find your father's people, that they might know and make claims. He has not yet returned."

"He has a long journey. It's yours, Mustaf. All yours. I ask but a horse and a small amount of coin with which to begin my ministry."

Mustaf was surprised. "Micah—"

"I am El Murid now. Micah al Rhami is no more. He was a boy who died in the desert. I have returned from the fiery forge as the Disciple."

"You're serious, aren't you?"

El Murid was surprised that there could be any doubt.

"For the sake of the friendship I bore your father, hear me now. Do not pursue this path. It can be naught but a way of tears and sorrow."

"I must, Mustaf. The Lord himself has commanded me."

"I should restrain you. I will not. May the ghost of your father forgive me. I will choose a horse."

"A white horse, if you have one."

"I have one."

Next morning El Murid again taught beneath the palms. He spoke with passion, of the scarcely restrained wrath of God losing all patience with his Chosen's neglect of their duties. The argument of the empty oasis was hard to refute. The fiery summer could not be discounted. Several of his younger listeners remained for a more scholarly question and answer session.

Three days later Nassef whispered from beyond El Murid's tent flap. "Micah? May I come in?"

"Come. Nassef? El Murid?"

"Sorry. Of course." The youth settled himself opposite El Murid. "Father and I have had an argument. About you."

"I'm sorry to hear that. It isn't a good thing."

"He ordered me to stay away from you. Meryem too. The other parents are going to do the same. They're getting angry. You're calling too many ideas into question. They tolerated you when they thought it was the desert madness talking. But now they're calling you a heretic."

El Murid was stunned. "Me? The Disciple? They accuse me of heresy? How can that be?" Had he not been chosen by the Lord?

"You challenge old ways. Their ways. You accuse them. You accuse the priests of Al Ghabha. They are set in their ways. You can't expect them to say, 'Yes, we are guilty.' "

He had not foreseen that the Evil One would be so cunning as to deflect his own arguments against him. He had underestimated his Enemy. "Thank you, Nassef. You're a true friend to warn me. I will remember. Nassef, I hadn't anticipated this."

"I thought not."

"Go, then. Do not give your father cause for a grievance. I will speak to you later."

Nassef rose and departed, a small, thin smile on his lips.

El Murid prayed for hours. He retreated deep into his young mind. At last the will of the Lord became clear to him.

He looked up the long, stony slope at Al Ghabha. The low hill was barren, as if the darkness up there might creep down to devour any goodness surrounding it.

It was there that his first and most important victory had to be won. What point to winning the el Habib if their traditional spiritual shepherds guided them back to the paths of wrongdoing the moment he traveled on?

"I'm going to the Shrine," he told one of the men of the village, who had come to see what he was doing. "I'm going to preach a sermon there. I shall show them the Truth. Then let them name me heretic to my face, and risk the wrath of the Lord."

"Will that be wise?"

"It must be done. They must declare themselves righteous, or tools of the Evil One."

"I'll tell the others."

El Murid began walking.

The desert religion had contained no real devil figure till El Murid named him. Evil had been the province of a host of demons, ghosts, and fell spirits without leadership. And the paternalistic God of Hammad al Nakir had been but the paterfamilias of a family of gods suspiciously resembling the extended families of the Imperial and desert tribes. The Lord's problems had tended to come from a black-sheep brother who meddled and politicked for the pleasure of causing discord. The religion had retained traces of animism, belief in reincarnation, and ancestor worship.

The scholars at the Rebsamen University in Hellin Daimiel believed the desert gods to be vague echoes of a family that had united the original Seven Tribes and had guided their migration into the land that would one day become the Empire, and later Hammad al Nakir.

El Murid's teachings banished animism, ancestor worship, and reincarnation. They elevated the family chieftain to the position of an omnipotent One True God. His brothers and wives and children became mere angels.

And the meddlesome brother became the Evil One, the master of djinn and ifrits and the patron of all sorcerers. El Murid railed against the practice of witchcraft with a vehemence his listeners found incomprehensible. His principal argument was that it had been sorcery that had brought on the doom of the Empire. The glory of Ilkazar, and a hope for its return, was a theme running through all his teaching.

The primary point of contention at El Aquila was a proscription against praying to the lesser gods. El Murid's listeners were accustomed to petitioning specialists. They were accustomed, especially, to approaching Muhrain, the patron of the region, to whom the Al Ghabha Shrines were dedicated.

The boy's path led him not to Al Ghabha but to the site

where the imam, Ridyah, had found him. He did not at first know what drew him thither. Then he thought that he was looking for something.

He had left something there, something that he had forgotten. Something that he had hidden in his last moment of rationality. Something that had been given him by his angel.

Visions of an amulet came in snatches. A potent wrist amulet bearing a living stone. It would be, his angel had told him, the proof he needed to convince unbelievers.

But he could not remember where he had concealed it.

He scrabbled round the sides of the wadi that had prevented him from reaching El Aquila on his own.

"What in the world are you doing?" Nassef asked from above.

"You startled me, Nassef."

"What're you doing?"

"Looking for something. I hid it here. They didn't find it, did they? Did they find anything?"

"Who? The priests? Only a ragged, desert-worn saltman's son. What did you hide?"

"I remember now. A rock that looks like a tortoiseshell. Where is it?"

"There's one over here."

The rock was just a yard from where al Assad had found him. He tried lifting the stone. He did not have the strength.

"Here. Let me help." Nassef nudged him aside. In the process he tore his sleeve on a thorn of a scraggly desert bush. "Oh. Mother's going to brain me."

"Help me."

"Father too, if he finds out I was here."

"Nassef!"

"All right! I'm here." He heaved on the rock. "How did you move it before?"

"I don't know."

Together they heaved the stone onto its back. Nassef asked, "Ah, what is it?"

El Murid gently extracted the amulet from the rocky soil, brushing dirt from its delicate golden wristlet. The stone glowed even in the brilliant morning sun.

"The angel gave it to me. To be my proof to the doubtful."

Nassef was impressed, though he seemed more troubled than elated. In a moment, nervously, he suggested, "You'd better come on. The whole village is going to be at the Shrine."

"They expect to be entertained?"

Noncommittally, Nassef replied, "They think it's going to be interesting."

El Murid had noticed this evasiveness before. Nassef refused to be pinned down. About anything.

They strolled up to Al Ghabha, Nassef gradually lagging. El Murid accepted it. He understood. Nassef had to get along with Mustaf.

Everybody was there, from El Aquila and Al Ghabha alike. The gardens of the Shrines had assumed a carnival air. But he received very few friendly smiles there.

Behind the merriment was a strong current of malice. They had come to see someone hurt.

He had thought that he could teach them, that he could debate the abbot and so expose the folly inherent in the old dogma and old ways. But the mood here was passion. It demanded a passionate response, an emotional demonstration.

He acted without thinking. For the next few minutes he was just another spectator watching El Murid perform.

He threw his arms up and cried, "The Power of the Lord is upon me! The Spirit of God moves me! Witness, you idolaters, you wallowers in sin and weak faith! The hours of the enemies of the Lord are numbered! There is but one God, and I am His Disciple! Follow me or burn in Hell forever!"

He hurled his right fist at the earth. The stone in his amulet blazed furiously.

A lightning bolt flung down from a sky that had not seen a cloud in months. It blasted a ragged scar across the gardens of the Shrine. Singed petals fluttered through the air.

Thunder rolled across the blue. Women screamed. Men clutched their ears. Six more bolts hurtled down like the swift stabbing of a short spear. The lovely flowerbeds were ripped and burned.

In silence El Murid stalked from the grounds, his strides long and purposeful. At that moment he was no child, no man, but a force as terrible as a cyclone. He descended on El Aquila.

The crowd surged after him, terrified, yet irresistibly

drawn. The brothers of the Shrine came too, and they almost never left Al Ghabha.

El Murid marched to the dry oasis. He halted where once sweet waters had lapped at the toes of date palms. "I am the Disciple!" he shrieked. "I am the Instrument of the Lord! I am the Glory, and the Power, incarnate!" He seized up a stone that weighed more than a hundred pounds, hoisted it over his head effortlessly. He heaved it out onto the dried mud.

Thunders tortured the cloudless sky. Lightnings pounded the desert. Women shrieked. Men hid their eyes. And moisture began to darken the hard baked mud.

El Murid wheeled on Mustaf and the abbot. "Do you label me fool and heretic, then? Speak, Hell serf. Show me the power within you."

The handful of converts he had earlier won gathered to one side. Their faces glowed with awe and something akin to worship.

Nassef hovered in the gap between groups. He had not yet decided which party was truly his.

The abbot refused to be impressed. His defiant stance proclaimed that no demonstration would reach him. He growled, "It's mummery. The power of this Evil One you preach . . . you've done nothing no skilled sorcerer couldn't have done."

A forbidden word had been hurled into El Murid's face like a gauntlet. A strong, irrational hatred of wizardry had underlain all the youth's teachings so far. It was that part of his doctrine which most confused his audiences, because it seemed to bear little relationship to his other teachings.

El Murid shook with rage. "How dare you?"

"Infidel!" someone shrieked. Others took it up. "Heretic!"

El Murid whirled. Did they mock him?

His converts were shouting at the abbot.

One threw a stone. It opened the priest's forehead, sending him to his knees. A barrage followed. Most of the villagers fled. The abbot's personal attendants, a pair of retarded brothers younger than most of the priests, seized his arms and dragged him away. El Murid's converts went after them, flinging stones.

Mustaf rallied a handful of men and intercepted them.

Angry words filled the air. Fists flew. Knives leapt into angry hands.

"Stop it!" El Murid shrieked.

It was the first of the riots which were to follow him like a disease throughout the years. Only his intercession kept lives from being lost.

"Stop!" he thundered, raising his right hand to the sky. His amulet flared, searing faces with its golden glow. "Put up your blades and go home," he told his followers.

The power was still upon him. He was no child. The command in his voice could not be refused. His followers sheathed their blades and backed away. He considered them. They were all young. Some were younger than he. "I did not come among you to have you spill one another's blood." He turned to the chieftain of the el Habib. "Mustaf, I offer my apologies. I did not intend this."

"You preach war. Holy war."

"Against the unbeliever. The heathen nations that rebelled against the Empire. Not brother against brother. Not Chosen against Chosen." He glanced at the young people. He was startled to see several girls among them. "Nor sister against brother, nor son against father. I have come to reunite the Holy Empire in the strength of the Lord, that once again the Chosen might take their rightful place among the nations, secure in the love of the one true God, whom they shall worship as befits the Chosen."

Mustaf shook his head. "I suspect you mean well. But riots and discord will follow wherever you go, Micah al Rhami."

"El Murid. I am the Disciple."

"Contention will be your traveling companion, Micah. And your travels have begun. I will not have this among the el Habib. I take no harsher action than banish you forever from el Habib lands because I consider your family, and your trials in the desert." And—unspoken—because he feared El Murid's amulet.

"I am El Murid!"

"I don't care. Not who you are, or what. I won't have you fomenting violence in my territories. I'll give you the horse and coin you asked, and whatever you need to travel. You'll leave El Aquila this afternoon. I, Mustaf abd-Racim ibn Farid el Habib, have spoken. Do not defy me."

"Father, you can't—"

"Be silent, Meryem. What were you doing with that rabble? Why aren't you with your mother?"

The girl began to argue. Mustaf cut her short. "I've been a fool. You're starting to think you're a man. That is ended, Meryem. From this moment forward you will remain with the women, and do the work of women."

"Father!"

"You heard me. Micah. You heard me too. Start moving."

His converts were ready to resume scuffling. He disappointed them.

"No," he said. "It's not yet time for the Kingdom of Peace to challenge the unrighteous controlling temporal powers, corrupt as they may be. Endure. Our hour will come."

Mustaf reddened. "Boy, don't push me."

El Murid turned. He faced the chieftain of the el Habib. He clasped his hands before him, right over left. The jewel in his amulet blazed at Mustaf. He met the chieftain's gaze without flinching or speaking.

Mustaf yielded first, his eyes going to the amulet. He swallowed and started toward the village.

El Murid followed at a slower pace. His acolytes orbited him, their mouths full of soothing promises. He ignored most of them. His attention was on Nassef, who again was drifting aimlessly between parties, drawn both ways.

Intuition told him that he needed Nassef. The youth could become the cornerstone of his future. He had to win Nassef over before he left.

El Murid was as ambivalent about Nassef as Mustaf's son was about El Murid. Nassef was bright, fearless, hard, and competent. But he had a dark streak in him that frightened the Disciple. Mustaf's son contained as much potential for evil as he did for good.

"No, I won't defy Mustaf," he told his imploring companions. "I've recovered from my debility. It's time I started my travels. I'll return in time. Carry on my work while I'm gone. Show me a model village when I return."

He began one of his gentle teaching sessions, trying to give them the tools they would need to become effective missionaries.

* * *

He did not glance back as he rode out of El Aquila. He had only one regret: he had had no opportunity to present Nassef with further arguments. El Aquila had been a beginning.

Not nearly as good a beginning as he had hoped, though. He had not been able to sway anyone important. Priests and temporal leaders simply refused to listen. He would have to find some way to open their ears and minds.

He took the trail that reversed the road his father's caravan had been traveling. He wanted to pause at the place where his family had died.

His angel had told him his work would be hard, that he would be resisted by those who had an investment in the old ways. He had not believed. How could they refuse the Truth? It was so obvious and beautiful that it overwhelmed one.

He was two miles east of El Aquila when he heard hoofbeats. He glanced back. Two riders were overtaking him. He did not immediately recognize them. He had noticed them only momentarily, when they had helped the stoned abbot flee the oasis. What were they doing? He turned his face eastward and tried to ignore them.

His worry would not leave him. It quickly became obvious that they were trailing him. When he looked again he found that they were just a dozen yards behind. Naked steel appeared in their hands.

He kicked his mount's flanks. The white stallion surged forward, almost toppling him. He flung himself forward and clung to the animal's neck with no thought of regaining control.

The riders came after him.

He now knew the fear he had had no time for in the ambush of his father's caravan. He could not believe that the Evil One would have become so desperate so soon.

His flight led him into and through the defile where his family had died. He swept round a mass of bizarrely weathered boulders.

Riders awaited him. His mount sank to its haunches to avoid a collision. El Murid tumbled off. He rolled across the hard earth and scrambled for cover.

He had no weapon. He had trusted in the protection of the Lord. . . . He began praying.

Hooves thundered down the defile. Men shouted. Steel rang on steel. Someone moaned. Then it ended.

"Come out, Micah," someone shouted into the ensuing silence.

He peeped between boulders. He saw two riderless horses and two bodies lying on the stony earth.

Nassef loomed over them on a big black stallion. His right hand held a bloody blade. Behind him were another three youths from El Aquila, and Meryem and another girl.

El Murid crept out. "Where did you come from?"

"We decided to come with you." Nassef swung down. Contemptuously, he wiped his blade on the chest of one of the dead men. "Priests. They send halfwits to do murder."

The brothers had not been priests themselves, only wards of the Shrine who had been cared for by the abbot in return for doing the donkey work around the monastery.

"But how did you get here?" El Murid demanded.

"Meryem saw them start after you. Some of us were arguing about what to do. That decided us. There's an antelope trail that goes over the hills instead of around. I took that, riding hard. I was sure they would let you get this far, then try to make it look like you'd run foul of bandits again."

El Murid stood over the dead brothers. Tears came to his eyes. They had been but tools of the Evil One, poor things. He knelt and said prayers for their souls, though he had little hope that the Lord would show them any mercy. His was a jealous, vengeful God.

When he had finished, he asked, "What are you going to tell your father?"

"Nothing. We're going with you."

"But . . ."

"You need somebody, Micah. Hasn't that just been proven?"

El Murid paused thoughtfully, then threw his arms around Nassef. "I'm glad you came, Nassef. I was worried for you."

Nassef reddened. The Children of Hammad al Nakir were often demonstrative, but seldom in the tenderer emotions. "Let's get going," he said. "We've got a long way to travel if we're not going to spend the night in the desert."

El Murid hugged him again. "Thank you, Nassef. I wish

you knew how much this means to me." Then he went round clasping the hands of the others, and kissing the hands of the girls.

"I don't rate a hug, eh?" Meryem teased. "Do you love Nassef more?"

Now he was embarrassed. Meryem would not cease playing her games.

He called her bluff. "Come down here."

She did so, so he hugged her. It aggravated Nassef and completely flustered the girl.

El Murid laughed.

One of the youths brought his horse. "Thank you."

So there were seven who began the long trail, the trail of years. El Murid thought it an auspicious number, but the number gave no luck. He would suffer countless nights of frustration and depression before his ministry bore fruit. Too many of the Children of Hammad al Nakir refused him, or were just plain Truth-blind.

But he persisted. And each time he preached he won a heart or two. His following grew, and they too preached.

Chapter Two

Seeds of Hatred, Roots of War

Haroun was six years old when first he encountered El Murid.

His brother Ali had found himself a perch in a gap in the old garden wall. "God's Whiskers!" Ali squealed. "Khedah. Mustaf. Haroun. Come and look at this."

Their teacher, Megelin Radetic, scowled. "Ali, come down from there."

The boy ignored him.

"How am I supposed to pound anything into the heads of these little savages?" Radetic muttered. "Can't you do anything?" he asked their uncle Fuad.

Fuad's severe lips formed a thin, wicked smile. *Can but won't,* that smile said. He thought his brother Yousif a fool for wasting money on a pansy foreign teacher. "It's Disharhun. What did you expect?"

Radetic shook his head. That was Fuad's latest stock answer.

This barbarous holiday. It meant weeks lost in the already hopeless task of training the Wahlig's brats. They had come damned near three hundred miles, from el Aswad all the way to Al Rhemish, for a festival and prayer. Foolish. True, some important political business would take place behind the scenes.

The scholars of Hellin Daimiel were notorious skeptics. They labeled all faith as farce or fraud.

Megelin Radetic was more skeptical then most. His attitude had generated some bitter arguments with his employer, Yousif, the Wahlig of el Aswad. Fuad had become part of the class scene as a result. Yousif's younger brother and chief bully remained on hand to assure the children's insulation from Hellin Daimiel's stronger heresies.

"Hurry!" Ali insisted. "You'll miss it."

All traffic passing through the Royal Compound, from the pilgrim camps to the Most Holy Mrazkim Shrines, had to follow the one dusty street beyond the wall of Radetic's courtyard-classroom. This was the first time any of his students had joined their fathers during Disharhun. They had never seen Al Rhemish or its holiday displays.

"High Holy Week," Radetic muttered sourly. "Spring Hosting. Who needs it?"

It was his first visit, too. In his quiet way, he was as excited as the children.

He had taken the teaching position in order to study the primitive political processes going on behind the Sahel. The unprecedented challenge of a messianic type like El Murid promised an interesting study of a culture under stress. His field was the study of the evolution of ideals in government, especially the monolithic state trying to survive by adapting to the changing perceptions of subjects believed to be politically disenfranchised. It was a subtle and tricky area of study, and one's conclusions were always subject to attack.

His deal with Yousif had been accounted a great coup at his college, the Rebsamen. The secretive people of Hammad al Nakir were a virgin territory for academic exploitation. Radetic had begun to doubt the opportunity was worth the pain.

Only little Haroun remained attentive. The others jostled Ali for vantage points.

"Oh, go on," Radetic told his one remaining pupil.

Haroun was the sole intellectual candle Radetic had found in this benighted wasteland. Haroun was the only reason Radetic did not tell Yousif to pack up his prejudices and head for Hell. The child had shown tremendous promise.

The rest? Haroun's brothers and cousins, and the children of Yousif's favored followers? Doomed. They would become copies of their fathers. Ignorant, superstitious, bloodthirsty savages. New swordbearers in the endless pavane of raid and skirmish these wild men accounted a worthy life.

Radetic would have confessed it to no man, and least of all himself. He loved the imp called Haroun. He followed the boy and for the thousandth time pondered the mystery of the Wahlig.

Yousif's station roughly equated with that of a duke. He was a cousin of King Aboud. He had every reason to defend the status quo, and much to lose by change. Yet he dreamed of ending the old killing ways, the traditional desert ways, at least in his own demense. In his quieter, less abrasive way, he was as revolutionary as El Murid.

One of the older boys boosted Haroun to the top of the wall. He stared as if smitten by some great wonder.

Radetic's favorite was slight, dusky, dark-eyed, and hawk-nosed, a child-image of his sire. Even at six he knew his station.

Because he was only a fourth son, Haroun was fated to become his province's chief *shaghûn,* the commander of the handful of sorcerer-soldiers serving with the family cavalry.

Yousif's Wahligate was vast. His forces were numerous, for they nominally included every man able to bear arms. Haroun's responsibilities would be large, his immersion in wizardry deep.

Already Radetic had to share his pupil with witch-teachers from Jebal al Alf Dhulquarneni, the appropriately named Mountains of a Thousand Sorcerers. The great adepts almost always began their studies at the time they were learning to talk, yet seldom came into the fullness of their power till they had passed their prime mating years. The young years were critical to the learning of self-discipline, which had to be attained before the onset of puberty and accompanying distractions.

Radetic wriggled his way into the pack of children. "I'll be damned!"

Fuad pulled him back. "Of that there's no doubt." He assumed Radetic's place. "Holy! . . . A bare-faced woman! Teacher, you might as well turn them loose. They'll never settle down now. I'd better go tell Yousif that they're here." Fuad's face had taken on the glassy look of a man in rut. Radetic did not doubt that he had an erection.

The ways of the desert were strange, he thought.

Speculation had haunted the Royal Compound for days. Would El Murid really dare come to the Shrines?

Radetic shoved himself into the gap again, staring.

The woman was younger than he had expected. She rode a

tall white camel. The fact of her facial nakedness completely eclipsed the presence of the wild-eyed youth on the white mare.

El Murid was, for that matter, overshadowed by the man riding the big black stallion.

That would be Nassef, wouldn't it? Radetic thought. The brawler who led El Murid's dramatically named bodyguard, the Invincibles, and who was the brother of the Disciple's wife.

"El Murid. You're a bold bandit, son," Radetic murmured. He found himself admiring the youth's arrogance. Anyone who thumbed his nose at priesthoods rated with Megelin Radetic.

"Boys. Get down. Go find your fathers. Do you want a whipping?"

Such was the punishment for gazing on a woman's naked face. His pupils fled.

All but Haroun. "Is that really El Murid? The one Father calls Little Devil?"

Radetic nodded. "That's him."

Haroun scampered after his brothers and cousins. "Ali! Wait. Remember when Sabbah came to el Aswad?"

Megelin suspected imminent deviltry. Nothing but bad blood had come of that ill-starred peace conference with Sabbah i Hassan. He stalked his pupils.

He had warned Yousif. He had cast horoscope after horoscope, and each had been blacker than the last. But Yousif had rejected the scientific approach in his own life.

There was a natural yet innocent cruelty in the Children of Hammad al Nakir. Their very language lacked a means of expressing the concept "cruelty to an enemy."

Haroun looked back. He paused when he noticed Radetic watching him. But the urge to impress his brothers overcame good sense. He seized his rudimentary shaghûn's kit and joined their rush into the street.

Radetic followed. He would not be able to prevent their prank, but might finally penetrate the veil of mystery that surrounded the collapse of the negotiations with Sabbah i Hassan.

Its simplicity was frightening.

A shaghûn was as much stage magician as true sorcerer. Haroun spent an hour a day practicing sleight of hand that would awe the credulous one day. Among his simple tools was a peashooter. He could conceal it within a fist and, with a faked cough, blow a pellet into a campfire or a dart at an unsuspecting enemy.

Haroun chose a dart, and put it into the white horse's flank.

She reared and screamed. El Murid fell at Haroun's feet. They locked gazes. El Murid looked puzzled. When he tried to stand, he fell. He had broken an ankle.

Haroun's brothers and cousins began mocking the injured youth.

A quick-witted priest shouted, "An omen! False prophets inevitably fall."

Others took it up. They had been lying in wait, hoping for a chance to embarrass El Murid. Pushing and shoving started between factions.

Haroun and El Murid still stared at one another, as if seeing the future, and seeing it grim.

Nassef spied the peashooter. His sword rang as it cleared his scabbard. Its tip cut a shallow slice an inch above Haroun's right eye. The boy would have died but for Radetic's quick action.

Royalist partisans roared. Weapons materialized. "It's going to get ugly. You little fool. Come up here." Radetic yanked Haroun off the ground and threw him over his shoulder, then hurried toward his employer's tent. During Disharhun everyone, whether making the pilgrimage to Al Rhemish or not, lived the week in tents.

Fuad met them in the street. He had heard a swift-winged rumor of murder. He was angry. A huge man with a savage reputation, Fuad in a rage was a ferocious spectacle. He had his war blade in hand. It looked big enough to behead an ox with a single blow.

"What happened, teacher? Is he all right?"

"Mostly scared. I'd better talk to Yousif." He tried hiding the bleeding. Fuad had less self-control than the usual volatile native.

"He's waiting."

"I should find an injured child every time I want to talk to him."

Fuad gave him a poisonous look.

The shouting and blade waving around El Murid had

turned ugly. Fighting was forbidden during Disharhun, but the Children of Hammad al Nakir were not ones to let laws restrict their emotions.

Horsemen bearing round black shields emblazoned with the crude red eagle of the Royal Household descended on the trouble spot.

Radetic hurried on to his employer's quarters.

"What happened?" Yousif demanded as soon as he had determined that Haroun's wound was minor. He had cleared his tent of the usual hangers-on. "Haroun, you tell it first."

The boy was too frightened to stretch the truth. "I . . . I used my blow tube. To hit his horse. I didn't know he would get hurt."

"Megelin?"

"That's the gist of it. A practical joke, in poor taste. I'd blame the examples set by his elders. I did, however, hear mention of Sabbah i Hassan beforehand."

"How so?"

"In the context, I believe, of a similar stunt. Your children, you know, are even more primitive and literal-minded than the rest of you."

"Haroun? Is that true?"

"Huh?"

"Did you do the same thing to Sabbah i Hassan?"

Radetic smiled thinly as he watched the boy struggle with the lie trying to break out of the prison of his mouth. "Yes, Father."

Fuad returned to the tent. He seemed to have calmed down.

"Teacher?"

"Wahlig?"

"What the hell were they doing running the streets? They were supposed to be in class."

"Be serious, Yousif," Fuad interjected. "Don't tell me you're already too old to remember being young." The Wahlig was forty-one. "It's Disharhun. The woman wore no veil. You think the man is a miracle worker?"

Radetic was amazed. Fuad had made it plain that he thought any teacher who did not teach the use of weapons was superfluous. A warrior chieftain needed no other education. Scribes and accountants could be enslaved.

Moreover, he disliked Radetic personally.

What had put him into so good a mood? It worried Radetic.

"Haroun."

The boy approached his father reluctantly, took his spanking without crying. And without contrition.

Yousif was angry. He never punished his children before outsiders. And yet . . . Radetic suspected that his employer was not entirely displeased.

"Now go find your brothers. Tell them to get back here and stay out of trouble."

The boy ran out. Yousif looked at Fuad. "Bold little brat, isn't he?"

"His father's son, I think. You were the same."

Haroun was Yousif's favorite, though the Wahlig hid it well. Radetic suspected that he had been hired specifically for the benefit of the one boy. The others had been tossed into his classes in a vain hope that a patina of wisdom might stick.

Haroun would have preferred a scholarly life. When away from older brothers he showed the temperament. In fact, he had told Radetic that he wanted to be like him when he grew up. Megelin had been pleased and embarrassed.

For a six-year-old Haroun showed remarkable determination to pursue the mission decreed for him by an accident of birth. He acted twice his age. He was possessed of a stern, stolid fatalism seldom seen in anyone under thirty.

Megelin Radetic hurt a lot for the fated child.

Fuad bubbled over. "Yousif, this is the break we've been waiting for. This time he's given us a good, rock-hard excuse."

Radetic was startled when he suddenly realized that Fuad was talking about El Murid. It was a revelation. He had not suspected that powerful men were actually afraid of the Disciple. Afraid of a fifteen-year-old who, like themselves, had come to Al Rhemish for the rites of Disharhun, and to see his infant daughter christened before the Most Holy Mrazkin Shrines.

They had been lying to him. And to themselves, probably. Just plain old-fashioned whistling in the dark.

All this fuss over religious nonsense.

"Wahlig, this is ridiculous. Barbarous," Radetic grumbled. "Even pathetic. The boy is a madman. He crucifies himself every time he preaches. You don't have to trump up charges. Let him have his High Holy Week. Let him talk. They'll laugh him out of Al Rhemish."

"Let me boot this fish-faced pimp," Fuad growled.

Yousif raised a silencing hand. "Calm down. He has a right to an opinion. Even a wrong one."

Fuad shut up.

Yousif virtually owned his younger brother. Fuad seemed to have no imagination or aspirations of his own. He was a mirror of Yousif, the Wahlig's far-reaching right hand, a sledge used to hammer out another's dreams. Which was not to say that he always agreed. He and Yousif sometimes argued bitterly, especially when the latter was pushing an innovation. Sometimes Fuad won his point. But once a decision had been handed down he would support it to the death.

"Wahlig—"

"Be silent a moment, Megelin. Let me tell you where you're wrong." Yousif rearranged his cushions. "This is going to be long-winded. Get comfortable."

Radetic considered Yousif's tent to be furnished in garish, barbarous taste. The Children of Hammad al Nakir, when they could afford it, surrounded themselves with intense color. The reds, greens, yellows and blues around Yousif so clashed that Radetic could almost hear their conflict.

"Fuad, see if you can find some refreshments while I start to educate our educator. Megelin, you're wrong because you're too convinced of the correctness of your own viewpoint. When you look around here you don't see a culture. You see barbarians. You hear our religious arguments and can't believe we take them seriously because you can't. I grant you, a lot of my people don't either. But the majority do.

"As for El Murid and his henchman, you see only a deranged boy and a bandit. I see a huge problem. The boy is saying things everyone wants to hear. And believe. And Nassef just might have the genius to carve out El Murid's new Empire. The two together might have an overpowering attraction for our children. Our children, otherwise, have no other hope than to relive our yesterdays.

"You see Nassef as a bandit because he has raided caravans. What makes him remarkable and dangerous isn't the fact of his crimes, but the skill with which he committed them. If he ever rises above theft in God's name to making war in God's name, then God help us. Because he'll probably destroy us.

"Megelin, nobody is going to laugh if El Murid speaks. Nobody. And as a speaker he is as dangerous as Nassef is as a fighter. His speeches are creating the weapons Nassef needs to rise above banditry.

"The boy's movement is at a crossroads. And he knows it. That's why he came to Al Rhemish this year. After Disharhun he'll either be discredited and fade away, or he'll begin sweeping the desert like a sandstorm. If we have to trump up charges to stop that, we will."

Fuad returned with a lemonade-like drink. Megelin and Yousif accepted their portions. Fuad seated himself quietly, out of the way.

Radetic, squatting on a scarlet pillow, took a sip, then said, "And Fuad wonders why I think you a barbarous people."

"My brother has never visited Hellin Daimiel. I have. I can believe that your people would laugh a messiah out of business. You're all cynics. And you don't need that kind of leader.

"We do, Megelin. The heart of me craves an El Murid. He's telling me exactly what my heart wants to hear. I want to believe that we're the Chosen People. I want to believe that it's our destiny to master the world. I want something, anything, to make the centuries since the Fall worthwhile.

"I want to believe that the Fall itself was the work of an Evil One. Fuad wants to believe. My cousin the King would like to believe. Unfortunately, we're old enough to recognize gossamer on the wind. A deadly gossamer.

"Megelin, that boy is a death merchant. He's put it in pretty packages, but he's selling another Fall. If we turn to him, if we break out of Hammad al Nakir in order to convert the pagan and resurrect the Empire, we'll be destroyed. Those of us who have been across the Sahel realize that the world out there isn't the one conquered by Ilkazar.

"We don't have the numbers, the resources, the arms, or the *discipline* of the western kingdoms."

Radetic nodded. These people would be hopelessly overmatched in any war with the west. Warfare, like everything else, evolved. The style of the Children of Hammad al Nakir had evolved in a direction suited only to the desert.

"But his jihad doesn't terrify me yet. That's a long way off," Yousif continued. "The struggle here is what frightens me. He has to win his homeland first. And to do that he will have to tear the belly out of Hammad al Nakir. So. I want to draw his fangs now. By fair means or foul."

"You live by different rules," Radetic observed. It was becoming a favorite saying. "I have to go think about what you've said." He finished his drink, rose, nodded to Fuad, and departed. He seated himself outside the tent flap, in the position for meditation. He listened while Yousif instructed Fuad how to approach King Aboud with news of this opportunity. Embittered by the foolishness of it, the injustice of it, he sealed them out, contemplated his surroundings.

The Royal Compound occupied five acres bordering the southwest flank of the Mrazkim Shrines, which were the religious heart of Hammad al Nakir. Today, because it was Disharhun, the compound was infested with royal relatives, favor seekers and sycophants. Most of the captains, sheiyeks and wahligs had brought their entire households. Traders and artisans, hoping to achieve some small advantage over their competitors, virtually besieged the Compound's boundaries. Ambassadors and foreign mercantile factors roamed everywhere. The smells were overwhelming. Men, animals, machines, and insects made noises which melded into an overpowering din.

And beyond the mad anthill of the Compound lay vast encampments of ordinary pilgrims. Their tents swept up the sides of the bowl-shaped valley containing the capital and Shrines. Thousands upon thousands more than customary had made the journey this year—because El Murid's visit had been rumored for months. They had come because they did not want to miss the inevitable collision between dissidence and authority.

Yousif was playing with fire, Radetic reflected as he watched Fuad stride toward Aboud's palatial tent. This monarchy, unlike its predecessor in Ilkazar, did not have the power to rule by decree. Today even the most obnoxious rabble-rouser could not be denied his hour in court, his opportunity to speak in his own defense.

A shy Haroun came to sit with his teacher. He put his hand into Radetic's.

"Sometimes, Haroun, you're too crafty for your own good." There was no rancor in Radetic's voice, though. The gesture touched him, genuine or not.

"I did wrong, Megelin?"

"There's some disagreement." Radetic surveyed the human panorama briefly. "You should think, Haroun. You can't simply act. That is your people's biggest handicap. They yield to impulse without ever considering the consequences."

"I'm sorry, Megelin."

"The hell you are. You're sorry you got caught. You don't care a whit how much you hurt that man."

"He's our enemy."

"How do you know? You never saw him before. You've never talked to him. He's never hurt you."

"Ali said—"

"Ali is like your uncle Fuad. He says a lot. His mouth is always open. And because of that, someday somebody else who doesn't think is going to shove his fist down Ali's throat. How often is he right? How often does pure foolishness come out of that open mouth?"

Radetic was letting his frustrations run wild. He had never encountered a student more unyieldingly unteachable than Ali bin Yousif.

"Then he isn't our enemy?"

"I didn't say that. Of course he is. He's your bitterest enemy. But not because Ali says he is. El Murid is an enemy in his ideals. I don't think he'd harm you physically if he had the chance. He'd just rob you of everything that's important to you. Someday, I hope, you'll understand just how gross a mistake your prank was."

"Fuad's coming."

"So he is. And he looks like an old cat licking cream off her whiskers. It went well, Fuad?"

"Beautifully, teacher. Old Aboud isn't as stupid as I thought. He saw the chance right away." Fuad's grin vanished. "You may be called to testify."

"Then, perhaps, we may be friends no more. I am of the Rebsamen, Fuad. I cannot lie."

"Were we ever friends?" Fuad demanded as he entered the tent.

A chill stalked down Radetic's spine. He was not a brave man.

He was disgusted with himself. He knew that he would lie if Yousif pressed him hard enough.

The court was convened as the traditional Disharhun Court of Nine, the supreme court of Hammad al Nakir. Three jurists were provided by the Royal Household, and another three by the Shrine priests. A final three were common pilgrims selected at random from among the hosts come for the High Holy Days.

It was a stacked court. El Murid was down eight votes before a shred of evidence had been presented.

Someone had bandanged Haroun heavily. He had been coached quickly and well. He lied with a straight face and defiantly traded stares with El Murid and Nassef.

Radetic nearly shrieked in protest when the Court voted to deny a request for permission to cross-examine.

A parade of pilgrims testified after Haroun stepped down. Their testimony bore little relation to the truth of what had happened. It seemed, instead, to follow religious predilection. No one mentioned seeing a peashooter or dart.

Radetic already knew this phase of desert justice well. He had reviewed judicial sessions at el Aswad. The disposition of most cases seemed to depend on which adversary could muster the most relatives to lie for him.

Megelin dreaded having to give his own testimony. His conscience had been ragging him mercilessly. He feared he would not be able to lie.

He was spared the final crisis of conscience. Yousif had passed the word. He was not called. He sat restlessly, and seethed. Such a travesty! The outcome was never in doubt. The decision had been made before the judges heard the charges. . . .

What *were* the charges? Radetic suddenly realized that they had not been formally declared.

They were trying El Murid. Charges did not matter.

El Murid rose. "A petition, my lord judges."

The chief judge, one of Aboud's brothers, looked bored. "What is it this time?"

"Permission to call additional witnesses."

The judge sighed and rubbed his forehead with the heel of

his left hand. "This could go on all day." He was speaking to himself, but half the audience heard him plainly. "Who?"

"My wife."

"A woman?"

A murmur of amazement ran through the gallery.

"She is the daughter of a chieftain. She is of the el Habib, who are of the same blood as the Quesan."

"Nevertheless, a woman. And one disowned by her family. Do you mock this Court? Do you compound your crimes by trying to make a farce of the administration of justice? Your request is denied."

Radetic's disgust neared the explosive point. And yet . . . to his amazement, he saw that even the El Murid factionalists in the audience were appalled by their prophet's suggestion.

Megelin shook his head sadly. There was no hope for these savages.

Fuad pushed a stiffened finger into his ribs. "Keep still, teacher."

The chief judge rose less than two hours after the trial's commencement. Without consulting his fellows privately, he announced, "Micah al Rhami. Nassef, once ibn Mustaf el Habib. It is the judgment of this Court that you are guilty. Therefore, this Court of Nine orders that you be banned forever from all Royal lands and protection, all holy places and protection, and from the Grace of God—unless a future Court of Nine shall find cause for commutation or pardon."

Radetic smiled sardonically. The sentence amounted to political and religious excommunication—with an out. All El Murid had to do was recant.

Had there been any genuine crime the sentence would have been scorned for its mildness. This was a land where they lopped off hands, feet, testicles, ears, and, more often than anything, heads. But the sentence fulfilled the Royal goal. Executed immediately, it would keep El Murid from preaching during Disharhun, to the vast gatherings this year's High Holy Week had drawn.

Radetic chuckled softly. Someone was scared to death of the boy.

Fuad gouged him again.

"My lords! Why hast thou done this to me?" El Murid asked softly, his head bowed.

He does it well, Radetic thought. The pathos in him. He'll win converts with that line.

Suddenly, proudly, El Murid stared the chief magistrate in the eye. "Thy servant hears and obeys, O Law. For does not the Lord say, 'Obey the law, for I am the Law'? At Disharhun's end El Murid shall disappear into the wilderness."

Sighs came from the crowd. It looked like the old order had won its victory.

Nassef shot El Murid a look of pure venom.

And why, Radetic asked himself, hadn't Nassef said a word in their defense? What game was he playing? For that matter, what game was El Murid playing now? He did not seem at all distressed as he laid himself open for further humiliation.

"The Court of Nine orders that the sentence be executed immediately."

That surprised no one. How else to keep El Murid from speaking?

"One hour from now the King's sheriffs will receive orders to seize any of the proscribed, or their families, found within any of the restricted domains."

"That," Megelin murmured, "is too much." Fuad jabbed him again.

Seldom was it that a pivoting point of history could be identified at the precise instant of turning. Radetic recognized one here. A band of frightened men had compounded an action of self-defense with one of spite.

They were trying to rob El Murid of a father's precious opportunity and inalienable right to have his child baptized before the Most Holy Mrazkim Shrines, during Disharhun. El Murid had already announced that he would dedicate his daughter to God on Mashad, the last and most important of the High Holy Days.

Radetic need be no necromancer to predict the long-term results. The meekest of the desert-born would have felt compelled to respond.

In later days El Murid's followers would say that this was the moment when the grim truth of reality finally burst through the curtain of ideals blinding the youth to the hypocrisies of his world.

Radetic suspected that that revelation had come a lot

earlier. The youth seemed secretly satisfied with the pronouncement.

Nevertheless, he reddened. The muscles in his neck stood out. "It must be God's will. May the Lord grant his Disciple an opportunity to return to grace."

He spoke softly, but his words were a threat, a promise and a declaration of schism. Henceforth the Kingdom of Peace would make war on heretics and the enemies of its future.

Radetic could smell the stink of blood and smoke drifting back across the years. He could not understand how El Murid's enemies could fail to see what they had done. Old cynic that he was, he studied El Murid intently. Behind the very real anger there was evidence that the youth had expected this.

He did detect a barely restrained glee in Nassef.

El Murid departed Al Rhemish meekly. But Meryem left word that her daughter would bear no name till she received it before the Mrazkim Shrines themselves. Fuad laughed when he heard. "Women making threats?" he demanded. "Camels will fly before she sees Al Rhemish again."

Yousif was not as sure. Megelin's naggings were forcing him to think. He did not like the thoughts that came to him.

The rioting started before the dust had settled on El Murid's backtrail. More than a hundred pilgrims died. Before the end of Disharhun, El Murid's partisans had defaced the Shrines themselves.

Yousif and Fuad were amazed.

"It's begun," Megelin told his employer. "You should have murdered them. Then it would've been over this week, and in a year he would have been forgotten."

Despite his earlier speech about the emotions involved, Yousif seemed stunned by the reaction of the Disciple's followers. He could not comprehend being so hated by people who did not know him. So the human tragedy goes, men hating without trying to understand, and unable to understand why they are hated.

Later in the week, Radetic cautioned his employer. "There was planning behind this. They anticipated you. Did you happen to notice that neither one of them really tried to defend himself? Especially Nassef? He never said a word through the whole trial. I think you've created a couple of martyrs, and I think you did exactly what they wanted you to do."

"Are you listening, Haroun?" the Wahlig asked. He was keeping the boy close. There were people in the streets who wanted to lay hands on him. "Nassef. He's the dangerous one."

"This rioting will spread," Radetic predicted. "It'll begin to show elements of class struggle, too. Common folk, artisans and merchants against priests and nobles."

Yousif looked at him oddly.

"I may not understand faith, Yousif. But I understand politics, vested interests and promises for tomorrow."

"What can they do?" Fuad demanded. "A handful of outlaws? The Little Devil's scattered converts? We can hunt them down like wounded jackals."

"I'm afraid Megelin might be right, Fuad. I think Aboud overdid it. He took away their pride. You can't do that to a man. He has to save face somehow. We sent them out like whipped dogs. They *have* to hit back. At least, Nassef does. He's the one with the ego. Think. What would you do if we'd done the same to you?"

Fuad did not think long. He replied, "I see."

Radetic added, "Messiahs tend to take what comes, I think. They see the abuse as part of their witnessing. I've begun to think the jihad El Murid preaches is a metaphoric concept, that he doesn't really see it in terms of blood and death. Not the way Nassef would look at it."

"Still," said Fuad, "all we have to do is go kill them if they try something."

Yousif replied, "I think I can guarantee that Nassef will. We'll just have to judge his strength and try to anticipate him. And, of course, try to kill him. But I have a gut feeling that he won't let us. I have an audience with Aboud tonight. I'd better light a fire under him."

The King, unfortunately, shared Fuad's thinking. For him the El Murid matter was closed.

Yousif and Radetic fussed and worried and, even so, were no less stunned when the blow finally fell.

Even they had grossly underestimated Nassef.

Chapter Three

A Minor Squabble in Another Land and Time

Twenty-three warriors stalked through falling snow, their shoulders downed with white. Ice stiffened the mustaches of those who had them. Towering pines loomed ahead, but here ancient oaks surrounded them like a convocation of gnarled, antlered frost giants squatting, dreaming of blood and fire. Snow masked the altar stone where the priests of the Old Gods had ripped the hearts from screaming virgins. Two boys, Bragi and Haaken, turtled their heads against their shoulders and hurried past.

The trailbreakers fought the deep, soft new snow in iron silence. An arctic wind drove frozen daggers through the heaviest clothing.

Bragi and Haaken had just begun to sport scraggly beards. Some of their companions had winter-white hair. Harald the Half had no shield arm. Yet each man wore the horn helm. Old and young, they were warriors.

They had a cause.

The wind moaned, winging the sad call of a wolf. Bragi shuddered. Some of his companions would be wolf meat soon.

His father Ragnar raised a hand. They stopped. "Smoke," said the man known across Trolledyngja as the Wolf of Draukenbring.

The odor drifted thinly from among the pines. They were near Thane Hjarlma's longhouse. As one, they sat on their hams to rest.

Minutes sped.

"Time," Ragnar said. He was also called Mad Ragnar, a crazy killer known for a thousand miles.

Men checked shields and weapons. Ragnar chose groups to go right and left.

Ragnar's son Bragi, his foster son Haaken and his friend Bjorn conferred with him briefly. The boys bore clay pots containing carefully nurtured coals. And within them the boys nursed grudges. Their father had ordered them to stay out of the fighting.

Ragnar muttered words of caution and encouragement. "Haaken, you go with Bjorn and Sven. Bragi, stay with me."

The last half mile was the slowest. Bragi kept remembering friendlier visits. And, last summer, spirited, clandestine tumbles with the Thane's daughter Inger. But now the old King was dead. The succession was in contest.

Hjarlma had declared for the Pretender. His strength had overawed most of his neighbors. Only Ragnar, Mad Ragnar, had remained visibly loyal to the Old House.

The civil war was shredding the tapestry of Trolledyngjan society. Friend slew friend. Ragnar's own father served the Pretender. Families that had been at each other's throats for generations now stood shoulder to shoulder in the battle line.

Every spring in Bragi's memory his father had gone reeving with Hjarlma. Sailing gunwale to gunwale, their dragonships had scourged the southern coasts. They had saved one another's lives. They had celebrated shared wealth. And, in the same chains, they had shared the despair of imprisonment by the Itaskian King.

Now they sought to murder one another, driven by the bitter blood-thirst only politics can generate.

The news had come south on rumor's lightning wings: the Pretender had taken Tonderhofn. The Old House was collapsing.

Hjarlma's men would be celebrating. But the raiders moved carefully. Hjarlma's men had wives, children, and slaves who would be sober.

They penetrated the trenches and stockades. They passed the outbuildings. Fifty feet from the longhouse itself Bragi turned his back into the wind. He dropped dried moss and tree bark into his jar, blew gently. His father and several warriors held out their torches. Others quietly splashed the longhouse with oil.

A man would be stationed at each window. The best fighters would hold the doorway. They would slaughter the drunken rebels as they tried to escape. The Old House's cause, here beneath the brooding, glacier-clawed northern slopes of the Kratchnodian Mountains, would revive at the eleventh hour.

That was Mad Ragnar's plan. It was as bold and ferocious a stroke as ever plotted by the Wolf.

It should have worked.

But Hjarlma was expecting them.

It was a great slaughter anyway. Hjarlma had gotten his warning only seconds before the blow fell. His people were still confused, still trying to shake the mead and find their weapons.

Fire whipped through axed-in windows.

"Stay put!" Ragnar growled at Bragi. "To me!" he thundered at the others.

"Yai! It's Ragnar!" one of Hjarlma's men wailed.

The blond giant attacked with sword in one hand, axe in the other. Not for nothing was he called Mad Ragnar. He went into insane killing rages, became an unstoppable killing machine. It was whispered that his wife, the witch Helga, had spelled him invincible.

Three, four, five of the drunkards fell for each of Ragnar's men. And still he could not win. The odds were too terrible.

The fire had become a liability. Without it driving them to save their families, Hjarlma's men might have surrendered.

Bragi went looking for Haaken.

Haaken's thoughts paralleled his own. He had secured a sword already. They had not been allowed to bring their own. Ragnar had not wanted them getting dangerous ideas.

"What now?" Haaken asked.

"Father won't run. Not yet."

"How did they know?"

"A traitor. Hjarlma must have bought somebody from Draukenbring. Here!"

A rebel, nearly disemboweled, crawled toward them. "Cover me while I get his sword."

They did what had to be done. And felt ghastly afterward.

"Who sold out?"

"I don't know. Or how. But we'll find out."

Then they became too busy to speculate. Several rebels, who had crawled out a window no longer held against them, stumbled their way.

The longhouse burned briskly. Women, children and slaves screamed inside. Ragnar's men fell back before the weight of their panic.

In a brief exchange, from ambush, Bragi and Haaken slew three men and sent a fourth fleeing into the pines. They received their own first man-wounds.

"Half of us are down," Bragi observed, after studying the main action. "Bors. Rafnir. Tor. Tryggva. Both Haralds. Where's Bjorn?"

Ragnar, roaring and laughing, stood out of the fray like a cave bear beset by hounds. Bodies lay heaped around him.

"We've got to help."

"How?" Haaken was no thinker. He was a follower and doer. A strong-backed, stolid, steadfast lad.

Bragi had all of his mother's intellect and a little of his father's crazy courage. But the situation had rattled him. He did not know what to do. He wanted to run. He did not. With a bellow imitative of Ragnar's, he charged. Fate had made his decision for him.

He had discovered what had become of Bjorn. Ragnar's lieutenant was charging him from behind.

No warning could reach Ragnar's blood-drugged brain. All Bragi could do was race Bjorn to his prey.

He lost the footrace, but prevented the traitor's blow from being fatal. Bjorn's deflected blade entered Ragnar's back kidney high. Ragnar howled and whirled. A wild blow from the haft of his axe bowled Bjorn into a snowdrift.

Then the Wolf's knees buckled.

The rebels whooped, attacking with renewed ferocity. Bragi and Haaken became too busy to avenge their father.

Then twenty rebels wailed.

Ragnar surged to his feet. He roared like one of the great trolls of the high Kratchnodians.

There was a lull as the combatants eyed one another.

The pain had opened the veil across Ragnar's sanity. "A crown has been lost here tonight," he muttered. "Treason always begets more treason. There's nothing more we can do. Gather the wounded."

For a while the rebels licked their wounds and fought the fire. But the raiders, burdened with wounded, gained only a few miles head start.

Nils Stromberg went down and could not get up again. His sons, Thorkel and Olaf, refused to leave him behind. Ragnar bellowed at all three, and lost the argument. They stayed, their faces turned toward the glow of the burning longhouse. No man could deny another his choice of deaths.

Lank Lars Greyhame went next. Then Thake One Hand. Six miles south of Hjarlma's stead, Anders Miklasson slipped down an icy bank into the creek they were following. He went under the ice and drowned before the others could chop through.

He would have frozen anyway. It was that cold, and the others dared not pause to light a fire.

"One by one," Ragnar growled as they piled stones in a crude cairn. "Soon there won't be enough of us left to drive off the wolves."

He did not mean Hjarlma's men. A pack was trailing them. The leader already had made a sally at Jarl Kinson, who kept lagging.

Bragi was exhausted. His wounds, though minor, nagged him like the agonies of a flensing knife in the hand of a master executioner. But he kept silent. He could do no less than his father, whose injury was much greater.

Bragi, Haaken, Ragnar and five more lived to see the dawn. They evaded Hjarlma and drove the wolves off. Ragnar went to ground in a cave. He sent Bragi and Haaken to scout the nearby forest. The searchers passed near the boys, but without slowing.

Bragi watched them go, Bjorn, the Thane and fifteen healthy, angry warriors. They were not searching. They were talking about waiting for Ragnar at Draukenbring.

"Hjarlma's not stupid," Ragnar said when he received the news. "Why chase the Wolf all over the woods when you know he has to return to his lair?"

"Mother—"

"She'll be all right. Hjarlma's scared to death of her."

Bragi tried reading behind his father's beard. The man spoke softly, tautly, as if he were in great pain.

"The war is over now," Ragnar told him. "Understand

that. The Pretender has won. The Old House is in eclipse. There's no more reason to fight. Only a fool would."

Bragi got the message. He wasn't to waste his life pursuing a lost cause.

He had had fifteen years of practice reading the wisdom behind Ragnar's terse observations.

"They'll abandon him as quickly as they flocked to him. Eventually. They say . . ." A shudder wracked his massive frame. "They say there's a demand for Trolledyngjans in the south. Over the mountains. Beyond the lands of the bowmen. Past the reeving kingdoms. There's war a-brewing. Bold lads, bright lads, might do well while awaiting a restoration."

Itaskia was the lands of the bowmen. The reeving kingdoms were the necklace of city states hugging the coast down to Simballawein. For half a dozen generations the Trolledyngjan dragonships had gone out when the ice broke at Tonderhofn and Torshofn, to run the gauntlet of the Tongues of Fire and plunder the eastern littoral.

"Under the shingle pine, beside the upper spring. The northwest side. An old, broken hearthstone marks it. You'll find the things you'll need. Take the copper amulet to a man called Yalmar at the Red Hart Inn in Itaskia the City."

"Mother—"

"Can take care of herself, I said. She won't be happy, but she'll manage. I only regret that I won't be able to send her home."

Bragi finally understood. His father was dying. Ragnar had known for a long time.

Tears gathered at the corners of Bragi's eyes. But Haaken and Soren were watching. He had to impress them with his self-control. Especially Haaken, on whose good opinion he depended more than he could admit.

"Prepare well," said Ragnar. "The high passes will be bitter this time of year."

"What about Bjorn?" Haaken demanded. The bastard child that Mad Ragnar had found in the forest, abandoned to the wolves, was not too proud to reveal his feelings.

"Ragnar, you've treated me as your own son. Even in lean years, when there was too little for those of your own blood. I've always honored and obeyed as I would a birth-father.

And in this, too, I must obey. But not while Bjorn Backstabber lives. Though my bones be scattered by wolves, though my soul be damned to run with the Wild Hunt, I won't leave while Bjorn's treachery goes unrepaid."

It was a proud oath, a bold oath. Everyone agreed it was worthy of a son of the Wolf. Ragnar and Bragi stared. Soren nodded his admiration. For Haaken, terse to the point of virtual non-communication, a speech of this length amounted to a total baring of the soul. He seldom said as many words in an entire day.

"I haven't forgotten Bjorn. It's his face, smiling, pretending friendship while he took Hjarlma's pay, here in my mind's eye, that keeps me going. He'll die before I do, Haaken. He'll be the torchbearer lighting my path to Hell. Ah. I can see the agony in his eyes. I can smell the fear in him. I can hear him when he urges Hjarlma to hurry and establish the Draukenbring trap. The Wolf lives. He knows the Wolf. And his cubs. He knows that his doom stalks him now.

"We'll leave in the morning, after we've buried old Sven."

Bragi started. He had thought that the old warrior was sleeping.

"A sad end for you, friend of my father," Ragnar muttered to the dead man.

Sven had served the family since the childhood of Bragi's grandfather. He had been friends with the old man for forty years. And then they had parted with blows.

"Maybe they'll be reconciled in the Hall of Heroes," Bragi murmured.

Sven had been a sturdy fighter who had taught Ragnar his weapons and had followed him in his southern ventures. More recently, he had been weapon master to Bragi and Haaken. He would be missed and mourned. Even beyond the enemy banners.

"How did Bjorn warn them?" Haaken asked.

"We'll find out," Ragnar promised. "You boys rest. It'll be hard going. Some of us aren't going to make it."

Six of them reached Draukenbring.

Ragnar gave the steading a wide berth, leading them on into the mountains. Then he brought them home from the south, down a knee of the peak they called Kamer

Strotheide. It was a pathway so difficult even Hjarlma and Bjorn would not think to watch it.

Hjarlma was waiting. They could see his sentries from the mountain.

Bragi looked down only long enough to assure himself that Hjarlma had indulged in no destruction.

His mother's witchcraft was held in great dread.

He did not understand why. She was as compassionate, understanding and loving a woman as any he knew.

Slipping and sliding, they descended to a vale where, in summer, Draukenbring's cattle grazed. They then traveled by wood and ravine toward the longhouse. They halted in the steading's woodlot, a hundred yards from the nearest outbuilding. There they awaited darkness and grew miserably cold.

The inactivity told on Ragnar most. He got stiff.

Bragi worried. His father had grown so pale. . . .

His mind remained a whirl of hope and despair. Ragnar believed he was dying. Yet he went on and on and on, apparently driven by pure will.

It darkened. Ragnar said, "Bragi, the smokehouse. In the middle of the floor, under the sawdust. A metal ring. Pull up on it. The tunnel leads to the house. Don't waste time. I'll send Soren in a minute."

Sword ready, Bragi ran to the smokehouse, stirred through greasy sawdust.

The ring was the handle of a trapdoor. Beneath, a ladder descended into a tunnel. He shook his head. He had known nothing about it. Ragnar had secrets he kept even from his own. He should have been called Fox, not Wolf.

Soren slipped into the smokehouse. Bragi explained. Then Haaken, Sigurd and Sturla followed. But Ragnar did not come. Sturla brought the Wolf's final instructions.

The tunnel was low and dark. Once Bragi placed a hand onto something furry that squealed and wriggled away. He was to remember that passage as the worst of the homeward journey.

The tunnel ended behind the wall of the ale cellar, its head masked by a huge keg that had to be rolled aside. It was a keg Ragnar had always refused to tap, claiming he was saving it for a special occasion.

The cellar stair led up to a larder where vegetables and

meats hung from beams, out of the reach of rodents. Bragi crept up. Someone, cursing, entered the room over his head. He froze.

The abuse was directed at Bragi's mother, Helga. She was not cooperating with Hjarlma's men. They, after the hardships they had faced in the forests, were put out because she refused to do their cooking.

Bragi listened closely. His mother's voice betrayed no fear. But nothing ever disturbed her visibly. She was always the same sedate, gracious, sometimes imperious lady. Before outsiders.

Even with the family she seldom showed anything but tenderness and love.

"Banditry doesn't become you, Snorri. A civilized man, even in the house of his enemy, behaves courteously. Would Ragnar plunder Hjarlma?" She was overhead now.

Bragi could not repress a grin. Damned right Ragnar would plunder Hjarlma. Down to the last cracked iron pot. But Snorri grumbled an apology and stamped away.

The trap rose while the doeskin larder curtain still swayed from Snorri's passage. "You can come up," Helga whispered. "Be quick. You've only got a minute."

"How'd you know?"

"Ssh. Hurry up. Hjarlma, Bjorn and three others are by the big fireplace. They've been drinking and grumbling because your father has taken so long." Her face darkened when Haaken closed the trap. Bragi had watched her hope die by degrees as each man came up. "Three more are sleeping in the loft. Hjarlma sent the rest out to look for your camp. He expects you to come in just before dawn."

The others prepared to charge. She touched Bragi, then Haaken. "Be careful. Don't lose me everything."

Helga was rare in many ways, not the least of which was that she had borne only one child in a land where women were always pregnant.

She held Bragi a moment. "Did he die well?"

He hated the misdirection. "Stabbed in the back. By Bjorn."

Emotion distorted her features momentarily. And in that instant Bragi glimpsed what others feared. The fires of Hell shown through her eyes.

"Go!" she ordered.

Heart pounding, Bragi led the charge. Fifteen feet separated him from his enemies. Three rebels had no chance to defend themselves. But Hjarlma was as quick as death and Bjorn only a split second slower. The Thane rose like a killer whale from the deeps, dumped a table in Bragi's path, hurled himself to where Ragnar's battle trophies hung. He seized an axe.

Regaining his feet, Bragi realized that the surprise was spent. Hjarlma and Bjorn were ready to fight. Haaken, Sigurd and Soren were already in the loft. That left only himself and Sturla Ormsson, a man well past his prime, to face two of Trolledyngja's most wicked fighters.

"The cub's as mad as his sire," Hjarlma observed, turning a swordstroke with ease. "Don't get yourself killed, boy. Inger would never forgive me." His remark was a sad commentary on the nature of Man. Had the Old King not died unexpectedly, Hjarlma would have become Bragi's father-in-law. The arrangements had been made last summer.

Don't think, Bragi told himself. Don't listen. Old Sven and his father had beaten those lessons into him with blunted swords. Don't talk back. Either remain absolutely silent or, as Ragnar did, bellow a lot.

Hjarlma knew Ragnar's style well. They had fought side by side too many times. He handled it easily in the Wolf's son.

Bragi entertained no illusions. The Thane was bigger, stronger, craftier and had far more experience than he. His sole goal became to survive till Haaken had finished in the loft.

Sturla had the same idea, but Bjorn was too quick for him. The traitor's blade broke through his guard. He staggered back.

Two pairs of ice-blue eyes stared into Bragi's own.

"Kill the pup," Bjorn growled. His fear was plain to hear.

As stately as one of the caravels the longships pursued down the southern coasts, Helga glided between them.

"Stand aside, witch woman."

Helga locked gazes with the Thane. Her lips moved without speaking. Hjarlma did not back down, but neither did he press. She turned to Bjorn. The traitor went pale, could not meet her terrible eyes.

Haaken jumped from the loft, snatched a spear from a far wall. Soren and Sigurd came down by the ladder, but nearly as fast.

"Time has run out," Hjarlma observed laconically. "We have to go." He directed Bjorn to the door. "Should've expected them to slip the picket." He whipped his axe past Helga, struck the sword from Bragi's hand, creased the youth's cheek on the backstroke. "Be more civil when I return, boy. Or be gone."

Bragi sighed as the wings of death withdrew. Hjarlma had done all he dared because of old friendship.

The fear of Ragnar haunted Bjorn's eyes throughout the encounter. He kept looking round as if expecting the Wolf to materialize out of fireplace smoke. He was eager to flee. He and Hjarlma plunged into the night, where the snow had begun to fall again.

Helga started tending Bragi's cheek and berating him for not having killed Bjorn.

"Bjorn hasn't escaped the storm yet," Bragi told her.

Haaken, Soren and Sigurd lingered near the doorway. They kept it open a crack. The women, children and old folks of the stead, who had done their best to remain invisible during the skirmish, tended Sturla or wept softly for those who had not returned.

There was no joy in Ragnar's longhouse, only the numbness that follows disaster.

Draukenbring had come to the end of its years, but the realization of that fact had not yet struck home. The survivors faced uprooting, diaspora and persecution by the Pretender's adherents.

The falling snow muted the cries and clanging of weapons, but not completely. "There," Bragi told his mother. One of his father's howling war cries had torn the belly out of the night.

Ragnar soon staggered through the doorway, bloody from chin to knee. Much was his own. He had his stomach opened by an axe stroke.

With a peal of mad laughter he held Bjorn's head high, like a lantern in the night. Bjorn's horror remained fixed on his features.

Ragnar mouthed one of his battle cries, then collapsed.

Bragi, Haaken and Helga were beside him instantly. But it was too late. His will had, finally, broken.

Helga plucked at the ice in his hair and beard, ran fingers lightly over his face. A tear dribbled down her cheek. Bragi and Haaken withdrew. Even in her loss the plunder-bride from the south could not shed her pride, could not reveal the real depth of her feelings.

Bragi and Haaken crowded the main fire, and shared their misery.

The funeral was managed in haste. It was an expediency, unworthy of the dead man, rushed because Hjarlma would return. It should have been a warrior's funeral with pyres and ricks, following a week of mourning and ritual.

Instead, Bragi, Haaken, Sigurd and Soren carried Ragnar up Kamer Strotheide, above the tree- and summer snow-lines, and placed him, seated upright, in a stone cairn facing both Draukenbring and the more distant Tonderhofn.

"Someday," Bragi promised as he and Haaken placed the last stone. "Someday we'll come back and do it right."

"Someday," Haaken agreed.

It would be a long tomorrow, they knew.

They shed their tears, alone together there, then went down the mountain to begin the new life.

"This is how he managed it," said Helga, while watching her sons chop at the frozen earth by the broken hearthstone. She held a golden bracelet, slim but ornately wrought. "It's half of a pair. Hjarlma wore the other. Each reacted to the other's approach. When Bjorn drew close, Hjarlma realized that Ragnar was coming."

Bragi grunted. He did not care now.

"I think I hit it," Haaken said.

Bragi started digging with his hands. He soon exposed a small chest.

Sigurd and Soren arrived with the packs. The four surviving warriors would go south from the shingle pine.

The chest proved to be shallow and light. It was not locked. Little lay within. A small bag of southern coins, another of gemstones, an ornate dagger, a small parchment scroll on which a crude map had been inscribed hastily. And a copper amulet.

"You keep the valuables," Bragi told his mother.

"No. Ragnar had his reasons for keeping these things together. And of treasure he left me plenty elsewhere."

Bragi considered. His father had been secretive. The forest round Draukenbring might be filled with pots of gold. "All right." He pushed the things into his pack.

Then came the moment he had dreaded, the time to take the first southward step. He stared at his mother. She stared at him. Haaken stared at the ground.

The cord was hard to cut.

For the first time in memory Helga revealed her feelings in public—though she did not exactly go to pieces.

She pulled Haaken to her, held him for nearly two minutes, whispering. Bragi caught the sparkling of a tear. She brushed it away irritably as she released her foster son. Embarrassed, Bragi looked away. But there was no evading emotion. Sigurd and Soren were, once again, parting with their own families.

His mother's embrace engulfed him. She held him tighter than he had thought possible. She had always seemed so small and frail.

"Be careful," she said. And what less banal was there to say? At such a parting, probably forever, there were no words to convey true feelings. Language was the tool of commerce, not love.

"And take care of Haaken. Bring him home." No doubt she had told Haaken the same thing. She pulled away, unclasped a locket she had worn for as long as Bragi could remember. She fastened it round his neck. "If you have no other hope, take this to the House of Bastanos in the Street of the Dolls in Hellin Daimiel. Give it to the concierge, as an introduction to the lord of that house. He'll send it inside. One of the partners will come to question you. Tell him:

> *'Elhabe an dantice, elhabe an cawine.*
> *Ci hibde clarice, elhabe an savan.*
> *Ci magden trebil, elhabe din bachel.'*

He'll understand."

She made him repeat the verse till she was sure he had memorized it.

"Good. No more can be done. Just don't trust anyone you don't have to. And come home as soon as you can. I'll be here waiting."

She kissed him. In public. She had not done that since he had been a toddler. Then she kissed Haaken. She had never done that at all. Before either could react, she ordered, "Now go. While you can. Before we look more foolish than we already do."

Bragi shouldered his pack and started toward Kamer Strotheide. Their way led round its knee. Sometimes he looked up toward Ragnar's cairn. Only once did he look back.

The women and children and old people were abandoning the steading that had been home to generations. Most would flee to relatives elsewhere. A lot of people were on the move during these times of trouble. They should be able to disappear and elude the spite of the Pretender's men.

He wondered where his mother would go. . . .

Forever afterward he wished that, like Haaken, he had refused to look. He could, then, have remembered Draukenbring as a place alive, as a last hope and refuge quietly awaiting him in the northland.

Chapter Four

A Clash of Sabers

Nassef looked back once. Heat waves made the bowl of Al Rhemish a tent city writhing beneath dancing ghosts. A muted roar echoed from the valley. He smiled. "Karim," he called gently.

A hard-looking man whose face had been scarred by the pox joined him. "Sir?"

"Go back down there. Visit our people. The ones who met us when we came in. Tell them to keep the riots going. Tell them I need an extended distraction. And tell them to pick five hundred willing warriors and send them after us. In small groups, so they're not noticed leaving. Understand?"

"Yes." Karim smiled. He was missing two front teeth. Another was broken at an angle. He was an old rogue. He had seen his battles. Even his gray-speckled beard seemed war lorn.

Nassef watched Karim descend the stony slope. The former bandit was one of their more valuable converts. Nassef was sure Karim's value would increase as the struggle widened and became more bitter.

He swung his mount and trotted after his sister and brother-in-law.

El Murid's party consisted of almost fifty people. Most were bodyguards, his white-robed Invincibles, who had been guaranteed a place in Paradise if they died in El Murid's behalf.

They made Nassef uneasy. They had eyes madder than those of their prophet. They were fanatically devoted. El Murid had had to bend the full might of his will to keep them from storming the Royal Compound after the trial.

Nassef assumed his post at El Murid's right hand. "It

went better than we hoped," he said. "The boy's attack was a godsend."

"Indeed it was. To tell the truth, Nassef, I was reluctant to do it your way. But only the intercession of the Lord Himself could have made it so easy. Only He could have brought about an attack so timely."

"I'm sorry about the ankle. Does it bother you much?"

"It pains me terribly. But I can endure it. Yassir gave me an herbal for the pain, and bound it. If I stay off it, I'll be good as new before long."

"During that farce of a trial . . . For a minute I thought you were going to give in."

"For a minute I did. I'm as subject as anyone else to the wiles of the Evil One. But I found my strength, and the lapse made the outcome sweeter. You see how the Lord moves us to His will? We do His work even when we think we're turning our backs on Him."

Nassef stared across the barren hills. Finally, he replied, "It's hard to accept a defeat hoping it will yield a greater victory someday. My friend, my prophet, they signed their death warrants today."

"I'm no prophet, Nassef. Just a disciple of the Lord's Way. And I want no deaths that can be avoided. Even King Aboud and the High Priests may someday seek the path of righteousness."

"Of course. I was speaking figuratively. Saying that by their actions they have doomed their cause."

"It is often thus with the minions of the Evil One. The more they struggle, the more they contribute to the Lord's work. What about the raid? Are you *sure* we can pull it off?"

"I sent Karim back to Al Rhemish. If our people do what we ask, if they keep the riots going and send us five hundred warriors, we can. There'll be no one to stop us. All the lords came to Al Rhemish to see our humiliation. The riots will occupy them through Mashad. We'll have a week's lead."

"I just wish we could have christened the baby."

"That was a pity. We'll return, Lord. We'll see it done, some Mashad. I promise it."

For once Nassef's words burned with total sincerity, with absolute conviction.

The by-ways of the desert were long, lonely and slow, especially for a man apart from other men. There was no one for El Murid to confide in, to dream with, except Meryem. The Invincibles were too much in awe of him, too worshipful. Nassef and his handful of followers remained engrossed in their scheming against tomorrow. The riders who overtook them, coming from Al Rhemish by tens and twenties, were all strangers. The fast friends who had been his first converts, the others who had come with him out of El Aquila, were all dead, sainted.

Nassef's struggles on his behalf took their toll.

The Disciple rode beside the white camel, his child in his lap. "She's such a peaceful, tiny thing," he marveled. "A miracle. The Lord has been good to us, Meryem." He winced.

"Your ankle?"

"Yes."

"You'd better let me take her back, then."

"No. These moments are too rare already. And they're going to become rarer still." After a minute alone with his thoughts, "How long will it be before I can set aside my staff?"

"What do you mean?"

"How long before our success is achieved? How long till I can settle down and lead a normal life with you and her? We've been riding these hidden trails for three years. It seems like thirty."

"Never, my love. Never. And as a wife I loathe to admit it. But when the angel spoke to you, you became El Murid for all time. So long as the Lord sees fit to leave you among the living, that long must you remain the Disciple."

"I know. I know. It's just the mortal within me wishing for something it can't have."

They rode without speaking for a while. Then El Murid said, "Meryem, I'm lonely. I don't have anyone but you."

"You have half the desert. Who brings us food and water from the settlements? Who carries the Truth into provinces we've never seen?"

"I mean a friend. A simple, ordinary, personal friend. Somebody I can just play with, as I did when I was a child. Somebody I can talk to. Somebody who can share the fears and hopes of a man, not somebody smitten by the dreams of El Murid. Surely you've felt the same things since Fata died."

"Yes. Being the woman of El Murid is lonely, too." After a time, "But you have Nassef."

"Nassef is your brother. I won't speak ill of him to you. I do love him as if he were my own brother. I forgive him like a brother. But we'll never be real friends, Meryem. We'll just be allies."

Meryem did not argue. She knew it was true. Nassef, too, had no one else in whom to confide. No friendship would blossom between her husband and brother while they remained unsure of each other.

It had been a long, hard ride. In the end, Nassef had pushed hard. Everyone was tired except Nassef himself, who seemed immune to fatigue.

"There it is," El Murid whispered in wonder. He forgot the pain in his ankle. "Sebil el Selib."

The light of a three-quarters moon illuminated the mountain-flanked meadow which was second only to Al Rhemish in the hearts of the Children of Hammad al Nakir. Long ago, it had been second only to Ilkazar in the hearts of their Imperial ancestors.

A very old fortress overlooked the meadow, and the shrine and cloisters it contained. There were no lights to be seen anywhere.

The name Sebil el Selib meant Path of the Cross. It had come into being because of the event memorialized by the shrine.

It was in that meadow that, on the first day of the Year 1 in the common dating, the Empire had been born. The first emperor had made himself secure in his power by crucifying a thousand opponents there. The path of the name was the trail winding through the pass, along which the doomed nobles had had to bear the instruments of their destruction. From the meadow that trail wound on, connecting the old Inner Provinces with the cities along the coast of the Sea of Kotsüm.

The weathered fortress, dating from the early Imperial era, guarded the pass, not the shrine and cloisters over which it brooded.

"Here the father of our dream found life," El Murid told Nassef. "Here the First Empire was born. Let our own gasp its first breath on the same bedclothing."

Nassef said nothing. He was looking with awe on a place drenched with history. It seemed too plain, too simple, to be so important.

Al Rhemish had given him the same feeling.

It amazed him that ordinary places could, in time, attain such a hold on men's imaginations.

"Nassef."

"Yes?"

"Are we ready?"

"Yes. Karim will take the Invincibles down first. They'll scale the walls and open the gate to the rest. I'll send smaller forces to seize the shrine and cloisters."

"Nassef?"

"I hear you."

"I'm no warrior. No general. I am but the instrument of the Lord. But I'd like to make a small adjustment to your plan. I'd like you to close the road to the coast. And to leave a detachment with me. I don't want anyone to escape."

Nassef thought that he had misunderstood. El Murid was always after him to spare and forgive their enemies.

"I thought about it all the way here. The Lord has no friends in this place. They're soldiers of the King and acolytes of the false path. Moreover, a clear, unequivocal message has to be sent to those who yield to the seductions of the Evil One. Last night I prayed for guidance, and it came to me that our Second Empire must also have its birth in the blood of its enemies, on the site where the First Empire was born."

Nassef was surprised, but not dismayed. "As you say, so shall it be."

"Slay them all, Nassef. Even to the babes in arms. Let no man, from this day forth, think that he can evade the wrath of the Lord."

"As you say."

"You may begin." But before Nassef had taken a dozen steps, El Murid called, "Nassef."

"Yes?"

"In this moment, before the armed struggle begins, I name you my war captain. I entitle you Scourge of God. Wear the title well."

"I will. Have no fear."

The attack went forth with the speed and precision that

had become hallmarks of Nassef's caravan raids. Many of the fortress's garrison died in their bedrolls.

El Murid sat his horse on the elevation and awaited fugitives or news. In his heart he nursed a black seed of fear. If he failed here, if the defenders of the fortress drove him away, then his mission might never recover. Nothing impressed the men of the desert so much as boldness and success. Nothing daunted them so much as failure.

No fugitives came. Neither did any news till, as dawn began coloring the sky over the mountains before him, Nassef's man Karim rode up.

"My Lord Disciple," said Karim, "your war captain sends me to report that the fortress, shrine and all cloisters are in our hands. Our enemies have been gathered in the meadow. He begs you to come accept them as a gift of his love."

"Thank you, Karim. Tell him I'm on my way."

Nassef awaited him on a knoll overlooking the captives. There were at least two thousand of them. Many were from the fortress, but most were from the cloisters, innocent pilgrims who had come here to celebrate Disharhun and who had not yet departed for their homes.

The garrison had been a large one. The only other useful pass through Jebal al Alf Dhulquarneni lay hundreds of miles to the north. The Hidden Ones permitted passage at no other points. The defense was big because the passage taxes were important to the Crown.

The stronghold's defenders lived their entire lives there. Some of the garrison families went back to imperial times. Women and children lived in the castle with the men.

El Murid looked down on the captives. They looked up at him. Few recognized him till Meryem, veilless, on her white camel, came up beside him. They began to buzz in excitement. An officer of the garrison shouted something placatory, offering his men's parole. El Murid peered at him. He searched his heart for mercy. He could find none. He gave Nassef the signal to begin.

The horsemen rode round the prisoners, chopping with their sabers. The prisoners screamed. They tried to run. There was nowhere to go except to climb atop one another. Some dashed through the circle of death, only to be ridden down by pickets awaiting them outside. A few warriors hurled themselves at the horsemen, trying to make a brave end.

Thus it was that a man named Beloul escaped the massacre.

He was one of the under officers of the garrison, a man about Nassef's age. He came of a family which traced its roots well back into the imperial era. Fighting like a demon, Beloul seized both horse and sword, then cut his way through the pickets. He bluffed a charge toward El Murid. While the Invincibles rushed to protect their prophet, he galloped through the pass into the desert.

Nassef sent four men after him. None ever returned.

Beloul carried the news to el Aswad. Messengers immediately streaked from the Wahlig's castle.

"Is this really necessary?" Meryem asked when the slaughter was halfway done.

"I think so. I think my enemies . . . the enemies of the Lord will find it instructive."

It took longer than he expected, and eventually proved more than he could stomach. He turned away when the Invincibles dismounted to drag the corpses of mothers aside to get at the children they had shielded with their bodies. "Let's look at the shrine," he said. "I want to see my throne."

Nassef came to report while he knelt, praying, before the Malachite Throne.

Ancient artisans had sculpted that seat from the boulder on which the first emperor had sat while watching the crucifixions of his enemies. It was the second most potent power symbol in Hammad al Nakir. Only the Peacock Throne, salvaged from the ruins of Ilkazar and transported to Al Rhemish, had a greater hold on men's minds.

Nassef waited patiently. When El Murid completed his prayers, his war captain told him, "It's done. I've ordered the men to rest. In a few hours I'll begin the burying. Tonight I'll send scouts back into the desert."

El Murid frowned. "Why?"

"We're within the domains of the Wahlig of el Aswad. They say he's decisive and smart. He'll attack us as soon as he hears what's happened."

"You know him?"

"By sight. So do you. That was his son who attacked you

in Al Rhemish. Yousif was the one who arranged our trial."

"I remember him. A thin, cruel-faced man. Eyes of jet, and hard as diamonds. A true champion of the Evil One."

"My Lord Disciple, do you realize what we've accomplished today?" A sudden awe filled Nassef's voice.

"We captured the Malachite Throne."

"And more. Much, much more. Today we became a major power in Hammad al Nakir. Because of the Throne, and its location. So long as we hold Sebil el Selib, we're a factor they have to reckon in every decision they make at Al Rhemish. So long as we hold this pass we virtually isolate the desert provinces from the coast of the Sea of Kotsüm. We deny Aboud all the strength and wealth of the coast in his struggle to defy the will of the Lord."

Nassef was right. The seacoast was the one area of the core Empire that had not suffered heavily during the Fall. It had not become a wasteland. In modern times its cities were virtually autonomous, though they shared the language and cultural roots of Hammad al Nakir. They paid lip service and tributary fealty to King Aboud and the Quesani, mainly so their wild cousins of the desert would leave them alone. Politically, they had little to gain by opposing El Murid, and would come up losers if they supported him.

If they did and he failed, they would have won the hatred of the ruling Quesani family. If they supported him and he succeeded, they would be expected to squander their wealth and manpower in his holy war against the infidel states surrounding Hammad al Nakir.

They could be counted on, for a while, to remain outside the power equation. Nassef's selection of Sebil el Selib as his first target had been the best possible.

Geopolitics and economics aside, the seizure should have a strong psychological effect. Thousands should turn to El Murid. Other thousands should cool toward the Royal cause.

"I have one question, Nassef. Can we keep what we've won?"

"These men will die for you."

"I know that. It doesn't answer my question. There's a field full of men who died for Aboud outside. They didn't hold the pass."

"We won't be taken by surprise."

Nassef was only half right. The Wahlig of el Aswad responded quicker than he expected.

The pickets had scarcely gone out when one on a lathered horse returned to say that several hundred horsemen were right behind him.

They swooped down from the northwest. Nassef had expected to be attacked from el Aswad, so had distributed his pickets and skirmishers to the southwest. But Yousif had heard about Sebil el Selib while coming home from Al Rhemish. He had decided to strike back immediately, using his escort.

The swift strike, the sneak attack, the hit and run, were traditional desert warfare, founded on centuries of tribal feuding.

Yousif arrived long before the pickets could be recalled, thereby denying Nassef a quarter of his strength.

Fighting raged through the pass and down into the meadow. Yousif's warriors were skilled and disciplined household troops who spent their lives in training and maneuver. The Wahlig was a master of light cavalry technique. He pushed Nassef's larger force into the fortress and cloisters.

El Murid and his Invincibles became isolated in the shrine, defending the Malachite Throne. As soon as he learned the Disciple's whereabouts, Yousif concentrated on the shrine. He wanted the serpent's head.

Facing the Wahlig across twenty feet of bloody floor, El Murid shouted, "We will die before we yield one inch, Hell serf. Though your master send up all the devils of his fiery abode. . . . Yea, though he hurl against us all the legions of the damned, we will not be dismayed. The Lord is with us. Ours is the confidence of the righteous, the assurance of the saved."

A big, muscular man said to the Wahlig, "I'll be damned. Yousif, he really believes that drivel."

"Of course he does, Fuad. Belief in himself is what makes a maniac dangerous."

El Murid was puzzled. Could they doubt his sincerity? The Truth was the Truth. They could accept or refuse it, but never brand it a lie.

"Slay them," he told the Invincibles, though they were grossly outnumbered.

The Lord would deliver them.

His fanatics attacked like hunger-maddened wolves. Yousif's warriors went down like wheat before the scythe. The Wahlig himself went to his knees with a grievous wound. His troops wavered.

Fuad rallied them with his war cries. His scimitar flickered like a mirage, so swiftly did it cut and stab.

The Invincibles did as El Murid said. They held each inch they had taken.

They did not yield, but they died.

Gingerly, still believing that the Lord would deliver him, El Murid descended from the Malachite Throne. He collected a fallen blade.

Now the Invincibles were falling like scythed wheat. El Murid began to doubt. . . . He would not! Were he to be martyred here, it would be the will of the Lord.

His sole regret was that he might leave this pale without seeing Meryem and his daughter again. They were trapped in the fortress with Nassef. . . .

But Nassef was trapped no longer. Yousif's assault on the shrine had given him time to organize. He went over to the attack. His sally scattered Yousif's forces on the meadow.

He, Karim and a score of their best burst into the shrine. The tide of fighting shifted.

"God is merciful!" El Murid thundered, daring to cross blades with a warrior. The man struck the weapon from his hand.

Nassef was there in an instant, turning the warrior's attack.

Fuad hurled that warrior aside and faced Nassef. "Let's see the color of your guts, bandit."

Nassef attacked. He wore a thin, cruel, confident smile.

Their blades danced a deadly morisco. Neither could penetrate the other's guard. Each seemed astonished by the other's skill.

"Fuad. Fuad," Yousif gasped from between supporting warriors. "Break off."

Fuad stepped back, wiped sweat from his face. "Let me finish him."

"We have to go. While we still have the strength to rescue our wounded."

"Yousif—"

"Now, Fuad. They've beaten us. All we can do here is die. And there'd be no point to that. Come on."

"Next time, bandit," Fuad growled. "I've seen the weakness in your style." He spit in Nassef's face.

The desert people could be demonstrative. Especially in matters of hatred and war.

"You won't live long enough to take advantage, son of a jackal." When Nassef reached a certain level of anger he achieved an icy self-control. He had done so now. Clearly, for the benefit of everyone present, he said, "Karim. Put an assassin into el Aswad. Let this heap of camel dung be the target. You. Hell serf Fuad. You think about that. Wonder when he—or she—will strike." He smiled his thin, cruel smile. "Karim. They wish to depart. Let them run like the whipped dogs they are. Let us amuse ourselves with the sight of them running with their tails between their legs."

Once the enemy had departed, El Murid sighed, limped back up and collapsed into the Malachite Throne. "That was close, Nassef."

"Too close. Why didn't you use the amulet? You could have destroyed one of our worst enemies."

El Murid raised his arm. He stared at the glowing jewel. He had not called on its power since his demonstration at El Aquila. The people of the el Habib were still talking about the day that he had restored their dry oasis.

"It didn't occur to me. It truly didn't. I suppose the Lord touched me, telling me that you were coming. I never doubted our victory."

"As you say, it worked out. And as long as you don't use it, they won't be reminded. They won't be trying to find ways to counter it."

"Why did you tell Karim to let them go?"

"We've lost too many men. There's no sense spending more lives after we've won. They'll be back, stronger than this time. We'll need every man then."

"What was that about an assassin?"

"A ploy. Let them become afraid to turn their backs on each other. Let them become frightened of shadows. Let fear sap their strength and will."

"How clever you are. Nassef, my brother, don't you ever speak without first calculating some long-term effect for your words?"

"With my friends. Isn't it one of your teachings that words are the mightiest weapons of the Kingdom of Peace?"

"That's true. Words of Truth. But, Nassef, sometimes I think you're mocking me. Even when you save my life . . ."

Nassef stared at the floor. "Forgive me, my Lord Disciple. It's my manner, my way of speaking. It's a curse. When I was little I couldn't tease the other children. I couldn't tell jokes. They always took me seriously. And when I was serious, they thought I was sneering."

"What are we to do now, Nassef? We have the Malachite Throne. We have Sebil el Selib. And that will bring all the enemies of the Lord upon us."

"We can defend ourselves and trust in the Lord. I'll send messengers to our supporters asking for warriors and arms. I'll strengthen our defenses. We'll erect another fortress here. The Throne has to be protected too."

"You're right. Nassef, I'm afraid we'll be here a long time. Sebil el Selib is a trap in a way. It's given us two astonishing victories, but to survive we'll have to hang on to what we've taken. I'm afraid they'll simply bottle us up here."

"They'll try. But they'll never manage it completely. Their own system will work against them. As long as they can summon the tribal levies for only forty-five days a year, we'll pretty much be free to come and go the rest of the time. Assuming I receive your blessing, I plan to have partisan bands hitting and running wherever we have willing converts. That'll keep the full-time warriors busy elsewhere. It'll give us a chance to build our foundation here."

El Murid peered at him thoughtfully. After a time he observed, "You seem to have your plans thoroughly worked out."

"I've lain awake during a lot of lonely nights these three years, Lord."

"I suppose you have. When are you going to take a wife, Nassef?"

Nassef was taken aback. "I haven't considered it. After we've established the Kingdom of Peace, maybe."

El Murid peered at him again. "Nassef, I'm tired. Tonight and tomorrow we rest. The next day we resume our work. You, your wars. Me, my preparations for the Kingdom they will establish. I'll want you to find me scribes and architects. I want to set down a code of laws, and I want a special palace built to house the Malachite Throne. Also, I want to erect a stele in the meadow. On it I'll inscribe the names of the faithful who fall in the Lord's cause, that their names be immortal both here and in Paradise."

"As you say. I like the stele. Perhaps if you set aside the top for the Invincibles?"

"Yes. Have somebody remember the names of everyone who died here. They'll be the first inscribed."

Later, before he retired, El Murid led Meryem, and carried his daughter, to the highest rampart of the old fortress. "My loves," he said, "one tiny splinter of the dream has come to life. The Kingdom of Peace exists, although its bounds lie no farther than I can see. Someday all the earth will acknowledge the Lord."

Cradling the baby in his left arm, he slipped his right around Meryem's waist. She leaned against him, shivering in the cool mountain breeze.

"Come," she said after a time. "Let me remind you that you're also a man." She smiled up at him. The spoiled brat of the el Habib had grown into a woman who loved him as a man.

That night they conceived a boy-child.

Chapter Five

A Fortress in Shadow

Megelin Radetic walked the stony slopes below the tired walls of el Aswad, the Eastern Fortress. Haroun tagged along, scattering his attention as small boys will, yet clinging to the one adult who had time for him. A scarred old veteran dogged them both, his sword always in hand.

Haroun had not spoken for days. He had become lost inside his own young mind. Now, at least, he chose to speak, as Radetic paused to stare out across the sere, inhospitable land. "Megelin, is Father going to die?"

"I don't think so. The physicians are hopeful."

"Megelin?"

"What?" It was time to be gentle. He knelt.

"Why did he kill them? The pilgrims at the shrine."

Radetic resumed walking. "I don't know. If anyone but El Murid had given the order, I'd guess for spite."

They moved round the flank of the mountain. On its eastern face they encountered Haroun's brother Ali. Ali was seated on a boulder. He stared at Jebal al Alf Dhulquarneni, as if his thoughts might conjure the Hidden Ones from their secret strongholds.

Radetic stared too. He wondered what the wizards of the mountains thought of recent events. Presumably they would pursue tradition and ignore their neighbors. They had been up there since time immemorial. They bothered no one who did not bring them trouble. Even the mighty Empire had let them be, and they had remained aloof from its death throes.

Haroun murmured, "Megelin, I'm afraid."

Ali started to make a cutting remark.

"He's right, Ali. It's a time for fear. We have to fear Nassef for his sword, and El Murid for his Word. They make a deadly combination. And we must fear this, too: that the Sword might become master of the Word, rather than the reverse. Go, then, and try to capture the whirlwind."

Ali frowned. Old Radetic was in one of his ambiguous moods.

Ali was cast more in the mold of his uncle than of his brother or father. He was no thinker. Haroun understood Radetic plainly.

Yousif had reached el Aswad only hours behind the returning family caravan. His force had been savaged, and he had come within a mouse's whisker of death.

The caravan had not come through unscathed. Yousif had left no guards. Disorganized bands of Nassef's pickets had tried their luck plundering.

Even Megelin Radetic had taken up arms in the running fight.

He gripped his left bicep. He had taken a light saber slash. The wound still ached.

He smiled. How he had amazed his assailant with his counterattack!

Fuad still could not assimilate the fact that his brother's tame intellectual knew which end of a sword to grab. Nor did he know what to make of the fact that the teacher had taken charge of old men, boys, women and camel drovers and had whipped hell out of tough young warriors.

Radetic found his incredulity amusing. He had told Fuad, "We study more than flowers at the Rebsamen." The remark referred to Fuad's bewilderment the time when he had discovered that Megelin was cataloging and making color drawings of desert wildflowers.

Ali descended from his perch. "Megelin?"

"Yes?"

"I'm scared too."

"We all are, Ali."

Ali glared at Haroun. "If you tell, I'll pound you."

Haroun snatched up a jagged rock. "Come on, Ali."

"Boys. Save it for El Murid."

"He asking for it," Haroun replied.

"You little snot—"

"I said knock it off. Haroun, come on. Ali was here first."

Ali stuck out his tongue.

Radetic strolled away wondering what Haroun did fear. People did not intimidate him. "Let's go back to the castle, Haroun. It's time we did a little studying."

El Aswad was a regional name which popular usage also applied to its capital fortress. The Imperial builders of the original featureless square stronghold had called it the "Eastern Fortress." Under the Empire it had been the headquarters of a major military command.

The castle was bigger now, though less important. Every generation did a little something to make it more impregnable. Rounded towers had been added to the original walls. Curtain walls and supporting towers had been appended to its north side, enclosing the whole of the mountaintop. Still farther north, connected to the main castle by the curtains, commanding the mountain's most gentle slope, stood a massive square sub-fortress.

The other three faces of the mountain were barren, rocky, and often precipitous. The surface rock was soft and loose. Weather had been gnawing away for ages. Tortuously curved layers of sedimentary rock showed the progress of ancient ages. The children of Yousif's courtiers and soldiers loved scrounging the slopes for fossils, for which Radetic paid a candy bounty.

Radetic found the castle a miserable place to live. It was either too cold and drafty, or too hot and stuffy. The roofs and walls leaked during the rare rains. The sanitary facilities were primitive, and furniture virtually non-existent. There was not one bath in the entire place. Hellin Daimiel was known for its communal baths. The only closable door he had ever seen was the one barring entry into the women's quarters.

He often longed for the comfort and privacy of his tiny apartment at the university.

Despite its drawbacks as a home, the castle served its intended function. Its granaries, cisterns and arsenals could support its garrison almost indefinitely. It commanded a view of vast territories. It had never been conquered by siege or storm.

Radetic paused at the gate and surveyed the miles of stony land surrounding the fortress. "Haroun, you know what I'd like to look out there and see? Just once? A tree."

Weeks passed. Fuad sent out a summons to the tribal

levies. On the morning they were to muster, Haroun wakened his teacher. "What do you want?" Radetic growled, squinting one-eyed at the dawn light crawling through his apartment window. "Better be good. No normal human being ought to be up at this hour."

"Uncle Fuad is going to meet the levies. I thought you'd want to be there."

Radetic groaned, swung his legs out of bed. "Want to? No. You've seen one mob of fellahin, you've seen them all. But I suppose I'd better go, if only to keep your uncle from doing anything he'll regret. How many showed up?" He had had doubts that a call from Fuad would elicit the same response as a call from the Wahlig.

Haroun looked disappointed. "Not good. But they're still coming in. Maybe some were delayed."

"Uh? Pretty bad, eh? Here. Hand me those sandals."

The levies were assembling on the slope leading to el Aswad's main gate. Not all had arrived, as Haroun had said, but the few dust clouds approaching indicated that Fuad would be disappointed by the response to his call. "Not a third of what he has a right to expect," Megelin observed.

"Some of those eaters of camel droppings have gone over to the bandits." Fuad had come out. He scowled at the assembling host. "Cowardice is spreading like the pox."

Radetic replied, "I wouldn't think them that fickle."

"They are, fishwife. And those that haven't deserted are hiding in their tents like old women, afraid to take a stand. Their excuse to my brother will be that he didn't issue the call himself. I ought to ride out and punish them. Bloody crones."

"Maybe you ought to wait a few days," Radetic suggested. "Send another round of messengers and have them talk tough."

"What good will that do? They want to hide behind their women's skirts, let them. I'll mock them when I return with El Murid's head on my lance. Beloul! Assemble the sheiyeks."

The captain Beloul inclined his head and descended the slope. He passed among the contingents. Chieftains started uphill by twos and threes. Fuad did not greet any of them warmly, though he knew them all and had been riding with them for years. His black scowl compelled them to hold their tongues and keep their distance.

When the last arrived, joining the circle surrounding Fuad, Radetic, Haroun and Fuad's officiers, Fuad turned slowly. "So this is it. Only you have the guts to face these boy bandits. Taha. Rifaa. Qaboos. All of you. I promise you my brother will remember this. And he'll not forget the faces we don't see here today."

Someone suggested, "Maybe we ought to give the others more time."

"More time, Feras? Will the Disciple give *us* more time? No! We strike. No game. No subtleties. We hit them like a hammer. And we bring their heads back to decorate the walls. Every motherlorn one."

Radetic muttered, "Fierce this morning, aren't we?"

Fuad rewarded him with an ugly look. "You'll find out fierce, teacher. Keep nagging. Beloul. Order the column according to plan. Just drop the places of the cowards who didn't show."

"Fuad," Radetic whispered, "I really think you ought to reconsider this."

"We ride when the column is in order," Fuad countered. "There will be no more discussion. We will be victorious or we will fail. I wouldn't want to be in the sandals of those cowards if we fail and I survive. Get away from me, teacher. You don't have anything to tell me."

Hours later Megelin watched the column pass out of sight. "I did what I could, Haroun. But he's too damned stubborn to hear reason."

"You don't think he'll win?"

Radetic shrugged. "Anything is possible. Maybe he'll get lucky."

A messenger located Megelin in his classroom two days after Fuad's departure. "The Lord Yousif has awakened. He asks your attendance."

Radetic was irritated by the interruption, but could not ignore the summons. "Ali. I'm leaving you in charge while I see your father. Keep on with the lesson."

Outside, the messenger chuckled. "You set them a grim taskmaster."

"I know. It's the only way I can get him to learn anything.

He doesn't want his students thinking they're smarter than he is."

"Would that I had had such an opportunity when I was young."

"Ah." Radetic smiled gently. Yousif's subterfuge was working. Before children could be educated their elders had to be convinced that there was some point to education. "How is he?"

"Quite well, considering. But he's tough. This is a tough family. The desert has never been kind here."

"I can see that." Megelin had heard the same remark so often, even where the desert had been kind, that he suspected it was a homily.

Yousif was sitting up, arguing with a physician who wanted him to lie down. "Ah. Megelin. Here at last. Save me from the mercies of this old woman."

"The old woman probably knows more about what your body needs than you do, Wahlig."

"You all stick together, don't you? Well, no matter. Come here. Take one of these cushions. I can't use them all."

Radetic sat. He could not conceal his discomfort. He was too old to adapt to the desert custom of sitting cross-legged on cushions.

Yousif ignored his discomfort. "I've been away from this world a long time. It makes a man take stock. You know what I mean?"

"I think so, Wahlig."

"My first job in this second life is to get you to stop acting like a servant. We have things to talk about, Megelin. I think the first should be friendship."

"Wahlig?"

"You brought my caravan through."

"Nonsense."

"I've spoken with Muamar. We won't argue it. I'm grateful. It hadn't occurred to me that I might be leaving enemies behind me."

"My life was in danger, too."

"That's one way of looking at it. Whichever view you choose, my wives and children came through safely. I consider your effort an act of friendship. I do as I'm done by, Megelin."

Radetic could not stifle a wry smile. "Thank you." The gratitude of princes was notoriously short-lived.

"Megelin, you show expertise in surprising directions. I value a man who has skills beyond those demanded by his profession."

"Score a point for education."

"Indeed. Tell me. What do you think of Fuad's expedition?"

"I haven't been over the ground, except on the chicken tracks you call maps. He had a thousand men. Maybe he'll get lucky."

"He outnumbers them three or four to one."

"The numbers might be enough to make his hammer blows more convincing than Nassef's finesse. Your brother isn't a thinker."

"How well I know. Tell me, why are you so impressed with Nassef?"

"He has the subtle touch of genius. In a western context his threat to send an assassin to el Aswad would have been brilliant. Here it's a waste of inspiration."

"I don't see it. That was just talk by somebody who got spit on."

"That's the flaw in his subtlety."

"What?"

"There's no one here subtle enough to see the implications of the threat. Is the assassin here already? If not, how will he get in? And so on."

"You westerners are a devious race. We're more direct."

"I've noticed. But Nassef and El Murid are working on a different level. Their behavior betrays careful calculation. They occupied Sebil el Selib knowing your strength and probable response."

"Meaning?"

"Meaning they're confident they can hold it. There's no point in their taking something they can't keep. Not at this point in their growth."

"You give them too much credit."

"You don't give them enough. Despite everything you told me at Al Rhemish, you haven't really convinced yourself that these people are anything more than bandits led by a madman. Do you recall what you said? About El Murid selling the snake oil everyone wants to buy? I've reflected on that, and I think it's even truer than you know."

"What would you have me do?"

"There are a lot of possibilities." Radetic suggested several, all of which Yousif rejected as impractical or politically unfeasible. "Then be direct. Murder El Murid. People will scream, but they will forget quickly enough. And Nassef won't be able to survive without him. Not at this point."

"I plan to try. Assuming Fuad fails. You haven't given me a thing."

"I know I'm overlooking the financial and political difficulties. You asked for options. I laid out what I see. Hell, it's even remotely possible we could ignore them till they all die of indifference."

"Megelin, my recovery wasn't spontaneous. I've been lying here for two days, aching more in mind than in body. I've thought of it all. And the only workable option is to fight and hope we get lucky. If we can't get lucky, then we'll try to keep them contained."

"This is depressing. We're talking ourselves into accepting a defeat before the event."

"Drop it, then. Megelin?"

"Yes?"

"You can do one thing to brighten my life."

"Wahlig?"

"Stay here when your contract is up. I may need the outsider's viewpoint desperately before this is over."

Radetic was surprised. This was the first time ever that Yousif had treated him with more than minimal respect. "I'll consider it, Wahlig. I'd better go. I left Ali in charge of my class."

Yousif chuckled. "Yes, you'd better."

"I'm a political historian, Haroun," Megelin explained. "That's why I'm going to stay. Why I have to stay. I can't leave during the political storm of the century, can I?"

The boy seemed slightly disappointed. Radetic understood, but did not have it in him to lay out the true, emotional bases for lengthening his stay. He did not understand all his motives himself.

"You see, I'm the only one here at the heart of it. History is written by prejudiced parties, Haroun. By winners, usually. This is a unique opportunity to capture the truth."

Haroun looked at him sideways, wearing an amused little smile. After a moment, Megelin chuckled. "You devil. You see right through me, don't you?"

He had his excuse, though. It would be good enough to prolong his stay as grim weeks piled into months and years.

Haroun whipped into Megelin's room, almost falling as he swung through the door, almost overturning the little table where the scholar was pouring over his notes, inscribing one of his regular missives to a friend in Hellin Daimiel. "What is it, child?"

"Uncle Fuad is coming."

Radetic asked his next question by raising an eyebrow. Haroun understood. "No."

Radetic sighed, pushed his papers back. "I didn't think so. There would have been messengers carrying his brags. Let's go down to the gate."

The troops were dragging in when Radetic arrived. Megelin located Fuad. The Wahlig's brother was tired, deflated and had exhausted his stock of contrariness. He answered questions dully, frankly, apparently not caring how bad the answers might make him look. "Just get it down the way it happened, teacher," he muttered at one point. "Just write it up the way it happened. We came up one company short. One stinking company. One fresh company, in reserve, and we would have had them." Stalking toward his brother's quarters, he added, "One company from any one of those whoreson sheiyeks who didn't show at muster. There's going to be some new chieftains in el Aswad."

Three months later Yousif issued his own call to arms. It took Megelin by surprise. "Why?" he demanded. "And why didn't you tell me?" He was severely piqued because the Wahlig had not consulted him.

"Because," Yousif replied, donning a teasing grin. "Because I wanted to deal with your protests at one sitting, instead of endlessly."

Hardly mollified, Radetic demanded, "Why this hosting? That's the important question."

"Because I need to assert my primacy over the tribes. They need to be shown that I'm still strong, that I remain in command. We children of the desert are a lot like your forest wolves, Megelin. I'm the leader of the pack. If I stumble, if I reveal any weakness, if I hesitate, I'm lost. I have no desire to attack El Murid. The time isn't right, as you no doubt would have told me endlessly had you been informed earlier. But the eyes of a hundred chieftains are on el Aswad, waiting to see my response to my wounding and Fuad's defeat. Not to mention the turnout for Fuad's hosting."

Megelin now recalled the busy comings and goings of recent weeks, movements he hadn't thought significant at the time. Messengers, of course. But, too, he had seen several of Yousif's most devoted captains leading sizable patrols into the waste. Not one of those had as yet returned. "I presume your representatives will be in place when the call reaches certain sheiyeks of questionable devotion."

Yousif chuckled. "Gently put, teacher. And true."

"I suppose my wisest course is to keep my mouth shut, then. It's an ancient truism: what is logical and practical isn't always politic. And vice versa."

"Truer in this land than anywhere else, Megelin. Truer here than anywhere. How have my son's lessons been progressing?" He did not clarify which son. They understood one another plainly on that score.

Radetic searched for the right words. He decided he could do no better nor worse than to be straightforward. There were no witnesses. The Wahlig was tolerant in private. "I say it's a pity he wasn't born in a civilized land. He's brilliant, Wahlig. Positively brilliant. The sorrow is, he has been shaped by this savage kingdom. Already. He could become a great man. Or a great villain. He has it in him. Let us direct that thrust to greatness."

Yousif harumphed, stared into the distance, finally remarked, "Were it not for the situation, I would consider sending him to your Rebsamen. Perhaps that can be accomplished later. After this wicked little devil is put down."

Radetic studied Yousif from the corner of his eye. There was a halo of destiny about the Wahlig at the moment, an aura, a smell, and Yousif sensed it himself. His stance said he knew the future he faced was not the one he had described.

Yousif's expedition against the usurpers of Sebil el Selib, though stronger than Fuad's, suffered the fate of his brother's. Once again the loyalists came up that one fresh company short of strength enough to recover the Malachite Throne. In his determination to retain an image as strong and hard, Yousif pressed his attack far longer than was reasonable, well beyond the point when it became obvious that he would fail.

The bitter fighting brutalized both loyalist and rebel. Its outcome generated repercussions which only injured the loyalist stance. As the news swept the desert ever more opportunists gravitated to El Murid's standard. Nassef sent out a call. Recruits drifted to him. He began teaching them his own devilish style of warfare.

Yousif adopted more reactionary tactics, screening the trails from Sebil el Selib, using his household warriors to pursue enemy bands moving in and out.

Spies sent disturbing reports about new fortifications.

"We can abandon any hope of ever rooting them out," Radetic prophesied one day three years after the loss of the pass. Intelligence had just been received concerning the rapid growth of the fortress-palace guarding the Malachite Throne. The report also claimed that El Murid now had a full-time following of a thousand warriors, half of whom belonged to the fanatic Invincibles.

Nassef and his henchman Karim had begun slipping in and out to advise and occasionally direct the marauders plundering the desert in El Murid's name.

"They're like ghosts," Fuad murmured one day. "Yousif, you should have let me kill Nassef when I had the chance. He's everywhere and nowhere, and I can't get him to fight."

"Do I detect a case of the guerrilla warfare blues?" Radetic asked. "Of course Nassef won't stand still. He'd get whipped if he did. Give him a target he can't resist. Have a surprise waiting."

"His spies would warn him two days before we decided to do it," Yousif replied.

"I know. The real hope is that you can get him or El Murid with a knife in the kidneys."

"We've tried," Fuad growled.

"Keep trying. We're losing a little ground every day. They're wearing us down. As long as Aboud looks at it as a scuffle between Yousif and El Murid, and won't see how it spills over into the rest of the kingdom, our best bet is to hang on and pray that they do something fatally stupid before we do."

"How's your monograph coming, Megelin?" Yousif asked.

The monograph's incompleteness was Radetic's stated excuse for staying on. He reddened. Gripping Haroun's shoulder, he replied, "Damned slow. The war keeps getting in the way. I hardly have time to teach, let alone get any writing done."

Time had made of Radetic much more than a tutor. In some ways he had become the power behind the Wahlig. Yousif sought his advice ever more often, and followed it with increasing frequency.

El Murid had recognized Radetic's new importance in a recent sermon, naming him as one of the thirteen Barons of Hell on Earth, minions the Evil One had sent up to abuse the faithful. Megelin had been surprised to discover his noble standing. He thought Yousif more deserving.

Radetic was guiding Yousif's policy into a Fabian mode, getting the Wahlig to husband his strength and buy time. He hoped the Crown would recover its senses, or that Nassef would do something to defeat himself.

He composed countless admonitory letters, over Yousif's seal, to virtually everyone close to Aboud. He found a few sympathizers, but Crown Prince Farid was the only one in any position to influence Royal policy.

Young Haroun was growing, though more in mind than in stature. His father had begun to fear that he would become the family runt. Megelin soothed him with remarks about late bloomers. He had abandoned any pretense of educating anyone else. He no longer had time to coax and coddle Yousif's stubborner sons and nephews.

His concentration on the one child won him no friends. Not when he took the boy away from his regular shaghûnry studies and chores to accompany him on botanical and geological field trips. Not when he answered questions about the other children's talents honestly.

Other than Yousif and Haroun, Megelin had just one real friend in el Aswad, his bodyguard, Muamar.

Muamar enjoyed the field trips and studies more than did

Haroun. For him they were play. The old warrior had reached that stage in life where mental challenges were more easily negotiated than physical. He responded to them with a heart never seen in the young.

In the fourth year the rebels made a small mistake. Fuad emerged triumphant, having trapped and slain nearly three hundred marauders. The victory guaranteed a respite from guerrilla activity. Yousif declared a holiday in his brother's honor.

Women were summoned from their quarters to dance. Yousif, Fuad and most of the captains brought out their favorite wives. The voices of kanoons, ouds, derbeckis and zils filled the hall with music. Radetic found it strident, harsh and discordant.

Laughter abounded. Even Radetic hazarded a few jokes, but his efforts were too esoteric for his audience. They preferred long-winded, intimately detailed tales about rogues who cuckolded pompous husbands and about nitwits who believed anything their wives and daughters told them.

There was no wine to modulate the merriment, but the air was sour with a mildly narcotic smoke produced in special braziers.

Haroun sat beside Radetic, taking it all in with wide, neutral eyes. Radetic wondered if the boy was becoming one of life's perpetual observers.

"Ho! Megelin! You old woman," Fuad called. "Get up and show us one of your infidel jigs."

Radetic was in a daring mood. He liberated a flute from a musician and danced a clumsy flamenco to his own abominable accompaniment. He laughed with the rest when he finished.

"Now you, Fuad. Put on the zils and show the ladies how it's done."

Fuad took the dare, without zils. He performed a wild sword dance which won a roar of applause.

The hall was packed with victorious warriors. With the women dancing, then the teacher and the Wahlig's brother doing their stunts, no one had any attention left over. Nobody noticed the slow drift of three men toward the leaders. . . .

Till they sprang, one each at Yousif, Fuad and Radetic.

Each lifted a silver dagger overhead. Fuad stopped his

with his dancing sword. Yousif evaded his by throwing himself into the screaming mob.

Muamar flung himself into the path of the third assassin. The silver dagger slashed his cheek as the killer desperately tried to reach Radetic.

Muamar's wound was bloody, but should have done no more than leave a thin scar. But the old warrior froze. His eyes grew huge. A gurgling whine crossed his lips. Then he fell, stone-dead.

The assassin drove toward Radetic again, struggling past grasping hands and flashing weapons. His dagger burned with a weird blue light.

"Sorcery!" a woman screamed.

The uproar redoubled.

Haroun kicked the assassin in the groin. It was as savage a blow as a ten-year-old could deliver. The knife wielder ignored him.

Neither he nor his companions seemed to notice the blows raining upon them. Six of Yousif's men perished before the assassins could be stopped.

Shaking, Radetic gasped, "I've never seen anything like it! What kind of men are they?"

"Back! Damn it, clear away!" Yousif bellowed. "Gamel! Mustaf! Beloul!" he roared at three of his captains. "Clear the hall. Get the women to their quarters. Don't touch them!" he snarled at a man who had rolled one of the assassins onto his back.

The three silver daggers lay on the dark stone floor, glowing blue.

Fuad crouched over the man who had come after him. He was pale. His hands shook. "Nassef said he would send an assassin."

"He waited long enough," Yousif growled.

"This isn't El Murid's style," Radetic murmured. "There's sorcery in this. It hasn't been six months since he preached that sermon against wizardry."

"Nassef. It has to be Nassef's doing," Fuad insisted.

Something about one assassin caught Radetic's eye. He dropped to one knee, lengthened a tear in the man clothing, gazed at his chest. "Come here. Look at this."

A tiny tattoo lay over the man's heart. It was not clear, but seemed to be two letters of the desert alphabet intertwined.

The tattoo faded away as they studied it.

"What the hell?" Fuad growled. He jumped to another assassin, hacked his clothing. "Nothing on this one." He went to the third. "Hey. This one's still alive." Again he cut cloth. "And he's got the same mark."

"Gamel. Send for the physician," Yousif ordered. "Maybe we can keep him alive long enough to get some answers."

While they were looking at the tattoo, Haroun collected one of the daggers. A blue nimbus formed round his hand. He held the flat of the blade to the light of a lamp.

"What are you doing?" Yousif demanded. "Put that down."

"It's harmless, Father. The light is just a spell unraveling."

"What?"

"There was a spell on the blade. This one includes Uncle Fuad's name. I'm trying to read the rest, if you'll let me. It's hard. It's fading away, and it's in the language of Ilkazar."

"If there's sorcery . . ."

"The blue is the sorcery giving up energy as it decays, Father. Because the knives cut the wrong men. They're just daggers now."

Haroun's assertions did not reassure Yousif. "Put the damned thing down."

"He just died," Fuad said of the third assassin. "Oh. There it goes."

The man's tattoo faded in thirty seconds.

"What are we into here?" Yousif asked the air. The air did not reply.

Haroun's shaghûnry instructors confirmed the boy's comments about the daggers. Spells had been placed on the blades to make even a slight cut fatal. But they could make nothing of the vanishing tattoos. Nor could they, with their most potent conjuring, determine whence the assassins had come.

The physician determined that the men had taken drugs. And everyone could see that they had bound their limbs and genitals tightly, severely restricting circulation. They had been both fearless and immune to pain when they had attacked.

"Whoever sent them has himself a potent weapon," Radetic observed. "Yousif, you'd better tell the gate watch to stay alert."

Once the excitement died and there was no other concern to stay him, Megelin knelt over Muamar and wept. "You were a true friend, old warrior," he murmured. "Thank you."

Fuad, of all people, placed a comforting hand on his shoulder. "He was a good man, Megelin. We'll all miss him."

The teacher glanced up. He was surprised to see a tear on Fuad's cheek. "He was my weapons master when I was Haroun's age. As he was Haroun's." For Fuad that seemed to be ample explanation.

The man called Beloul, who, subjective centuries ago, had escaped the disaster at Sebil el Selib, examined the dead men. He was now one of Yousif's most savage captains. In his time, too, he had gone back into Sebil el Selib as one of the Wahlig's spies.

"These are El Murid's men," he said. "This one is Shehab el-Medi, a captain of the Invincibles. He was almost as crazy as the Disciple."

"So," said Yousif. "The mystery deepens. They're El Murid's special bullies. Nobody gives them orders but the man himself. And yet it's only been six months since he outlawed any kind of sorcery. Curious."

The Disciple had, in fact, declared a death sentence upon all witches, warlocks, shamans, shaghûns, diviners and anyone who practiced any kind of occultism. He had charged Nassef with the eradication of sorcery wherever his troops found it.

"He's insane," Beloul observed. "He doesn't have to be logically consistent."

Radetic had thought at the time that the Disciple's declaration made a grim kind of sense. The Kingdom of Peace had won no converts among the wise. Men with the Power were almost universally his enemies. They aided the Royal cause where they could. That they were generally ineffectual reflected the level of competence of the sorcerers of Hammad al Nakir. The talent had been very nearly eradicated during the fury of the Fall.

Radetic again thought of the Hidden Ones. Would El

Murid be fool enough to try expelling them from Jebal al Alf Dhulquarneni?

That was too much to hope. Like most of the Children of Hammad al Nakir, he probably did not think of them at all.

El Aswad buried its dead and went on, as it had done for years. A month later a spy brought news which illuminated the assassination attempt.

El Murid had instructed his Invincibles to found a secret order within the bodyguard. The available details convinced Radetic that it was a mystery cult. It called itself the Harish, and was extreme in its secrecy. Members were organized in pyramided "brotherhoods" of three men, only one of whom knew any cultist above the three in the hierarchy. The tattoo was El Murid's personal seal. It was formed from the initial letters of "Beloved of God," and meant that the bearer was guaranteed a place in Paradise. It supposedly faded when the cultist's soul ascended.

"That's spooky," Fuad observed, and seemed perfectly willing to write the idea off as another example of El Murid's insanity.

"It is," Yousif agreed. "It's also damned dangerous if they're all as willing to die as our three were."

They were. Dredging the dark corners of his mind, El Murid had created a dread new instrument for the furthering of his mission.

Nine weeks later Radetic received a long letter from an old schoolmate, Tortin Perntigan, who had become a professor of mercantile theory. Meaning he was a glorified accounting instructor.

He mulled it for days before taking it to Yousif.

"You look strange," the Wahlig told him. "Like a man who's just seen his best friend and worst enemy murder each other."

"Maybe I have. I've received a letter from home."

"An emergency? You don't have to leave?" Yousif seemed alarmed by the prospect. Megelin's pride responded warmly.

"No. I'm not going anywhere. The letter . . . It'll take some explanation." Quickly, Megelin explained that Perntigan was a long-time friend, that they had been close since entering the Rebsamen together nearly three decades ago.

"He's the one costing you so much when I send my fat packets of mail." Yousif was a tight man with a copper, like all his desert brethren, and repeatedly protested the expense of Megelin's communications with his distant colleagues. "I've been sending him fragments of my monograph as I write it, along with my natural observations, notes, thoughts, speculations and what have you. To ensure that not everything will be lost if tragedy strikes. Knowledge is too precious."

"I seem to recall having heard that argument."

"Yes. Well. Perntigan, old gossip that he is, responds by keeping me informed of the latest from Hellin Daimiel."

Sourly, Yousif observed, "It gratifies me no end that you're able to stay in touch. Though it beggars me. Now, what piece of foul gossip has this expensive excuse for scholarly chitchat brought me?"

"As you are aware, Hellin Daimiel is the financial axis of the west—though the standing is being challenged by Itaskian consortiums—"

"Get on with it, Megelin. Bad news is like a dead camel. It gets no pleasanter for being let lie."

"Yes, Wahlig. Perntigan is obsessed with a phenomenon the bankers have begun calling 'the Kasr Helal Gold Seam.' Kasr Helal is a fortified Daimiellian trading village on the edge of the Sahel. The same one where, I believe, the Disciple's father traded for salt—"

"Megelin! You're still dancing around it."

"Very well. Of late large amounts of new specie have been reaching Hellin Daimiel, channeled through Kasr Helal. Thus the name Kasr Helal Gold Seam. According to Perntigan, the House of Bastanos—the largest of the Daimiellian international banks—has accepted deposits equalling a million Daimiellian ducats. And that's just one bank. He sent a long list of queries about what is happening inside Hammad al Nakir. His excuse is that he is a student of finance. His motive, of course, is that he hopes somehow to profit."

"Can't we somehow get to the point of all this? What're you getting at? The fact that this money is coming out of the desert?"

"Exactly. Which is the root of the mystery. There is a trader's axiom that says specie is as scarce as frog fur in the desert. In this land debts are almost always paid in service or kind. Are they not? What silver and gold there is has a tendency to remain motionless." Radetic indicated the rings and bracelets Yousif wore. They formed a considerable portion of the Wahlig's personal fortune. The men of Hammad al Nakir customarily wore or hid whatever valuable metals they possessed. They yielded them up only in the direst extremity. "The movement out of the desert of fortunes of the scale Perntigan describes represents a huge financial anomaly. There is a great deal of trepidation among the bankers, though they profit. They foresee some titanic economic disaster."

Yousif simply looked puzzled. Half of what Radetic was saying had to be couched in the tongue of Hellin Daimiel. The desert language hadn't much of a financial vocabulary. And, though Yousif spoke some Daimiellian, he did not comprehend merchants' cant.

"Perntigan questioned his contacts in the banking establishment. He assembled a list of names associated with the suspect deposits. Along with another list of questions. You put everything he wrote together and it implies a rather disturbing process."

"I see that somebody is sending a hell of a lot of wealth out of the kingdom."

Radetic nodded. Finally. About five minutes behind, but finally. "Exactly. The whos and whys are what make the news interesting."

Yousif puzzled for a few seconds, then started to speak. Haroun tugged at his clothing. "Father? May I?"

The Wahlig grinned. "Of course. Let's see if this old fussbudget is worth his keep. Show us what he's taught you."

Radetic smiled too. The boy was showing signs of overcoming his innate reserve.

Haroun proclaimed, "There are only two people who could have that much money. The King and El Murid."

"Your reasoning?" Radetic demanded.

"The King because he accepts money instead of service. Also, he collects some rents and trade taxes. And El Murid because he has been looting people for years."

Yousif peered at Radetic. "Well? I take it from your look that he's wrong. Explain."

"Not really. He just hasn't reasoned closely enough.

Tortin indicates that the Quesani family did make a big deposit. It was used to purchase properties on the Auszura Littoral. That's a stretch of seacoast north of Dunno Scuttari. It's a sort of elephant's graveyard of deposed princes. The purchase makes it look like somebody at Al Rhemish is covering the Quesani bets."

"Not Aboud. He doesn't have the foresight."

"Farid, perhaps? No matter. That was only a small part of the flow, and not what was bothering Tortin. What did bother him came from two other sources. The loot Haroun mentioned without carrying his reasoning to the point where he mentioned that it hasn't been El Murid doing the pillaging. The depositors have been Karim, el-Kader, el Nadim and that bunch."

"Nassef's bandits-turned-generals. That's good news, Megelin. We could make the Scourge of God damned uncomfortable by spreading that around. In fact, the Invincibles might end his tale if he's been slipping something over on El Murid."

Radetic was not cheered by the opportunity. "Our side is vulnerable too."

"Aboud's money? It's his. He can do what he wants with it. Besides, he isn't looting the realm."

"Not Aboud. The priesthood. They've been sending out as much bullion as Nassef's gang. Which means they're stripping the holy places and melting the gold and silver down. What would the faithful do if they found out that they're being robbed by their own priests? El Murid can explain Nassef, more or less. Soldiers pillage their enemies. We can't shed ourselves of the priesthood.

"A lot of people already damn Nassef without damning El Murid. They consider him the Disciple's compromise with fate. They figure he'll disappear if El Murid's Kingdom of Peace becomes a reality."

"Looks like Nassef is worried about it too. He and his boys are putting a little away for their old age."

"Don't you think the priesthood's behavior will win El Murid a lot of converts?"

"Absolutely. I'll write Aboud."

"Who is under the thumbs of the priests. Who will give you the same answer he's been giving you since this mess started. If he bothers to answer at all."

"You're right. Of course. We'll just have to intimidate a few priests. Cover it up." Yousif closed his eyes wearily. "Megelin, what do you do when your allies are more trouble than your enemies?"

"I don't know, Wahlig. I really don't. Stupidity and incompetence create their own special rewards. All I foresee is deterioration and more deterioration, and most of it moral. Maybe Hammad al Nakir *needs* the purifying flame of an El Murid."

Haroun gripped Radetic's elbow. "Don't give up yet, Megelin."

The boy's face had assumed an expression of stubborn determination. It made him seem far older than his years.

Radetic thought it a pity that a child had to grow up in the fires of this particularly chaotic furnace.

Chapter Six

Into Strange Kingdoms

Gaunt, shivering, Bragi and Haaken paused at the crest of the last high pass.

"Already spring down there," Bragi observed. He extended an arm to support his brother. "That green must be a hardwood forest."

"How long?" Haaken croaked.

"Three days? Five? Not long."

"Hah!"

There had been days when they had not made a mile. Like yesterday. After burying Soren in the hard earth, they had fought the snowy mountain till exhaustion had forced a halt.

Sigurd had passed almost a month ago. The crossing had taken two months.

"Can't make it," Haaken gasped. "Go on without me."

He had suggested it before. "We've got it whipped now, Haaken. All downhill from here."

"Tired, Bragi. Got to rest. Make it while you can. I'll catch up."

"Come on. Step. Step. Step."

The foothills were hot compared to the high range. The boys camped there a week, regaining their strength. Game was scarce.

They had begun to encounter signs of the foothill tribes. Once they passed the ruin of a small log fortress. It had been burned within the month.

"We should be near Itaskia's Duchy Greyfells," Bragi said around a rabbit's leg. "This trail should run into the highway Father called the North Road. That's a straight run to Itaskia the City."

Itaskia the kingdom and its capital bore the same name. This was the case with several states. Each had grown round a strong city-survivor of the Fall.

"Wish you'd stop being so damned optimistic," Haaken grumbled. He attacked the rabbit like a starved bear. "We can't even speak the language. And we're Trolledyngjans. If bandits don't get us, the Itaskians will."

"You should ease up on the pessimism. Damned if I don't think all you'd see is a hernia if we found a pot of gold."

"Can't go through life expecting everything to work out. You expect the worst, you're ready for anything."

"What do *you* want to do?"

"I stopped making plans when Father died."

Bragi had no plan either, beyond following his father's sketchy suggestions. What happened after they found this Yalmar?

"Haaken, all I know is what Father said."

"Then we just have to keep on till something happens."

It happened next morning.

Haaken paused to urinate. Bragi ambled on ahead and was alone when the hillmen leapt out of the brush.

Their stone-tipped spears turned on his mail shirt, which his father had told him to wear whenever he traveled. They pulled him down and drew knives.

Haaken arrived, axe whining. He slew two before the others realized he was there.

Bragi scrambled away, regained his feet, finally used his sword.

A survivor tried to flee. Sword and axe stopped him.

"What the hell?" Haaken gasped.

"Meant to rob me, I guess," Bragi wheezed, shaking. "That was too close."

"I warned you."

"Let's ditch them and get out of here."

"Listen!"

Hoofbeats. Approaching.

"Into the brush," Bragi said.

"Up a tree," Haaken countered. "Ragnar said people never look up."

Within a minute they were high in an old oak. Their packs seemed weightless during the climb.

The dead still lay scattered on the trail.

Six horsemen appeared. An officer, four soldiers and one civilian.

"Itaskians," Bragi whispered.

"What the hell?" the officer demanded, reining in. The youths did not understand Itaskian, but guessed his meaning.

The soldiers drew swords. The civilian dismounted, examining the battleground.

"Majneric's men. They ambushed two travelers. Within the past few minutes. The travelers are in a black oak about thirty feet to your left."

"Who'd be out here when Majneric's loose?"

"You'll have to ask. Use bows. They shouldn't resist the invitation."

"Just so. Sergeant."

The soldiers sheathed their blades, readied bows. Bragi and Haaken exchanged looks.

"Nobody ever looks up, eh?" Bragi growled, looking down four shafts. The scout beckoned.

When Bragi reached the ground he found his foster brother with axe in hand, defiant.

"They're just pups," the sergeant observed.

"These were the two?" the officer asked.

"The same," said the civilian. "Look like Trolledyngjans. They teach them young up there." The woodsman held out his palms. "Let's talk in peace," he said in accented Trolledyngjan.

"What's going to happen?" Bragi asked. Shakes threatened to shame him.

"Depends on you. What happened here? What brings you south?"

Bragi told it all. The scout translated.

The Itaskians chattered briefly, then the interpreter said, "Sir Cleve is inclined to generosity. Because of those." He indicated the dead. "We've been after their band for weeks. We deliver their heads to the Duke, we'll get off patrol for a while. But he doesn't know about this Pretender. He wants to look in your packs."

Haaken growled softly.

"Easy, son. We won't rob you."

"Do what he says, Haaken."

A minute later, "Good. Now move back five paces."

The leader examined their things. Bragi's heirlooms generated questions.

"Our father gave them to us before he died. He told us to take them to a man in the City."

"What man?"

"Someone named Yalmar."

The officer asked, "You think they're telling the truth?"

"Too scared not to. This Yalmar probably fences for the coast raiders. Their father probably saw this succession crisis coming and made arrangements."

"What should we do with them?"

"We have no quarrel with them, sir. And they've done us a favor."

"They're Trolledyngjans," the sergeant observed. "Ought to hang them as a warning to the next bunch."

"A point," the officer agreed. "But I've no stomach for it. Not children."

"These children killed four men, sir."

"Majneric's men."

"What's going on?" Bragi asked nervously.

The scout chuckled. "Sergeant Weatherkind wants to hang you. Sir Cleve, on the other hand, is willing to let you go. Provided you let him have these bodies."

"That's fine by us."

"Watch that sergeant," said Haaken. "He'll get us killed yet." The soldier was arguing something with his commander.

"He wants Sir Cleve to confiscate your packs."

"Friendly sort."

"He's from West Wapentake, where the raiders strike first every spring."

"Look out!" Haaken dove into Bragi's legs.

But the sergeant's arrow was not meant for his brother. It brought a howl from down the trail.

Twenty hillmen charged from the forest.

The youths and scout braced for the charge. And Bragi marveled at the way it melted before the Itaskians' arrows.

It was a lesson he would not forget.

A few of those hillmen bore stolen weapons, mail and

shields. The first to reach Bragi was one such, and skilled with his blade. Haaken's axe, screaming across after slashing a spearman, saved Bragi.

While Sir Cleve and his soldiers sorted themselves out, the youths and woodsman dropped three more hillmen.

The remainder scattered before the horsemen, who harried them into the forest. "Finish the wounded before they escape," Sir Cleve called back.

"This is some day's work," the scout observed once the grisly business ended. "A quarter of Majneric's men dead within an hour. Makes a week spent chasing them worthwhile."

"Why?" Bragi asked.

"What? Ah. Hard times in the hills. Majneric brought his bucks down to raid. Can't really hate them for it. They're trying to take care of their families. At the expense of ours. We caught them near Mendalayas, killed a dozen. They scattered. We started hunting them down. Have to make this raiding too expensive for them."

The soldiers returned. They had corpses across their saddles and prisoners on tethers. Sir Cleve spoke.

"He says thanks for the help. Some of us would've been killed if you hadn't been in their way."

Even the sergeant seemed well disposed.

"Now's the time to make any requests. He's happy. He'll be in good odor when the Duke hears about this."

"Could he give us some kind of traveling pass? To get us to the City?"

"Good thinking, lad. I'll see."

They were ready to travel when the knight finished writing.

Later, after his lips stopped quivering, Bragi started whistling. But his brother never stopped looking back.

Haaken was still watching for a change of heart when they reached the capital.

The Red Hart Inn was a slum tavern. It was large, rambling, boisterous and appeared on the verge of collapse. Evening shadows masked its more disreputable features.

The clientele fell silent at their advent. Fifty pairs of eyes stared. Some were curious, some wary, some challenging, none friendly.

"I don't think we belong here," Haaken whispered.

"Easy," Bragi cautioned, concealing his own nervousness. "Yalmar?"

No response.

He tried again. "Is there a man named Yalmar here? I come from Ragnar of Draukenbring."

The Itaskians muttered amongst themselves.

"Come here." A man beckoned from shadows at the rear.

The murmur picked up. Bragi avoided hard eyes. These were men Haaken and he had best not offend.

"In here."

The speaker was lean, stooped, ginger-haired, about thirty-five. He limped, but looked as tough as the others.

"I'm Yalmar. You named Ragnar of Draukenbring. Would that be the Wolf?"

"Yes."

"So?"

"He sent us."

"Why?"

"How do we know you're Yalmar?"

"How do I know you're from Ragnar?"

"He sent proof."

"A map? A dagger, and an amulet of Ilkazar?"

"Yes."

Yalmar's grin revealed surprisingly perfect teeth. "So. How is the crazy bastard? We swung some profitable deals, us two. I picked the ships. He took them. I fenced the goods."

Haaken grunted sullenly.

"What's with him?"

"Ragnar's dead. He was our father."

"The infamous Bragi and Haaken. You've got no idea how he bored me silly bragging you up. Passed over, eh? I'm sorry. And not just for the loss of a profitable partnership. He was my friend."

Neither youth responded. Bragi studied the man. This was an honest innkeeper? How far could he be trusted?

Their silence unsettled Yalmar. "So. What do you want? Or are you just going to sit there like a couple of clams?"

"I don't know," Bragi said. "Father was dying. He said to go to you, you owed him. We're here."

"I noticed. Better begin at the beginning, then. Maybe give me an idea what he was thinking."

Bragi told the story. It did not hurt as much now.

"I see," Yalmar said when he finished. He pinched his nose, tugged his golden chin whiskers, frowned. "You got any skills? Carpentry? Masonry? Smithery?"

Bragi shook his head.

"Thought not. All you people do is fight. Not your safest way to make a living. And it don't leave you many openings here. Been at peace for fifteen years. And nobody in my business would use you. Too visible. And bodyguarding is out. Not enough experience. Tell you what. Give me a couple days. I'll put you up meantime. Upstairs. Try to stay out of sight. I'll put the word out that you're protected, but that won't keep the drunks from cutting you up. Or the police from breaking in to find out why I'm keeping Trolledyngjans."

With no better option available, Bragi and Haaken agreed.

They spent a week at the Red Hart. Yalmar told them things about Ragnar they had never heard at home. The Itaskian proved likable, despite an overpowering tyranny when he made them study his language.

Strange, hard men visited Yalmar late at night, though he steadfastly denied their existence. It finally dawned on Bragi that Yalmar did not trust them completely either.

One night he asked, "About the amulet, map and dagger . . ."

Yalmar laid a finger across his lips. He checked the windows and doors. "They're why I owe your father. If I have to run, I can go knowing he provided means elsewhere. Now forget about it. The Brothers would be displeased. There's honor on the Inside. There's fear or friendship. Your father and I were friends."

Later, he told them, "I'm sorry. There's nothing for you here. I'd say go south. Try to catch on with the Mercenary's Guild. High Crag is taking on recruits."

Next afternoon, Haaken grumped, "This loafing is getting old, Bragi. What're we going to do?"

Bragi touched his mother's locket. "There's Hellin Daimiel. I'll talk to Yalmar."

The day following Yalmar announced, "I've gotten you guard jobs with a caravan leaving tomorrow. There's a job you can do for me while you're at it. A man named Magnolo will be traveling with the caravan. He'll be carrying something for me. I don't trust him. Watch him." He added some details. "If he takes the package to anyone but Stavros, kill him."

Grimly, Bragi nodded.

"Bragi?" Haaken asked.

"Yeah?" Bragi poked the coals of their campfire, watched them glow briefly brighter.

"I kind of wish we didn't kill that guy Magnolo."

The man Yalmar had set them to watch had delivered the Itaskian's package to a house in the fanciest quarter in Hellin Daimiel. In their enthusiasm to fulfill their charge the youths had not only killed Magnolo, they had injured the gentleman he had visited and had killed one of the bodyguards. Aghast, panicky, they had fled the city.

"I'm hungry," Haaken complained.

"Don't seem to be much game in these parts, does there?"

They had made camp on a rocky hill eight miles northeast of Hellin Daimiel, in the only uncultivated area they could find. Hellin Daimiel was an old city. Its environs had been tamed for ages. Small game, especially agricultural pests, had been eradicated. The youths had eaten nothing but fish for three days, and those were treasures hard-won from irrigation canals.

"What're we going to do?"

Haaken sounded a little frightened.

Bragi did not mention it. He was scared too. They were on their own in a foreign, indifferent land.

"I don't know. I really don't."

"We don't have too many choices."

"I know."

"We can't just stay here. Not only will we starve, we're Trolledyngjan. Somebody's going to jump us for that."

"Yeah. I know." They had had their run-ins already. Trolledyngjans were not popular anywhere near the sea.

"We could go ahead and try the Mercenary's Guild."

"I just don't like the sound of that. All that marching around and saying 'Yes sir, no sir, by your leave, sir.' I don't think I could take it. I'd pop somebody in the snot box and get myself hung."

"It doesn't sound so bad to me. We could try it. They say

you don't have to stay if you don't like it. It isn't like joining a regular army."

"Maybe. Okay? I've been thinking about something else." Bragi rose and moved to a large boulder. He leaned against it and peered out across the plain surrounding Hellin Daimiel.

Even by night the view reflected the studious planning characteristic of these peculiar people. The lights of the planned villages where the farm laborers lived made points on the interstices of a grid. The grid was more clearly discernible by day, in the form of carefully maintained roads and irrigation canals. The city itself was a galaxy in the background.

A whippoorwill struck up its repetitive commentary somewhere downslope. Another vocalized agreement from a distance. A gentle breeze climbed the slope, bringing with it scents of crops still a few weeks short of being stealably ripe.

The lights died away till Bragi was alone with the darkness and stars. They formed an immense silver girdle overhead. He stared at them till one broke free and streaked down the sky. It raced toward Hellin Daimiel.

He shrugged. An omen was an omen. He went and sat across the coals from his brother, who seemed to be asleep sitting up. Softly, he said, "I wonder where mother is now."

Haaken shook all over, and for a moment Bragi was scared something had happened. Haaken was the sort who could become deathly ill without saying a word.

His concern was short-lived. There was enough light in the fire to betray the tears on Haaken's cheeks.

Bragi said nothing. He was homesick too.

After a time, he remarked, "She gave me this locket." He waited till he had Haaken's attention. "She told me we should take it to some people in Hellin Daimiel. To the House of Bastanos."

"That's not people. That's what they call a bank. Where rich men go to borrow money."

"Oh?" He had to think about that. After a few seconds, "People run it, don't they? Maybe that's what she meant. Anyway, we could find out about it before we tried the Guild."

"No. It's too hot down there. They'll hang us. Besides, I

don't think Mother wanted us to go there. Not really. Not unless there was nowhere else we could go."

"The excitement should have died down."

"You're fooling yourself, Bragi. I say try the Guild."

"You scared of Hellin Daimiel?" Bragi was. The city was too huge, too foreign, too dangerous.

"Yes. I don't mind admitting it. It's too different to just jump into. Too easy for us to get into something we can't handle because we don't know better. That's why I say go with the Guild."

Bragi saw Haaken's reasoning. The Guild would provide a base of safety while they learned southern ways.

He fingered his mother's gift, battled homesickness and temporized. "In the morning. We'll decide after we've slept on it."

He did not sleep well.

Chapter Seven

Wadi el Kuf

El Murid stalked around Sebil el Selib like a tiger caged. Would this imprisonment never end? Would that villain Yousif never crack? The desert was on his side, if his advisers were to be believed. Nassef claimed he could stamp his foot and twenty thousand warriors would respond.

Why, then, did the Kingdom of Peace still extend no farther than he could see? Like the Lord Himself, he was running short on patience.

The pressure had been building for months. He was growing increasingly frustrated, increasingly suspicious of Nassef and his gang of self-made generals. He had told no one, not even Meryem, but he had begun to believe that Nassef was keeping him here intentionally, isolating him from his people. He was not sure why Nassef should want it that way.

Sometimes he took his son or daughter along on his walks, explaining the wonders of God's handiwork to them. Over Nassef's objections he had had several scholars brought in to explain some of the less obvious miracles of nature. And he had begun learning to read and write so that he could promulgate his laws in his own hand.

But usually he roamed alone, accompanied only by the Invincibles. The Invincibles were necessary. The minions of the Evil One had tried to murder him a dozen times. Sometimes it seemed his enemies had more men in his camp than he did.

He would greet soldiers by name, study the ever growing barracks-city or inspect the new truck gardens being terraced into the hillsides. The army was devouring the available flatland. The gardens did not provide enough, but they helped. Every vegetable raised here meant one fewer that had to be bought on the coast and transported through the pass. And the fieldwork kept idle hands from turning to the Evil One.

It rained the day El Murid decided to end his confinement. It was not a pleasant rain, but one of those driving, bitter storms that beat down the spirit as easily as they beat down grass and leaves. The rains passed, but left the sky and his mood low, gray and oppressive, with the potential of turning foul.

He summoned the captains of the Invincibles.

His bodyguard now consisted of three thousand men. It formed a personal army independent of that which Nassef commanded. The quiet, mostly nameless men who formed its brotherhood were absolutely faithful and completely incorruptible.

They had, for the past year, been undertaking operations of their own out in the desert. Unlike Nassef's men, they did not concentrate on attacking and looting loyalists. They moved into preponderantly friendly areas and stayed, assuming both administrative and defense functions. They spoke for the Lord, but contained their enthusiasm, proselytizing by example. They did not bother local loyalists as long as the loyalists observed a strict pacifism and tended their own business. The areas they occupied were largely free of strife. They had skirmished with Nassef's men on several occasions because they refused to allow anyone to disturb the peace of their lands.

Once the commanders assembled, El Murid said, "My brother, the Scourge of God, has returned. Has he not?"

"Last night, Disciple," someone volunteered.

"He hasn't come to see me. Someone go get him."

A half minute after an emissary departed, the Disciple added archly, "I'd be indebted if someone could manage to borrow a Harish kill dagger." Though he knew who the senior members of the cult were, and had several in his presence, he wanted to allow them their secrecy. They were useful. "We'll leave it lying around as a reminder of where the final authority lies."

El Murid's formal audience chamber, before the Malachite Throne, was large and formularized. He had a bent toward show and structure. Petitioners had to come before him and stand at one of several podium-like pieces of furniture, wait their turn to be recognized, then present their plea and any important evidence.

At twenty-two El Murid was a hard, strong-willed, dictatorial leader—once he had suffered through his private hells of indecision. He no longer brooked defiance. The men and women of Sebil el Selib lived to the letter of his laws.

Less than two minutes passed before an Invincible placed a kill dagger on an evidence stand near the chief petitioner's podium. El Murid smiled his approval and suggested that the man move the blade slightly, so that it could not be seen from the Malachite Throne.

They waited.

Nassef stalked in sullenly. His lips were tight and pale. The Invincible accompanying him wore a smug look. El Murid guessed that there had been an argument, and Nassef had been compelled to concede.

Nassef strode to the central petitioner's podium. He was too angry to examine his surroundings immediately. El Murid could almost read the complaints marshaling behind his brow.

Then Nassef noticed the Invincibles standing stiffly in the shadows. Some of his anger and arrogance deserted him.

"Your war-general at your command, my Lord Disciple."

Nassef went through a further subtle deflation when he spied the kill dagger. Its placement made it appear to be a personal message from the cult, unknown to El Murid himself.

There was a quiet power struggle developing between Nassef and the Invincibles. El Murid, scarcely as ignorant as some of his followers thought, was aware of it, and hoped to use it to dampen Nassef's tendency toward independence.

Sometimes he thought that his brother-in-law was trying to carve out his own private empire.

What El Murid really wanted was a lever on Nassef that he could use to pry himself free of Sebil el Selib.

He could not stand to remain tied down much longer.

He mentioned none of the real grievances he had with his war general. "Scourge of God, you've boasted that you could muster twenty thousand warriors with a word."

"That's true, Enlightened One."

El Murid controlled an impulse to grin. Nassef was going

to lay it on heavy. "War general, speak that word. Gather your warriors. I've decided to move on Al Rhemish."

Nassef did not reply immediately. He surveyed the Invincibles. He found no sympathy in their eyes. They were El Murid's hounds. They would respond to his will no matter what he commanded. He looked at the dagger. He looked at El Murid. "It shall be as you command, my Lord Disciple. I'll send the summons as soon as I leave." He chewed his lower lip.

El Murid was mildly surprised. He had not expected Nassef to yield this easily. "Go, then. I'm sure you have a lot to do. I want to start as soon as possible."

"Indeed, Enlightened One. Moving an army to Al Rhemish will take a great deal of preparation. The desert is no friend to the soldier."

"It's a work of the Evil One. Naturally, it serves him. But it can be conquered, even as he can."

Nassef did not respond. He bowed and departed.

El Murid kept tabs. Not all the Invincibles wore white robes and mustered with their companies. A few remained secret members of the fraternity, providing intelligence for their commanders.

Nassef kept his word. He sent his messengers. He gathered his captains. They plunged into the problems inherent in marching a large army across a wasteland.

Satisfied, El Murid almost forgot him.

Then he stole one of his rare evenings with his family.

The Disciple's private life would have scandalized the conservative Invincibles. But he had learned from his attempt to have Meryem testify at his trial. He and she kept their abnormal equality concealed behind closed doors.

His New Castle apartments were sumptuous. Though it would serve as a cistern in time of siege, he even had a large pool in which to relax and bathe.

Meryem met him with the excited smile that had come to mean so much to him. "I was afraid something would keep you."

"Not tonight. Tonight I need you more than they need me." He closed the door and kissed her. "You're a patient woman. A miracle. You've changed so much since El Aquila."

She smiled up at him. "Men change us. Come on. There's no one but family tonight. I'm even doing the cooking myself so the outside can't get in."

He followed her into the next room—and stiffened.

Nassef sat with his son Sidi and the still unnamed girl, telling them some outrageous tale of the desert. El Murid pursed his lips unhappily, but settled to his cushion without a word. Nassef was Meryem's brother, and the children loved him. Especially the girl. Sometimes she would sneak out and follow her uncle all over the valley. She could not believe that her father's enemies were capable of attacking him through her.

"It'll be a while," Meryem told him. "Why don't you relax in the pool? You haven't had a chance all week."

"Me too!" Sidi yelped.

El Murid laughed. "You're going to grow scales like a fish if you spend any more time in the water. All right. Come on. Nassef, when we reach the sea we'll make Sidi our admiral. I can't keep him away from the water."

Nassef rose. "I'll join you. This old skin hasn't been clean for two months. Sidi, I've got a job for you. Show me how to swim. I might need to know if your father is going to take us to the sea."

"What about me?" the girl demanded. She hated the water, but did not want to let her uncle out of her sight. She was beginning to remind her father of her mother at an earlier age.

"You're a girl," Sidi told her. His tone suggested that that was cause enough for her to be thrown into stocks, let alone banned from the bath.

"You might melt, sugar," her father told her. "Let's go, men."

Lying in the cool water, letting it buoy him up, allowed him a relaxation that was missing even in Meryem's arms.

Her relaxed for half an hour. Sidi and Nassef squealed and splashed and laughed and dunked one another. Then he said, "All right, Nassef. Now."

His brother-in-law did not pretend to misunderstand. He hoisted Sidi to the edge of the pool. "Time to get out. Dry yourself off, get dressed and go help your mother."

"How come I have to leave whenever anybody wants to talk?"

"Do as he says, son," El Murid told him. "And make sure you're good and dry before you get dressed."

Sidi was gone in a minute. Nassef said, "I'm beginning to be sorry that I never married. I miss having children."

"You're not too old."

"No. But I'm in the wrong business. Taking a wife would be tempting fate too much, wouldn't it? Fuad would catch me the first time I took the field."

"Maybe you're right. Maybe a soldier shouldn't marry. Too much strain on the family."

Nassef said nothing for several seconds. Then, "We're alone. No ears to hear. No hearts to offend. Can we speak as brothers? As the two who rode out of El Aquila together, and who fought the desert side by side? Simply as Nassef and Micah, men who have too much in common to be at odds?"

"It's a family occasion. Try to keep it at a family level."

"I will. You married my sister, who is my only true friend in this world. I am your brother.

"I'm deeply troubled. We're embarking on a doomed enterprise. My brother, I tell you this out of my love for you, and for no other reason. We can't take Al Rhemish. Not yet."

El Murid conquered his anger. Nassef was following the rules. He could do no less. "I don't understand why not. I look and I listen. I see hosts pass through Sebil el Selib. I hear that we can summon a horde to our banner. I'm told that much of the desert is with us."

"Perfectly true. Though I can't say how much of the desert is on our side. More with us than with our enemies, I think. But it's a big desert. Most people don't care one way or the other. What they really want is for us and the Royalists both to leave them alone."

"Why, then, do you urge me to delay? That's the argument you want to present, isn't it? And I remind you of your own observation that we're alone. You can be as frank as you like."

"All right. Stated simply, twenty thousand warriors don't make an army just by gathering in the same place. My forces are only now beginning to coalesce. My men aren't used to operating in large groups. Neither are the Invincibles. And the men from areas that we've controlled a long time have lost their battle edge. Moreover, there isn't a man among us, myself included, who has the experience to manage a large force."

"Are you claiming we'll be defeated?"

"No. I'm telling you that we'd be risking it, and that the risk will go down every day that we put off fighting them on their own terms. Which we would be. They would know we were coming. They have their spies. And they have men who *do* know how armies work."

El Murid said nothing for a minute. First he tried to assess Nassef's sincerity. He could not fault it. Nor could he challenge his brother-in-law's arguments. His frustration at being trapped in Sebil el Selib returned.

He could stand his containment no more. He would tolerate it not one minute longer than it would take to assemble the host.

"My heart tells me to go ahead."

"That's your decision? It's final?"

"It is."

Nassef sighed. "Then I'll do everything I can. Maybe we'll be lucky. I do have one suggestion. When the time comes, take command yourself."

El Murid scrutinized his brother-in-law narrowly.

"Not because I want to shirk responsibility for any defeat. Because the warriors will fight harder for the Disciple than they will for the Scourge of God. That might be the margin between victory and defeat."

Again El Murid had the feeling that Nassef was being sincere. "So be it. Let's go see if Meryem is ready for dinner."

It was a quiet family meal, with few words spoken. El Murid spent much of it examining his ambivalent feelings toward Nassef. As always, Nassef was hard to pin down.

Nassef had argued no harder than a man of conscience should have. Had El Murid misjudged his brother-in-law? Was the news reaching him becoming distorted by the Invincible minds through which it passed?

His frustration mounted as the days turned into weeks. The army grew, but the process was so damnably slow! His advisers frequently reminded him that his followers had to come long distances, often pursued by Royalists, and as they approached Sebil el Selib they had to contend with Yousif's patrols.

But the time came at last. The morning when he could kiss Meryem good-bye and tell her that when next they met it would be within the Most Holy Mrazkim Shrines themselves.

More than twenty thousand men responded to Nassef's call. Their tents were everywhere. Sebil el Selib reminded El Murid of Al Rhemish during Disharhun.

Yousif's people had been quiet for nine days. They had ceased contesting the passage of the warrior bands. Nassef had been telling anyone who would listen that he did not like it, that it was a sign that the Wahlig had something up his sleeve.

Then the news came. Yousif had mustered every man he could, some five thousand, and had installed himself at the oasis near Wadi el Kuf. His neighbors had loaned him another two thousand men.

"We'll have to fight him there," Nassef told El Murid. "There's no choice. We can't get to Al Rhemish without watering there. This is what he's been waiting for all these years. The chance to get us into a conventional battle. It looks like he wants that chance so badly that he doesn't care about the numbers."

"Give him what he wants. Let's rid ourselves of him once and for all."

Nassef guessed right most of the time. But he had erred in calling in all of El Murid's supporters. By so doing he stripped the desert of his sources of intelligence. He and El Murid would not learn the truth about Yousif's stand till it was too late.

Nassef selected twenty thousand men. El Murid took twenty-five hundred Invincibles. They left a substantial force to defend the pass in their absence.

It was a morning many days after departure. The sun hung low in the east. They moved up on the waterhole by Wadi el Kuf.

The wadi was a shallow, broad valley a mile and a half east of the waterhole. It was filled with bizarre natural formations. It was the wildest badland in all Hammad al Nakir.

Nassef and El Murid raised the Lord's standard atop a low

hill a mile south of the oasis, and an equal distance from the wadi. They studied the enemy, who was waiting on horseback.

"They don't seem impressed by our numbers," Nassef observed.

"What do you suggest?"

"It seems straightforward. Hold the Invincibles here, in reserve. Send the rest in one wave and overwhelm them."

"This is a strange land, Nassef. It's so silent."

The stillness did seem supernatural. Thirty thousand men and nearly as many animals faced one another, and even the flies were quiet.

El Murid glanced at the wadi. It was a shadowy forest of grotesque sandstone formations: steeples, pylons, giant dumbbells standing on end. He shuddered as he considered that devil's playground.

"We're ready," Nassef said.

"Go ahead."

Nassef turned to Karim, el-Kader and the others. "On my signal."

His captains trotted their horses down to the divisions they commanded.

Nassef gave his signal.

The horde surged forward.

Yousif's men waited without moving. They had arrows ready on the strings of their saddle bows.

"Something's wrong," the Scourge of God muttered. "I can feel it."

"Nassef?" El Murid queried in a voice gone small and tentative. "Do you hear drums?"

"It's the hoofbeats. . . ."

El Murid did hear drums. "Nassef!" His right arm stabbed out like a javelin thrust.

The devil's garden of Wadi el Kuf had begun to disgorge a demon horde.

"Oh, my God!" Nassef moaned. "My God, no."

King Aboud had harkened to Yousif's importunities at last. He had sent Prince Farid to Wadi el Kuf with five thousand of the desert's finest soldiers, many of them equipped after the fashion of western knights. With Farid, in tactical command, was Sir Tury Hawkwind of the Mercenary's Guild. Hawkwind had brought a thousand of his brethren. They were arrayed in western-style lances of a heavy cavalryman, his esquire, two light and one heavy infantrymen.

Nassef had time to think, to react. Heavy cavalry could not charge at breakneck speed across a mile of desert and up a slight hill. And Hawkwind obviously meant to bring his shock power to bear.

"What do we do?" El Murid asked.

"I think it's time for the amulet," Nassef replied. "That's the only weapon that will help now."

El Murid raised his arm. Without a word he showed Nassef his naked wrist.

"Where the hell is it?" Nassef demanded.

Softly, "At Sebil el Selib. I left it. I was so excited about coming, I forgot it." He had not worn the amulet for years, preferring to keep it safe within the shrines.

Nassef sighed, shook his head wearily. "Lord, choose a company of Invincibles and flee. I'll buy you all the time I can."

"Flee? Are you mad?"

"This battle is lost, Lord. All that remains is to salvage as much as we can. Don't stay, and deprive the movement of its reason for existing."

El Murid shook his head stubbornly. "I see no defeat. Only more trouble than we anticipated originally. We still outnumber them, Nassef. And no matter what, I won't leave the field while men are dying for me. Not when they have it in their hearts that I am commanding them. What would they think of my courage?"

Nassef shrugged. "We can but die with honor, then. I suggest you form the Invincibles to meet the coming charge." A moment later, after studying the enemy banners, he murmured thoughtfully, "I wonder what Hawkwind is doing here."

"Trust in the Lord, Nassef. He will deliver them unto us. We have the numbers, and Him on our side. What more could we ask?"

Nassef stifled an angry response. He helped guide the Invincibles into a new disposition.

At the oasis, at least, it seemed that El Murid's confidence was justified. Yousif's force was surrounded.

"Who's this Hawkwind?"

"A Guildsman. Perhaps their best general."

"Guildsman?" El Murid's ignorance of the world outside Hammad al Nakir was immense.

"A brotherhood of warriors. Not unlike the Invincibles. Called the Mercenary's Guild. They're also a little like the Harish, and yet like nothing we know. They own no allegiance except to one another. After Itaskia, they're probably the greatest military power in the west, yet they have no homeland but a castle called High Crag. When their generals frown, princes cringe. Just their decision to fight for someone sometimes stops a war before it starts."

"How do you know? When have you ever had time to learn?"

"I pay people to learn things for me. I've got spies all over the west."

"Why?"

"Because you want to go there someday. I'm preparing the way. But it's all irrelevant if we don't get out of this alive."

Hawkwind's force was close enough to start increasing its pace.

None of the Invincibles had seen knights before. They neither understood nor sufficiently feared what they faced. When their master gave the signal, they charged. They trusted in the Lord and their name.

Hawkwind increased his pace again.

The long lances and heavy horses hit the Invincibles like a stone wall. The Royalists passed through and over them, and crushed them, and in ten minutes were turning and forming for a charge into the rear of the horde beleaguering Yousif.

Neither Nassef nor El Murid said a word. It was even worse than Nassef had expected. The Wahlig of el Aswad was in a bad way. But once help arrived the battle became a rebel slaughter.

Hawkwind placed a screen of infantry between himself and the remnants of the Invincibles. He placed another of light horse between himself and the oasis, with extended and slightly C-shaped wings. Then he started hammering with his armored horsemen. Charge. Melee. Withdraw. Reform. Charge.

El Murid was too stubborn to accept reality. Nassef's

troops, down in the witch's cauldron, were too confused to realize what was happening.

Hawkwind set about systematically exterminating them.

At one point Nassef wept. "My Lord," he pleaded, "let me go down there. Let me try to break them out."

"We can't lose," El Murid murmured in reply, more to himself than to his war general. "We have the numbers. The Lord is with us."

Nassef cursed softly.

The sun moved to the west. Hawkwind extended his wings, completing a thin encirclement against which Nassef's warriors collided randomly, like flies against the walls of a bottle. He put more and more strength into the circle, daring El Murid to try something with his battered Invincibles. The Wahlig's men filtered out of the cauldron and became part of the circle.

Some of Nassef's men tried to surrender, but Prince Farid had ordered his to take no prisoners.

"They have taken away our last ounce of choice," Nassef moaned. "We have to throw these pitiful few hundreds in to give those men down there a chance to escape."

"Nassef?"

"What?" The voice of the Scourge of God was both sorrowful and angry.

"I'm sorry. I was wrong. The time wasn't right. I listened to myself instead of to the Voice of God. Take command. Do what you can to save what you can. O Lord Almighty, forgive me for my arrogance. Pardon me for my vanity."

"No."

"What? Why?"

"I'll tell you what to do, but you do the leading. This is no time to show weakness. Salvage some respect from the disaster. Do that and we can always say that they tricked us, that the Evil One blinded our eyes."

"Nassef! You're right, of course. What should we do?"

Fifteen minutes later the survivors of the Invincibles hurled themselves against Hawkwind's circle. They did not strike toward the center, but cut a shallow chord meant to break the widest possible gap.

Nassef's warriors began flooding through while the gap was still opening.

El Murid and his brother-in-law rode at the head of the charge.

El Murid flailed about him with his sword. The clash of weapons, the screams of horses and men, were overwhelming, maddening. The dust choked him. It stung his eyes. A horse plunged against his, nearly unseating him. A wild sword stroke, partially turned by Nassef, cut his left arm, leaving a shallow, bloody wound. For an instant he was amazed at the lack of immediate pain.

Nassef struck about himself like some war djinn just released from Hell. The Invincibles did their desperate best to keep their prophet from coming to harm, but . . .

"Now!" Nassef shrieked at him. "Give the order to fly. To the wadi. We can lose them in the rocks." Most of Nassef's men were away. The circle was collapsing toward El Murid and the Scourge of God.

El Murid vacillated.

A random swarm of arrows rained from the cloudless sky. One buried itself in his mount's eye.

The beast screamed and reared. El Murid flew through the air. The earth came up and hit him like a flying boulder. A horse trampled his right arm.

He heard the snapping of bone over his own shriek. He tried to rise. His gaze met that of a Guild infantryman who was calmly working his way through the chaos, braining wounded Invincibles with a massive war hammer.

"Micah!" Nassef screamed at him. "Get up! Grab hold of my leg!"

He found the will and strength. Nassef started away.

"Hang on tight. Bounce high."

He did.

Behind him, another hundred Invincibles gave their lives to make sure he got away.

Once into the wadi, Nassef flung himself from his mount, seized El Murid's left hand. "Come on! We've got to disappear before they get organized."

The sounds of battle died swiftly as they fled deeper into the grotesque wilderness. El Murid did not know if distance or final defeat were responsible, but he feared the worst.

They kept to terrain no horse could penetrate. Their enemies would have to come for them on foot if they insisted on pressing the pursuit.

It was almost dark when Nassef found the fox den. Two badly wounded warriors crowded it already, but they made room. Nassef did his best to eliminate traces outside.

The first hunters came only a short time later. They were in a hurry, chasing game still on the wing. Other parties passed during the next few hours. Occasional shouts and metallic clashings echoed through the wadi.

During each stillness Nassef did what he could for the two warriors. He did not expect either to live. When it seemed that the pursuit had ended, he worked on El Murid's arm.

The fracture was not as bad as it had seemed. The bone had broken cleanly, without being crushed.

It was midnight when the pain subsided enough for El Murid to ask, "What do we do now, Nassef?" His voice was vague, his mind airy. Nassef had given him an opiate.

"We start over. We build it again, from the ground. We don't hurry it. At least we won't have to capture Sebil el Selib again."

"Can we do it?"

"Of course. We've lost a battle, that's all. We're young. Time and the Lord are on our side. Be quiet!"

He was at the mouth of the den, masking the others with his body and dark clothing. He could see the flickering light of torches playing among the rocks.

Men followed the light.

One complained, "I'm tired. How long do we have to keep this up?"

Another replied, "Until we get them. They're in here and I don't intend to let them out."

Nassef knew that second voice. It belonged to that stubborn brother of the Wahlig, Fuad. Hatred welled within him.

One of the wounded warriors chose that moment to die. His comrade thought quickly enough to smother his death rattle with a corner of his robe.

"Why didn't you bring the damned amulet?" Nassef demanded testily, after the danger had passed. "It would have made the difference."

The Disciple barely heard through his pain. He gritted the truth between clenched teeth. "I was a fool, wasn't I? The angel gave it to me for moments like those. Why didn't you say something before we left? You knew I was keeping it safe in the shrine."

Chapter Eight

The Castle Tenacious and Resolute

"There is great rejoicing in Sebil el Selib," Fuad snarled as he stalked toward Yousif, Radetic and the Wahlig's captains. A heavy layer of trail dust covered him. "Nassef and the Disciple have returned. They survived."

The cords in Yousif's neck stood out. His face darkened. He rose slowly, then suddenly hurled his platter across the room. "Damn it!" he roared. "And damn that fool Aboud! When they finally take Al Rhemish and strangle him, I hope I'm there to laugh in his halfwit's face."

Wadi el Kuf had been the limit of Royal aid. Nothing Yousif had done or said had been sufficient to excite Prince Farid into exceeding his orders and following through. The opportunity had been there, to pursue and slay, to recover Sebil el Selib. But Farid had had his instructions, and had been satisfied himself that El Murid and Nassef were dead.

Farid's father was old and fat and none too bright. He loved his comforts and could see nothing beyond tomorrow. He did not want his son wasting money or lives.

There had been a time when Aboud had been a renowned warrior and captain. He had driven the Throyens from the disputed territories along the northern end of the eastern shore. But that had been long ago. Time, that old traitor, slows and weakens all men, and makes them less inclined to seek hazard.

"Thank God for Farid," Yousif sighed, his rage spent. "No one else could have gotten us the help we needed at Wadi el Kuf. Megelin? What now?"

"We step back a few years and go on."

"The same thing?"

"The same. And don't count on them making any more

mistakes. They've had their one and gotten away with it. El Murid will take the lesson to heart. He'll listen to Nassef now."

Nearly eight thousand of Nassef's men had escaped Wadi el Kuf. They were back in the desert now, stunned, but a foundation for a new guerrilla infrastructure.

"We should have attacked Sebil el Selib while they were still demoralized," Yousif growled. "We should've hit them and kept on hitting till they gave up. None of the leaders were there."

"Hit them with what?" Fuad asked caustically. "We were lucky they didn't come after us."

Yousif's forces had been battered and exhausted after the battle. Getting themselves home had been the most difficult task they could handle.

Fuad added, "They would have if anybody had been there to tell them what to do."

Yousif's anger evaporated. He could not sustain it in the face of the truth.

The years had taken their toll. El Aswad was approaching its limit. Yousif had done all he could, but his best had not been enough. From Wadi el Kuf onward he foresaw nothing but a downhill slide. His last hope had been that El Murid and his generals had perished. But Fuad's news accounted for the last of the missing leaders. They were all alive. The fury of Wadi el Kuf had consumed none but the expendable.

"Megelin," Yousif said, "think for the enemy. What will he do now?"

"I don't know, Wahlig. They say Nassef is vindictive. We'll probably get a lot of attention. Beyond that guess, you might as well read sheep's entrails."

Yousif said nothing for several minutes. Then, "I'm going to concede the initiative again. We'll keep up the patrols and ambushes, but avoid contact most of the time. We'll stall. Concentrate on surviving. Try to lure them into a debilitating siege of the Eastern Fortress. Aboud is old. He's got the gout. He can't live forever. I talked to Farid. He's on our side. He'll be less sedentary. He can see the shape of things. He'd give us what we need if he wore the Crown."

But neither fate nor Nassef would play the game according to Yousif's wishes. In the year after Wadi el Kuf Yousif's men seldom saw their enemies. They could not be found even when hunted. Nassef seemed to have forgotten that el Aswad existed. With the exception of the patrolled zone immediately before the mouth of Sebil el Selib, security and peace reigned in the Wahligate.

The quiet drove Yousif and Fuad to distraction. They worried constantly. What did the silence mean?

Haroun and Radetic went on their first fieldtrip in almost two years. Megelin wanted to look for rare wildflowers. His search took them into a canyon which meandered deep into Jebal al Alf Dhulquarneni.

Haroun worried about offending the Hidden Ones. He tried to mask his nervousness behind uncharacteristic chatter. That generally took the form of trying to get Radetic to illuminate the enemy's behavior.

Exasperated, Radetic finally growled, "I don't know, Haroun. The Sword rules the Word these days. And Nassef is a big unknown. I can't begin to guess his motives, let alone predict his moves. One minute he looks like El Murid's most devoted follower, the next like a bandit looting the desert, and a second after that he seems to be a man quietly finagling himself an empire. All I can say is wait. He'll make everything painfully clear someday."

One painful piece of news had sullied a restful winter. El Murid had appointed Nassef commander of the Invincibles for a period of five years. Spies said that the Scourge of God had launched an immediate purge, that Nassef was redesigning the bodyguard to his own specifications.

The Sword apparently mastered the Word completely now.

Nassef's campaign plans became less murky once Haroun and Radetic returned to el Aswad. They were given no chance to recuperate from the hardships of the trail. Guards hustled them directly to the Wahlig.

"Well, he's finally made a move, Megelin," Yousif declared as they approached. "He's shown his hand. And it was the last thing anybody expected."

Radetic dropped gingerly to a cushion. "What did he do?"

"All that strength he's been gathering? That's been piling up so fast our spies figured he was going to take a stab at us this summer? He used it to attack to the east."

"The east? But—"

"Souk el Arba has fallen already. He's besieging Es

Souanna. His riders have reached Ras al Jan. Souk el Arba didn't resist. They sent a committee to welcome him. Our agents say our cousins on the coast are tripping over each other they're so eager to join him. He's promising everybody the loot of Al Rhemish and the Inner Provinces."

"In other words, the east has decided its future lies with El Murid."

"They've had a lot of time to preach there. And to make deals. Aboud hasn't done much to hold their loyalties. In fact, I expect Throyes to cut us off completely now."

The only way Al Rhemish could reach its eastern supporters was by using the same narrow, northern pass which gave desert merchants access to Throyes. The Throyens were racially and linguistically akin to the Children of Hammad al Nakir, but had not recognized an external suzerainty since the Fall. The city had been founded as a naval and mercantile port by Ilkazar.

There had been no fighting for years, but the city still claimed territories on the northern shores of the east coast. Since Sebil el Selib Throyes had been nibbling away at the lands Aboud had reconquered in his youth. The Royal lines of communication now had to pass through areas patrolled by unfriendly troops.

"I imagine they'll occupy in earnest as soon as they hear what's happened," Radetic agreed. "How strong a garrison did Nassef leave? Did El Murid go with him?"

"Fuad's checking it now."

Fuad was doing more than checking. He was conducting el Aswad's first assault on the pass in years. His initial progress report arrived early next day.

Haroun came to drag Radetic out of his quarters. "Come on, Megelin! Uncle Fuad took them by surprise. Get up! Father needs you."

Radetic rubbed sleep from his eyes. "Fuad did what?" He began to dress, donning desert-style clothing. The last of his own western garb had gone to rags years earlier. "Never going to get used to this women's wear," he muttered. "Maybe I should have something sent out. Bah. That would make it too easy for assassins to find their target."

"Come on!" Haroun bubbled. "He surprised them. He got through their picket lines and cut them off so nobody knew he was coming. He caught them working in their fields and killed a whole lot. Come on. Father needs to know what you think we should do."

Haroun could not stop jabbering. He revealed most of Yousif's surprise before he and Radetic located the Wahlig in the parapet of the tower on the north wall. Yousif was staring northward, toward Sebil el Selib.

With a mixture of luck, planning and cunning, Fuad had outmaneuvered El Murid's patrols and had broken into Sebil el Selib. He had killed or captured hundreds before the survivors could seal up the two fortresses, and had killed and captured hundreds more afterward, because in their panic the gatekeepers had locked them out. Fuad and the survivors were trading stares over the walls of the castles. Fuad did not have the strength to storm either. While he awaited advice from home he was destroying everything he could. He expected Nassef to send help soon. He wanted to leave the enemy nothing when he withdrew.

"What do you think we should do, Megelin?" Yousif asked.

"Send for help. Especially to Prince Farid. Explain the situation. Tell him that if he hurries we have a chance to cut them off on the coast. That might be as good as killing them."

"I've done that. I was thinking in more direct terms. What can we do up there? While we're waiting for Farid and Nassef?"

Radetic considered. "I'd have to see the fortresses myself. I might notice a weakness you've overlooked."

The western style of warfare was more given to castles and siegework than that of Hammad al Nakir. The men of the desert were inclined to run away when outnumbered rather than to retreat into a fortress. Most of the extant fortifications were Imperial hand-me-downs weak from long neglect.

"You can join me, then. I'm leaving in an hour. Taking every man who can hoist himself onto a horse."

"Father?"

Yousif eyed his son. He knew what the boy wanted, but made him ask anyway. "What, Haroun?"

"Can I go? If Megelin does?"

The Wahlig glanced at Radetic, who said, "It's all right with me if it's all right with you."

"Go get your things, son."
Haroun left with the excitement of a small whirlwind. Radetic observed, "It's time he got a glimpse of the realities."
"That's why I told him he could go. He accused me of letting Ali have all the fun this morning. I want him to see that Ali isn't enjoying himself."
"How much more muscle can you give Fuad?"
"Not much. Maybe three hundred men."
"Hardly enough."
"Then hope that my messengers get lucky."
Two days later Megelin saw Sebil el Selib for the first time. He was surprised. He had been hearing about it for eight years. He had built a mental picture that only vaguely resembled reality.
"How easy it is to destroy," he told Haroun. "You see what your uncle has done? In a few days he's undone the labor of years."
Fields had been ruined. Hillside terraces had been undermined and allowed to collapse. Fuad's men were still forcing their prisoners to destroy, daring the inmates of the two fortresses to try stopping them. Fuad was saving the vast barracks-city east of the new fortress to become a burning greeting for Nassef's return.
Radetic studied the situation for several hours. Then he located Fuad and asked, "Is El Murid here?"
"Went with Nassef. To preach to new converts. He left his family, though. They're in the New Castle."
Radetic glanced at the huge fortress. "We couldn't take that. The old stronghold we might. We can pound it a little, anyway. If we can come up with the lumber to build siege engines."
Fuad found the lumber in the barracks.
Radetic gathered the Wahlig's officers. "We probably won't have time for much before Nassef returns," he told them. "But we won't get anywhere if we don't try." Those men had been involved in the war so long that other ways of life now seemed alien. "What the Wahlig wants is a low-risk assault on these fortifications. We're likely to have little luck with the New Castle. It's up to modern standards and it's in good repair. The old castle isn't. It'll be our primary target.
"We'll build a variety of siege engines, beginning with

trebuchets and mangonels. We'll start gathering suitable stones, lumber and so forth, right away.

"We'll work on the old castle wall a few yards to the left of the barbican. That's a recent addition, and they weakened the wall during construction.

"I'll want to keep several things going at once. Especially some obvious practice with scaling ladders, turtles, rams and siege towers. We'll build the turtles right away and bunch them in the meadow as close to the old castle as we can. We'll use them to conceal the head of a mine we'll run under the weak section of wall. We'll dispose of the earth at night."

Radetic's siege strategy was extensive. It would require every available body, including Fuad's prisoners. But as he revealed it, the faces of Yousif's officers darkened. He was asking warriors to do the work of slaves. It was beneath their dignity. He considered their hostile faces. "Haroun," he whispered, "fetch your father."

The Wahlig did his convincing for him.

Yousif came to Megelin three days later, while Radetic was inspecting his projects. "How long till you drop that wall, Megelin? We're running out of time. Nassef should be on his way by now." There was little force in the Wahlig's voice. He seemed dazed.

"I'm having trouble. The soft earth doesn't run all the way to the foundations. I'm running a mine to the New Castle, too, but I don't have much hope for it. Those walls were engineered by westerners. You can tell that from the camber of the base."

"What?"

"The way it slopes out at the bottom. Instead of coming straight down. It increases the thickness and coherence of the wall, making mining difficult."

"Nevertheless, Megelin."

"Yes, Wahlig. We'll persist. Any news from Al Rhemish?"

Yousif became more sour. His lined, rugged, aquiline face darkened. "The messenger returned an hour ago."

Radetic watched as his hastily constructed trebuchets hurled a barrage against the old castle. One of the engines groaned and fell apart. The rocks rumbled against the castle. The wall shuddered. A merlon stone slid off the battlements and plunged downward. Cracks had begun to show in the wall. "The engines might be enough. If I can keep them working. What's the bad news?"

"Aboud says we have to chase Nassef off the coast. He was pretty definite about it."

"Did he have any suggestions? How much help is he going to send?"

"None. And no ideas either. Just a flat-out order to do the job."

Radetic peered at Yousif. The Wahlig's face had gone gray with despair.

"This is the beginning of the end, Megelin. Unless you can produce a miracle here. They've abandoned us."

Radetic thought he understood. "You could pretend the letter never arrived. You can't commit suicide."

"Megelin, I can't. I'm a man of honor. I don't think I could explain that to a westerner. Even a westerner who has been around as long as you. You see my men there? They know I'm fighting a losing battle. But they stick with me year after year. They don't see that they have any choice. Neither have I. Pledges of honor have been made. Aboud's orders leave me no room for maneuver. I have to try to beat Nassef even when I know that I can't."

"Haroun? Are you listening?"

"Yes, Megelin." The youth was as close as Radetic's shadow. As always. He followed his teacher everywhere, watching with those wide, curious eyes, logging every detail of the siegework in an infallible memory.

"Pay attention to this. Listen to your father. He's talking about paying the price of an absolute and inflexible concept of duty. Don't ever push a man into the corner he's in. And don't ever let yourself get shoved into one like it. Yousif, there has to be a way around destroying yourself because of Aboud's stupidity."

"It's our way, Megelin. It's mine. I have to do *something*."

"Isn't this something?" Radetic swept an arm round to include everything happening in Sebil el Selib. "Isn't this enough? We've been bled white. We just don't have our strength anymore. Yousif!"

The Wahlig stepped back from his sudden intensity. "What?"

"I get the feeling you're thinking about going on through the pass. To meet Nassef and martyr yourself in some big last battle. Don't do it. Don't waste yourself."

"Megelin—"

"At least set your schedule so you can do it after you've finished here. Would that violate the spirit of Aboud's orders? Only a fool leaves behind an enemy who can close a trap on him later."

Yousif mused. "You're right, of course. You always are. I'm not thinking this morning. I'm so tired of fighting and Aboud's indifference that part of me just wants to hurry the end."

"Have you explored the pass? Is there a narrow passage where you could ambush Nassef? Where you could roll boulders down on him? This is our last great cry of defiance, Yousif. Why don't we make it memorable *without* getting ourselves martyred?"

"All right."

The Wahlig departed. He seemed less depressed.

Radetic watched as the trebuchet crews cranked the arms of the engines back to throwing position. They were clumsy and slow. "Damn!" he muttered. "What I wouldn't give for a company of Guildsmen."

Fuad materialized. "I don't know what you said to Yousif, but thanks. He was ready to throw himself on his sword."

"Not much, really."

"He told you the news?"

"That Aboud isn't going to help? Yes. Damn the fool anyway. I thought sure Farid would talk him into sending us something."

"The Crown Prince won't be talking anybody into anything anymore. Didn't he tell you? Farid is dead."

Very carefully, like an old cat searching for just the right place to curl up, Radetic looked round and chose himself a stone on which to sit. "He's dead? Farid?"

Fuad nodded.

"He had help making his exit? The Harish finally got him?"

The cult was trying to exterminate the Quesani family. They failed more often than they succeeded, but scared hell out of the family by trying. Farid had become a favorite target. He had escaped their attentions three times.

"Not this time. This time Nassef sent his own expert. He slipped Karim and a couple of hundred Invincibles into the wastes north of Al Rhemish. Last week they ambushed Farid while he was lion hunting. It was a big hunt."

"That's sad. It really is. Sometimes I think there really is a God who's on El Murid's side."

"You don't know how sad it is. They didn't just kill Farid. I said it was a big hunt. They got most of his brothers, his retainers, a bunch of Aboud's officers and ministers and the Wahlig of Es Sofala and a lot of his people."

"Good heavens. A disaster."

"A hell of a coup if you're Nassef. He's carved the heart out of the Quesani. You know who's left? Who our beloved Crown Prince is now? Ahmed."

"Ahmed? I don't know the name."

"With reason. He's a nothing. I wish I didn't know him. He's a damned woman, if you ask me. I wouldn't be surprised if he prefers boys."

"No wonder Yousif was so grim."

"Megelin?" Haroun piped. "Does that mean it's over? Uncle Fuad? Did we lose the war when we weren't looking?"

Fuad laughed sourly. "A good turn of phrase, Haroun. A fine way to say it. Yes."

"No," Radetic countered. "It's never over till you surrender. In your own heart."

Fuad laughed again. "Bravely spoken, teacher. Fine talk. But it doesn't change the facts."

Radetic shrugged. "Haroun, let's see if they're ready with that spoon trebuchet."

The crew was cranking the machine for a test shot when they arrived. Radetic watched while they ignited a bundle of brush, tipped it into the spoon, then flipped the blazing missile over the New Castle wall.

"Will it start a fire, Megelin?"

"Probably not. But it'll keep them nervous."

"Why do it, then?"

"Battles can be won in men's minds, Haroun. That's what I meant when I told your uncle it's not over till you surrender in your heart. The sword isn't the only weapon that will wear an enemy down."

"Oh." Haroun's face took on that look he got when he wanted to remember something forever.

Two days passed. And still Nassef did not come. Megelin could feel the contempt radiating from the coast. Nassef did not consider them dangerous.

He would learn.

Megelin sent for Yousif, who wore a bright expression when he appeared. The Wahlig seemed to have made peace with himself.

"I'm going to bring her down now," Radetic told him. He gave a signal. "Fuad, get the men ready. The way we rehearsed it."

Fuad muttered something uncomplimentary and stalked off. A gust of activity swept the valley. It became a gale. Yousif's warriors gathered for the assault.

The trebuchets ceased pounding the old castle. The wall had held, but barely.

The engine crews dragged their machines around to face the New Castle.

An hour passed. Yousif became impatient. "When's something going to happen?" he demanded.

Radetic indicated smoke trailing out of cracks at the base of the wall. "When you mine a wall you have to shore it up with timbers. When you're ready to bring it down you fill the chamber underneath with brush and set it afire. It takes time for the timbers to burn through. Ah. Here we go."

A deep-throated grinding assailed the air. The cracks grew. Pieces of masonry popped out of the wall. Then, with a startling suddenness, a twenty-foot-wide section dropped straight down, virtually disappearing into the earth.

"Perfect!" Radetic enthused. "Absolutely perfect. Fuad!" he shouted. "Go ahead! Attack now!" He turned to Yousif. "Don't forget to watch the New Castle for a sally."

The gutting of the old fortress took under four hours. It was almost a disappointment. There weren't enough defenders to slow the assault.

Radetic turned his attention to El Murid's New Castle immediately. The capture of the old was barely complete when word came that an enemy column was in the pass. Yousif roared off to spring the ambush Radetic had suggested.

The tardiness and weakness of the relief column underscored Nassef's contempt for el Aswad. He did not come himself. He sent el Nadim and two thousand green recruits from the coast. Yousif carved them up.

Nassef himself came four days later. He brought twenty thousand men and did not spare their lives. It took him just eight days to reverse roles and surround el Aswad.

The siege of the Eastern Fortress persisted for thirty months and four days. It was as cruel to the enemy as Yousif had hoped. El-Kader, in command of the besiegers, though nearly as competent as Nassef himself, simply could not overcome Yousif, his environment and the sickness that ravaged his camp.

El-Kader's own most potent weapon, starvation, remained untested because Nassef was unable to spare the besieging army sufficiently long.

Nassef himself remained on the coast. After the successes at Es Suoanna and Souk el Arba he found the going more difficult. The narrow, rich, densely populated littoral was nearly four hundred miles long. Those miles revealed a lot of towns and cities with no sympathy for El Murid's cause.

And there was Throyes.

El Murid was compelled to fight a foreign war before he had won over his own people.

When it came, the Throyen land grab was so brazen and extensive that El Murid found it politically unendurable. The nationalist sentiment it generated forced him to react.

Nassef's need for warriors on that front drew the besiegers away from el Aswad. He left just a thousand men in the province, commanded by Karim. They were to distract Yousif from Sebil el Selib.

Once his environs were open Yousif began corresponding with neighbors and Royalists whose thinking paralleled his own. The Kasr Helal Gold Seam was reborn. Trustworthy friends and acquaintances of Megelin Radetic made quiet arrangements in the west.

To an extent, the defenders of the Eastern Fortress had surrendered in their hearts.

Yousif stood in a windswept parapet watching the smoke of a brush fire burning twenty miles south of el Aswad. It was a huge blaze. Fuad was using it to herd one of Karim's battalions into a deathtrap. Haroun, practicing his shaghûnry at last, was with his uncle.

The boy had been a tremendous asset since the end of the siege. He always accompanied his uncle now. His shaghûnry instructors said he had enormous potential. They had taken him to their limits without pushing him to his own.

The Wahlig spied a rider coming from the northwest. Another whining message from Aboud? He did not bother going down to find out.

His royal cousin was becoming a royal aggravation. His bluster, wishful thinking and vain edicts would not alter the situation one iota.

Radetic joined him a few minutes later. He looked grim. He was becoming ever more dour and remote as el Aswad's position became ever less tenable.

"Another command to victory?" Yousif asked.

"More like a petition this time. But he has started to realize what's happening. After all this time. I mean, Nassef has got to be more than a bandit if he can fight a war with Throyes. Doesn't he?"

"Eh?" Yousif turned. "You mean he said something positive? That he's going to take us seriously? Now that it's too late?"

"A little. A little too little too late. He's hired Hawkwind again. He's sending him out here."

"Hawkwind? Why a mercenary?"

"He didn't explain. Maybe because no one else would come. The messenger says the negotiations have been on since Prince Farid's death. For three years! Hawkwind was reluctant. But Aboud finally made a sufficiently convincing presentation to the Guild generals, and paid over a handsome retainer. And he put huge bounties on El Murid, Nassef, Karim and that lot. Hawkwind is on his way already."

Yousif paced. "How many men?"

"I don't know. I was told a substantial force."

"Enough to change anything?"

"I doubt it. We both know there will be no more victories like Wadi el Kuf."

"But why won't he send Royal troops?"

"I think all is not well in the Royal camp. Some wahligs apparently refuse to send men into the witch's cauldron.

They want to sit tight and let El Murid come to them. It seems if he wanted to send anyone, it had to be mercenaries. He did the best he could in the circumstances he faces."

"But not enough." Yousif smote the weathered, lichened stone of the parapet.

"No. Not enough." Radetic studied the smoke from the brush fire. "Is Haroun out there?"

"Yes. Fuad says he's doing well. Is there more news? You looked grim when you arrived."

Radetic kept his own counsel for a few minutes. Then, "Prince Hefni was killed."

"A pity. The Harish again?"

"Yes."

Hefni had been the last of Aboud's sons, excepting Crown Prince Ahmed. He had been much like his brother Farid. There were rumors that Aboud wished Hefni were Crown Prince instead of Ahmed, and that Ahmed was being pressured to abdicate in his favor.

"The Quesani are going to become extinct."

"Wahlig . . ."

Yousif turned slowly. "Don't tell me any more bad news, Megelin. I don't think I could stand what I think you're going to say."

"I don't want to. But I have to. Now or later."

Yousif peered at the fire. In time, he murmured, "Out with it, then. I don't want to break down in front of everybody."

"Your sons, Rafih and Yousif. They were killed in the attack on Hefni. They acquitted themselves well."

The two had been in Al Rhemish for several years, serving in the royal court. It was a common practice for nobles to send junior sons to court.

"So. Now I have only Ali and Haroun." He stared. For a moment it seemed the cloud of smoke was a response to his baleful glare. "Look away from me, teacher."

Radetic turned his back. The man had a right to solitude while he shed his tears.

After a time, Yousif remarked, "Aboud won't be able to handle this. He'll do something stupid." He sounded like a man begging for help. He was not talking about Aboud.

Radetic shrugged. "The behavior of others has always been beyond my control. Unfortunately."

"I'd better go tell their mother. It's not a task I savor."

Megelin moved nervously, came to a decision. "Would you look at this first?" He offered Yousif a chart on which he had penned names, titles and connecting lines in a tiny, tight hand. It constituted a who's who of Hammad al Nakir.

"A chart of succession?" Over a period of ten years Yousif had sneakily picked up enough reading ability to puzzle his way through simple texts. He was good at names.

"Yes."

"So?" Every nobleman kept one. The chart was critical in determining precedence and protocol.

"Permit me." Radetic laid the chart out on a merlon. He produced a stick of drawing charcoal. "Let's scratch out the names of people who aren't with us anymore."

His hand moved like the swift-stabbing hand of Death.

Dolefully, Yousif remarked, "That many? I hadn't realized. It's bad, isn't it?"

"Anything apparent?"

"The better classes are being slaughtered."

"Yes. But that's not what I wanted you to see."

Yousif leaned closer to the chart, then backed away. His eyes were weakening.

"I see," he said. His voice was sadder than ever. "All of a sudden I'm third in the succession. If anything happens to Ahmed . . ."

"Some of our most devoted allies might expedite his meeting with the angels."

The Crown Prince had all of his father's faults, and none of the virtues that had made Aboud a respected king earlier in his reign. He was thoroughly disliked. Some of his enemies even accused him of being a secret adherent of El Murid.

His life would become worthless the moment Aboud's health started to fail. The behind-the-scenes manipulators at Al Rhemish would hold an "abdication by dagger."

"And," Radetic added, "going by the way you people figure these things, Ali is fourth in line, Haroun fifth, Fuad sixth, and his sons in line after him."

"Megelin, I know how you think. You've got a double-level puzzle here. You're getting at something more. Out with it. I'm not in the mood for intellectual gymnastics."

"All right. If by some ill fortune your family is destroyed—say during a successful siege—the succession would shift to the western cousins of the Quesani. Specifically, to a certain Mustaf el Habib, who must be pretty old by now."

"So?"

"This particular gentleman is the father of a rebel named Nassef."

Yousif seized the chart. He stared and stared. "By damn! You're right. How come nobody ever saw it before?"

"Because it's not exactly obvious. Mustaf el Habib is a damned obscure royal relative. And Nassef is as cunning as El Murid's Evil One. His moves remain strictly explicable within the context of his service to the Disciple. Why should anyone expect a threat from this direction? Would you like to bet that El Murid hasn't the vaguest notion that the Scourge of God could become King?"

"No. Hell no. Megelin, somebody has got to kill that man. He's more dangerous than El Murid."

"Possibly. He does think on his feet. El Murid was ready to set the Harish on him before Wadi el Kuf. Six months later he took over the Invincibles."

"Well, I've got a surprise for both of them. It'll so amaze them that they'll waste six months trying to figure it out. It might even panic Nassef into abandoning his eastern wars." Yousif laughed a little madly. "How soon will Hawkwind arrive?"

"I couldn't guess. They should be coming by now, but it's a long haul from High Crag."

"I hope it's soon. I do hope it's soon."

Chapter Nine

Ripening Soldiers

High Crag was an ancient, draughty stone pile surmounting a wind- and sea-battered headland.

"The Gates of Hell," Bragi gasped as his training company double-timed uphill, toward the fortress. For three months he and his brother had been in the hands of merciless veterans. Seldom had they had a moment to call their own.

They had found themselves a new friend. He was the only other Trolledyngjan in their Itaskian-speaking company. He called himself Reskird Kildragon. "It was just a small dragon," he was wont to say. "And thereby hangs a tale." But, though Reskird almost never shut up, he never told that tale. He hailed from Jandrfyre, a town on the Trolledyngjan coast opposite the Tongues of Fire. He was as loquacious as Haaken was reticent.

"No," Kildragon replied to Bragi's remark. "Hell would look good from here."

"Knock off the chatter up there," Sergeant Sanguinet thundered. "You barbarians got breath to waste, I'll send you round the course again."

Kildragon had come south with a raiding fleet the previous summer. It had been one of the few to sail during the succession troubles. An Itaskian warship had rammed it off Libiannin. He had managed to swim to shore, the only survivor. Of necessity, he had learned southern ways fast.

"Still a scroungy-looking lot you've got there, Torc," the gatekeeper called as they double-timed into the Guild stronghold.

"I'll get them weeded out yet, Andy."

The three months had been a pitiless weeding through exhaustion of body and will.

"Wichard's about had it," Reskird murmured as the Itaskian ahead of him stumbled.

Bragi grunted. He and Haaken had weathered the grind well. Trolledyngja had schooled them for it. Haaken seemed right at home. The structured military life suited him perfectly. Bragi was less comfortable. He just did not like a Yes sir, No sir, Do it by the numbers approach to life.

"We'll get him through. He's got guts," Bragi whispered. Despite his reservations, Ragnarson had been designated recruit corporal in charge of his squad. He had a sneaking suspicion that the assignment was more of Sanguinet's torment, though the sergeant claimed he had been given the position because he could yell louder than anyone else.

After bathing and shaving they mustered for Recruits' Mess. Their mealtimes were one of the few occasions when they could relax and talk.

Haaken was in a mood. "You want to leave, Bragi?"

"Leave? What?"

"The Guild."

A recruit could do so whenever he decided the life was not for him. Any Guildsman could leave. But few who survived the training and shielding abandoned the brotherhood. The preliminary weeding was thorough.

The Citadel wanted no physical or moral weaklings in its command.

"Hell no. With six days to go? I'll finish if I have to do it walking on my hands."

The name Guild was a popular misnomer. The organization was not a Guild at all. It was a brotherhood of warriors bound together by honor, discipline and an exaggerated set of military codes. It showed elements of monasticism, though it bowed to neither god nor prince. It was a kingdom spanning scores of kingdoms, consisting of men from countless lands who had renounced every allegiance save that to their brothers in arms.

The ruling council of nine generals, all of whom had once entered the Guild as the recruits were now, had reached their stations on merit. A complete contempt for quality of birth was one of the cultural chasms separating the Guild from the rest of the world. There were princes in the ranks and farmers' sons in the Citadel.

The Guild had phenomenal political leverage. The fates of principalities turned on High Crag's decision to accept or reject a commission offering. The order was wealthy. Its services were not cheap. It often accepted payment in lands and livings. It held income properties everywhere. If the nine old men in the Citadel became unhappy, princes hastened to learn how they had offended. Elite, powerful, the Guild was like nothing else in existence. It held a strong attraction for youths seeking a mission, a place in something bigger than themselves. Just belonging set a man a notch above his contemporaries. It marked him as the best.

The brotherhood was also a mystery cult. It had seven circles of initiation. Certain promotional levels demanded a prior passage to a circle closer to enlightenment. The nine generals were the truly illuminated.

An organization so powerful and secretive naturally accumulated detractors. Those claimed that the true nature and goals of the brotherhood were known only to the old generals in the Citadel.

There was truth in the allegation, but not enough to make the order an object of terror or reprisal.

Bragi, Haaken and Reskird did not care how others saw the Guild. They had bought the message of pride sold them from the moment they had entered High Crag's gate.

In six days they would belong.

"Where do you think we'll be posted?" Reskird asked.

They had been sent to barracks immediately following supper. Their companions were abuzz, speculating about the unprecedented event. They used the time to catch up on their brass and boot polishing. Sergeant Sanguinet was obsessed with shininess.

"All I want is out of this dump," Haaken grumbled. "Penny to a pound, this is what Hell is like."

"Think we'll get lucky?" Reskird persisted. He smoothed straight, fine ginger hair that refused to stay in place. "One of the famous outfits? We're doing good."

Kildragon did not look Trolledyngjan. He was tall but on the lean side, with delicate features and feminine hands. He seemed more typically Itaskian.

"Hawkwind? Lauder? The White Company?" he babbled.

Bragi shrugged. "Wickhard's got a chance at the White. If we can get him through. It's spooky, the way he can use a bow."

"It's the regiments for us," Haaken grumbled. "Lauder and Hawkwind don't take Greens."

"I'd guess the regiment in Simballawein," Bragi said. "That's where the war scare is."

"Farther south," Haaken complained. "And it's still summer."

"Me," said Reskird, "I think we ought to kiss Sanguinet's ass so he'll recommend us for Octylya." Sardygo, the Prince of Octylya, maintained a Guild bodyguard consisting entirely of Trolledyngjans.

A demonic creature looking nine feet tall and seven wide lumbered into the barracks room. "Kiss it all you want, boy. I'm still getting rid of you before you get your shield."

Ragnarson squawked a startled, " 'Ten-shut!"

"Failing that, Kildragon, I'll get you the honeybucket concession for the whole damned castle."

Reskird did not cringe. This was what passed for light banter with the sergeant.

Sanguinet stalked round the cramped little room occupied by Bragi's squad. He poked fingers into cracks. He thumped hammocks. He hunted mercilessly, and could find nothing to bitch about.

"Ragnarson!"

"Sir?"

"You making fun of me, boy?"

"Sir? I don't understand, sir."

"You're playing some kind of game. It's too perfect. Your squad is always too perfect." He grinned wickedly. "So maybe I'll change the rules."

Corporal Trubacik stuck his head in the doorway. "Sarge? The Old Man wants you. Said make it yesterday."

"What is it now?"

"Another messenger came in. Looks set. He's expecting word from the Citadel."

"Damn it all to Hell! The rumor was right. And us stuck with Greens." The demon stalked out in the wake of his apprentice.

"What was that all about?" Bragi wondered. Haaken and Reskird shrugged.

Kildragon said, "We've got to give him something to gnash his teeth on, Bragi. He's foaming at the mouth because you won't give him anything."

"Not going to, either. I don't like his game. As long as I'm stuck with it, I'm going to play it better than he does. All that growl is just for show, anyway. My father did the same thing. Bet you he isn't half a hardass once we've won our shields."

"Hrumph!" Haaken opined.

Rumors flew like panicky pigeons at breakfast. The old men in the Citadel had accepted a big commission. The drill instructors did not deny that. The recruit company would be included. The noncoms would not confirm or deny that. Going on from that point, virtually every imaginable possibility was aired. Sanguinet and Trubacik apparently knew the truth, but they weren't talking. The sergeant was pale, and he roared more than normal. He altered the training routine to include more weapons practice and drill to battlefield signals.

"We're going," Bragi guessed, stomach heavy. "And he expects action. The enemy won't be anybody who'll fold when he hears we're in the field."

Haaken grunted affirmatively. Reskird observed, "He's scared."

Bragi grumbled, "Hell, you can't blame him. His life will depend on us. And we've never been in combat."

"He should have more faith in his ability as an instructor."

"Would you, in his boots?"

Reskird shrugged. "No. You never know what a man will do till he's stuck in a situation. We're the only ones in the outfit who've ever been in a real fight."

There was no official comment till evening parade. Then a Colonel from the Citadel addressed the assembled troops, veterans and recruits alike. He said, yes, a commission had been accepted. A thousand men would be involved. General Hawkwind would command. Details he kept to himself, perhaps for security reasons. He urged all brothers not actively participating to remember Hawkwind's force in their prayers.

"Hawkwind!" Reskird enthused. "What a break. First time out and we get the grand master. You hear what he did at Balewyne last year? Beat the whole Kisten army with five hundred men."

Bragi grunted. "With five hundred veterans from his own and the White Company."

"You're as bad as Haaken. Know that? What about Wadi el Kuf? Fifteen thousand enemy dead on the field. He's never lost a battle."

"Always a first time," Haaken grumbled.

"I don't believe you. How soon you think we'll head out?"

The word passed through the barracks that night: the recruit company would complete its training. Five days of Hell remained.

"So much for marching off to war, Reskird." Bragi whispered after lights out. "You're full of it, you know that? Enjoy the obstacle course."

One regular company departed two days later, bound for a rendezvous with Hawkwind somewhere to the south. Word spread quickly: the recruit company would have to catch up on the road. Grim faces appeared. The pace would be hard. Graduation would provide no respite.

Corporal Trubacik was amused. "You're all young men. In prime shape, I hear. You should be able to do it walking backward."

Bragi said little the next few days. He went through the exercises and drills numbly. Haaken finally asked, "You all right? Sure you don't want to bow out?"

"I started it. I'll finish it. I just have trouble when I think about dying out there. Wherever." They had not been told where they were going.

Bragi could not buy all the brotherhood of the Guild. He felt solidarity with his squad and company, of course. That was one function of the training program. A group went through Hell together and learned to depend upon one another. But the larger belonging that made the Guild had not infected him. The honor and nobility had not become tangible to him. And that worried him. Those things were important to both his superiors and to his comrades. They made the Guild what it was.

He tried hard to sell himself. It was like trying to force sleep. Self-defeating.

It seemed to take forever arriving, but Shielding Day did

come. All the grand old men, the great and famous generals, came down from the Citadel to review the recruits and make speeches. They kept their remarks refreshingly brief. The Castellan, the senior member of the order present, apologized because the recruits would have no opportunity to enjoy the leave traditional after completing training.

Then came the final ceremony, when each new Guildsman was awarded the shield of a Guild footsoldier. Each had to go before the assembly to accept. Trainees who had excelled received honor ribbons with their shields. Bragi was awarded one for having had the best squad during inspections.

The award embarrassed him terribly. He hustled back into line. His comrades grinned wolfishly. He knew he would not hear the end of it soon. He examined shield and ribbons, found a lump rising in his throat, felt his pride swelling. "Damn," he murmured. "They got to me after all."

Corporal Trubacik bellowed, "Up and at them, lads. Up and at them. It's another glorious day in the outfit." He whipped blankets off the new young soldiers. "Let's go. Let's go. You know the drill. Company formation in half an hour." Out the door he went, leaving the lamp turned a little higher.

"Damn," Reskird said. "Ain't nothing changed. I hoped we'd at least get to sleep in."

Bragi did not say anything. He got his soap and razor and stumbled to the lavatory. His head was stuffed up and his temper was foul. He washed and shaved in silence, refusing to respond to jibes about his ribbon.

"Fall in!" Trubacik bellowed across the parade yard. "Platoon leaders, report!" The platoon sergeants turned and bellowed for reports from the squads. Bragi reported all present and accounted for without checking. Nobody had missed muster yet.

He was more interested in a number of men lounging behind Sanguinet. Why were they here? What were they up to?

Minutes later his heart sank. The hangers-around proved to be veterans assigned as squad leaders. Though he had known it vain, he had hoped to retain that status himself.

Each squad departed as it received its new corporal.

Bragi's went to a wiry little Itaskian named Birdsong, who led them to the quartermasters. He did not have much to say at first, just watched while the quartermasters replaced gear worn or damaged during training. Each recruit received an extra pair of boots.

"I don't like this," Reskird grumbled. "Extra boots means somebody figures us to wear out a lot of shoe leather."

Bragi glanced at Birdsong. The little corporal smiled. Smiling made his mustache wiggle like a brown caterpillar.

The armorers came after the quartermasters. They exchanged training weapons for battle weapons. Breastplates were issued. Bragi and Haaken went two rounds with an armorer who wanted to relieve them of the swords they had brought down from Trolledyngja. Birdsong interceded. He understood the importance of heirloom blades.

"But they're not standard!" the armorer protested.

And Birdsong, "But your budget will come up on the long side."

End of dispute.

There were two more stops. The kitchens, for field rations, where Reskird moaned at the size of the issue, and the paymaster, where Reskird's protests were noteworthy by their absence.

Individual Guildsmen did not receive a large stipend. Not compared to other troops. Belonging was their great reward. But on this occasion the old men in the Citadel had awarded a substantial bounty because the trainees had been deprived of graduation leave. Each man also received a month's advance, which was customary on taking the field.

Then it was time to gather in the courtyard again. There were other squads passing through the system. Birdsong took the opportunity to acquaint himself with his men. He proved to be a tad pompous, a lot self-conscious, a little unsure of himself. In short, he suffered the usual insecurities of anyone new to a supervisory role.

Bragi told Haaken, "I think I'm going to like him."

Haaken shrugged, indifferent. But Reskird threatened to drag his feet because he thought Bragi should have retained the squad leader's post.

Bragi told him, "You do and I'll crack your back."

Sanguinet returned to the drill yard on horseback, accompanied by Trubacik and the other noncoms who had guided the company through training. They wore new belts and badges proclaiming their elevated status. Sanguinet had been promoted to lieutenant.

"Fall in!" Sergeant Trubacik roared. "We're moving out." And in five minutes, with the sun still barely above the horizon, the march began.

It was rougher than any training hike. Dawn to dusk, forty and fifty miles every day, eating pemmican, dried fruit and toasted grain, drinking only water, and occasionally nibbling such fruits as could be purchased from wayside farmers. Living off the land was prohibited, except catch-as-catch-can in the forests. Guildsmen did not plunder, even to support themselves. They were schooled to consider themselves gentlemen, above the savageries of national soldiers.

Kildragon complained. The northern custom was totally opposite.

Day followed day. Mile followed mile. They headed south, ever south, into ever warmer lands. They gained on the veteran company, but couldn't seem to catch it.

A horse troop joined them south and east of Hellin Daimiel. Their dust filled the lungs, parched the throat, and caked upon dried, cracking lips.

"I don't like this," Haaken grumbled as they reached a crossroads and turned eastward. "There ain't nothing out this way."

Kildragon grumped back. "What I don't like is getting screwed out of my shielding liberty. I had plans."

"You've said that a hundred times. If you can't sing a new song, don't sing at all."

"We'll make up for it," Bragi promised. "After the victory, when we're heroes." He laughed a laugh he did not feel. That morning Sanguinet had assigned the Birdsong squad to the primus, or front battle line.

Sanguinet had grinned over the announcement, explaining, "You do good, gentlemen, you work hard, and you reap your reward."

Thus Bragi learned a basic fact: the more a man does, and the better he does it, the more is expected of him. The rewards and gratifications come either as afterthoughts or as carrots meant to get the old mule moving after it realizes that it has been taken.

Bragi was no coward. There was little that he feared. But he had not inherited his father's battle lust. He was not eager to remain in the primus, which bore the brunt of combat.

"Look on the bright side," Reskird said. "We get to loaf around on guard duty when the other guys have to dig the trenches and pitch camp."

"Bah! Some silver lining." Bragi had a broad lazy streak, but in this case did not feel that escape from the drudge work was sufficient compensation.

Birdsong watched over his shoulder, mustache wriggling. Bragi bared his teeth and growled. Birdsong laughed. "You know what they say. A bitching soldier is a happy soldier."

"Then Reskird is the happiest fool on earth," Haaken grumbled. "A hog up to his collar in slops."

Birdsong chuckled. "Every rule has its exceptions."

"Where are we going, Corporal?" Bragi asked.

"They haven't told me yet. But we're headed east. There isn't anything east of here but the border forts facing the Sahel."

"The Sahel? What's that?"

"The outer edge of Hammad al Nakir. That means the Desert of Death."

"Oh, that sounds great."

"You'll love it. Most godforsaken land you'll ever see." His eyes went vague.

"You been there?"

"I was at Wadi el Kuf with the General. We took this route then."

Bragi exchanged glances with his brother.

"Ha!" Reskird cried, suddenly enthusiastic. He started babbling cheerfully about Hawkwind's victory.

Bragi and Haaken had listened to other veterans of the battle. It hadn't been the picnic Reskird thought. Haaken suggested Kildragon attempt a difficult autoerotic feat.

They finally overhauled the other infantry company a day from the assembly point, a fortified town called Kasr el Helal. The veterans grinned a lot during night camp. They had made the overtaking intentionally difficult.

Hawkwind and the remainder of the regiment were waiting at Kasr el Helal. Also on hand were several caravans hoping to slip into Hammad al Nakir in the regiment's safety shadow, and two hundred Royalist warriors sent to guide the Guildsmen. Bragi and Haaken found the desert men incredibly odd.

Hawkwind allowed a day's rest at Kasr el Helal. Then the savage march resumed. Bragi soon understood why extra boots had been issued. Rumor said they had eight hundred miles to march, to some place called the Eastern Fortress. The actual distance was closer to five hundred miles, but it was long enough.

The pace started slowly enough, passing through the wild, barren hills of the Sahel. The desert riders ranged far afield. The column traveled ready for combat. The primitive locals were fanatic adherents of the enemy, somebody called El Murid.

The natives never offered battle. The Guildsmen never saw them. They saw almost no natives anywhere during the first twenty-seven days of the desert crossing.

Hawkwind conducted repeated exercises during the march. The heavy support train acquired at Kasr el Helal was a severe drag on speed. Yet its professional camp followers, cooks and workers made military life easier to bear. Hawkwind, though, kept those people as segregated as he dared, fearing an infection of indiscipline. Their discipline was pure chaos compared to that of the Guildsmen.

The youths from the north examined the barrens day after day. "I'll never get used to this," Bragi said.

Haaken admitted, "It scares me. Makes me feel like I'm going to fall off the world, or something."

Bragi tried to see a bright side. "Somebody wants to attack us, we'll see them coming."

He was only partly right. Twenty-seven days out of Kasr el Helal, Reskird suddenly yelled, "Pay up, Haaken."

"What?"

"The van riders are coming in." Kildragon pointed. The native outriders were rushing toward the column like leaves aflutter on a brisk March wind. "That means a fight."

Bragi looked at Haaken meaningfully. "You suckered him out of a month's pay, eh?" An hour earlier word had come back that they could expect to be within sight of their destination before nightfall. Haaken had begun crowing about how he had hornswoggled Reskird into betting they would see action before they arrived.

Haaken suggested they both attempt the sexually impossible. He grumbled, "Those Invincibles wouldn't be this close to the castle anyway."

"They're between us and the Fortress," Reskird said. "We have to break through. Pay me now, Haaken. Be hard to collect if you get taken dead."

"Don't you ever shut up? You got a mouth like a crow."

"You do have a way with words, Reskird," Bragi agreed.

Horsemen indistinguishable from the outriders crested a ridgeline ahead. They studied the column, then flew back the way they had come.

Hawkwind halted. The officers conferred, dispersed. Soon Bragi and his companions were double-timing into the selected formation, which was a broad, shallow line of heavy infantry with the native horsemen on the flanks. Bowmen scattered behind the infantry. The heavy horse, still donning armor and preparing mounts, massed behind the center. The camp followers circled wagons behind them to provide a fortress into which to retreat.

Birdsong dressed the squad. "Looking good, lads," he said. "First action. Show the Lieutenant we can handle it." Sanguinet insisted they couldn't whip their weight in old women.

"Set your shields. Stand ready with spears. Third rank. Stand by with your javelins."

Bragi watched the ridgeline and worried about his courage. This was no proper way for a man to fight. . . .

Riders crested the hill. They swept toward the Guildsmen, hoofbeats rising into a continuous thunder. Bragi crouched behind his shield and awaited the order to set his spear. Some of his squadmates seemed to be wavering, certain they did not dare hold against the rush.

The riders sheered off toward the flanks. Arrows from short saddle bows pattered against shields, crossing paths with a flight from longer Guild bows. Horses screamed. Men cursed and wailed. Bragi could see no casualties on his side.

An arrow chunked into his shield. A quarter inch of sharp steel peeped through. A second shaft caromed off the peak of his helmet, elicited a startled curse behind him. He scrunched down another inch.

The earth shuddered continuously. Dust poured over him. The taunting riders were racing past just thirty yards away.

He could not restrain his curiosity. He popped up for a peek over the rim of his shield.

An arrow plunked him squarely, smashing the iron of his helmet against his forehead. He tumbled onto his butt, losing his shield. Another arrow streaked through the gap in the shield wall, creased the inside of his right thigh. "Damn," he muttered, before it started hurting. "An inch higher and . . ."

Reskird and Haaken shifted their shields, narrowing the gap till a man from the second rank could assume Bragi's place. Hands grabbed Ragnarson, dragged him backward. In a moment he was cursing at the feet of the bowmen. One shouted, "Get back to the wagons, lad."

He didn't make it halfway before the encounter ended. The enemy tried to turn the flanks. The friendly natives pushed them back. Trumpets sounded. Hawkwind led the heavy horse through aisles in the infantry, formed for a charge. The enemy flew away, vanishing over the hill as swiftly as he had come. He remembered Wadi el Kuf, and had no taste for another bout with the men in iron.

Though Bragi had perceived their undisciplined rush as an endless tide, there had been no more than five hundred of the riders. Outnumbered by a disciplined foe, they had done nothing but probe. Even so, several dozen fallen comrades were left scattered across the regiment's front. Bragi was one of only four casualties on the Guild side.

The camp followers rushed out to cut throats and loot. The Guildsmen remained standing at arms while their native auxiliaries went scouting again.

Bragi settled down with his back against a wagon wheel, cursing himself for the stupidity that had gotten him hurt. All he had had to do was keep his head down, just as he had been taught.

"Some people will do anything to get out of walking."

He looked up, lips taut. His wound hurt bad now.

Sanguinet dropped to one knee. "Might have known you'd be the first one hurt. Let me look at it." He grinned. "Close, eh? Don't look that bad, though." He squeezed

Bragi's shoulder. "There's a reason behind every lesson we try to teach. Hope you learned something today. You paid a cheap enough price." He smiled. "I'll send the surgeon around. You'll need stitches. Ride the chow dray the rest of the way in."

"Do I have to do KP? Sir?"

"Got to pull your weight somewhere."

"I'll walk, then. Just stay with my squad."

"You'll do what you're told, son. Laziness isn't a good enough excuse for losing a leg."

"Sir—"

"You have your orders, Ragnarson. Don't compound foolishness with more foolishness." Today Sanguinet spoke as a Guildsman to a brother, not as a drillmaster belittling a recruit.

Birdsong let Haaken and Reskird drop back to visit the afternoon the regiment started the long climb up the slope leading to the Eastern Fortress. They lifted him down off the chow wagon so he could look at the castle.

"Gods. It's big," he said.

"They call it the Eastern Fortress," Reskird told him. "Been here for like eight hundred years, or something, and them all the time adding on."

Bragi looked around. How did the people of Hammad al Nakir survive in such desolation?

The castle turned out its garrison in welcome. Ranks of silent men, dark of eye and skin, often beakish of nose, observed them without expression. Bragi sensed their disdain. The were all old, weathered veterans. He tried hard not to limp.

If he could impress them no other way, his size ought to stir some awe. He was six inches taller and fifty pounds heavier than the biggest.

Nowhere did he see a woman, and children were scarce. "This is the reception the old-timers talk about when Guildsmen come to the rescue?" he muttered. "Where are the flowers? Where are the cheers? Where are the eager damsels? Haaken, I'm not going to like it here. I've seen brighter people at funerals."

Haaken had his shoulders hunched defensively. He grunted his agreement.

The column passed through the castle gate, into a

stronghold as spartan as its defenders. Everything inside looked dry and dusty, and was colored shades of brown. Dull shades of brown. The companies fell in one behind another in a large drill yard, under the hard eyes of a group watching from an inner rampart. "Those guys must be the ones who hired us," Bragi guessed. He studied them. They did not look any different from their followers. To him, very strange.

Reskird murmured, "Two things I'd give up what Haaken owes me to see. A tree. And a smile on just one of their ugly faces."

The group on the wall came down and joined Hawkwind. Time passed. Bragi wished they would get on with it. After all that desert all he wanted was a gallon of beer and a soft place to lie down.

Things started moving. Men led the horses away. The front company filed through an inner gate. Bragi surveyed the fortress again, scowled. Not damned likely to be any comfortable barracks here.

One by one, the companies ahead marched away. Then it was the recruits' turn. A lean native youth approached Sanguinet and spoke briefly. The Lieutenant turned and started bellowing. The company filed out.

The quarters were worse than Bragi had imagined. Two hundred men had to crowd into space meant for maybe seventy. Only a serpent would be able to slide in or out after taps. He tried not to think of the horror consequent to an alarm sounding after dark.

Even officers and noncoms got shoved into that over-crowded cage. There was no room at all for gear. That they left outside.

The growling and cursing died a little. Reskird muttered that he didn't have room enough to get breath to bitch. Their youthful guide said, "I offer my father's apologies for these quarters. You came earlier than expected, and at a time when many of our warriors are away, fighting the Disciple. You will be moving to better quarters as soon as they can be furnished. Some may move tomorrow. Your commander is already meeting with my father concerning duty rosters. Men who are assigned stations far from here will be moved nearer immediately." He spoke Itaskian with a nasal accent, but much more purely than Bragi or his brother.

His gaze crossed Bragi's. Both youths stared for a moment, startled, as if seeing something unexpected. Once their eyes moved on, Bragi shook his head as though trying to clear it.

"What's the matter?" Haaken demanded.

"I don't know. It's like I saw . . . I don't know." And he didn't. And yet, the impact had been such that he was now sure this slim, dark, strange young man would play an important part in his life.

Haaken was intrigued. There was more life in his eyes than there had been for months. "You've got that look, Bragi. What is it?"

"What look?"

"The same look Mother got when she was Seeing."

Bragi snorted, making light of their mother's alleged ability to see the future. "If she'd been able to See, Haaken, we wouldn't be here."

"Why not? She could've known. She wouldn't have said anything if there wasn't anything she could do. Would she?"

"That was all bullshit. She just put on an act to scare people into doing things her way. She faked it, Haaken."

"Who's bullshitting who? You know better than that."

"Want to hold it down back there, you Ragnarsons?" Sanguinet bellowed. "Or at least speak Itaskian so the rest of us can get in on it?"

Bragi reddened. He glanced at the Lieutenant, averted his gaze from the man's taut face. His eye fell on the young guide again. Again he had that *frisson,* and the youth seemed to have suffered a similar response. He was just regaining his equilibrium. Curious. Maybe his mother was in his blood after all.

The youth said, "I am Haroun bin Yousif. My father is Wahlig of el Aswad. What you would call a duke. During your stay here, unless I am needed elsewhere, I will remain attached to your company as interpreter and go-between. Is there a word for that in Itaskian?" he said in an aside to Sanguinet.

The Lieutenant shrugged. Itaskian was not his native tongue either.

"Liaison," Sergeant Trubacik volunteered.

"Yes. I recall now. Liaison. If you have problems requiring communication with my people, see me. Especially in matters of dispute. We are of contrasting cultures. Probably my people seem as strange to you as you do to them. But we must stand side by side against the Disciple. . . ."

"Rah rah rah," Reskird muttered, a little too loudly. "Three cheers for our side. Why doesn't he tell us what's so special about this El Murid character?"

In a voice dripping with honey, easygoing Corporal Birdsong said, "That will be four hours of extra duty, Kildragon. Want to try for more?"

Reskird gulped, sealed his lips.

Haroun continued, "I, and my tutor, Megelin Radetic, whom I shall introduce later, are the only men here who speak Itaskian. If you find yourself desperate to communicate, and you can speak Daimiellian, try that. Many of our men have worked the caravans and speak a little Daimiellian. But talk slowly, and be patient."

Haaken lifted a hand. "Back here. Where can we get something to drink?"

"There is a cistern." Haroun turned to Sanguinet, who expanded upon the critical question in a soft voice. He looked puzzled. Then he said, "The drinking of spirited beverages is forbidden. Our religion does not allow it."

Grumble mumble growl. "Holy shit," somebody shouted. "What the hell kind of hole is this? No women. No booze. Hot and dirty. . . . Hell. For this we should risk our lives?"

The youth looked baffled. He turned to Sanguinet for help. Bragi prodded Haaken, who was within reach of the loudest complainer. Haaken took hold of the man's shoulder muscle and squeezed. His protests died.

Sergeant Trubacik called out, "Any problems, you see me or Haroun here. At ease. Settle in. Lieutenant suggests you roam around and get to know the place. Duty assignments will come out tomorrow. That's it."

"You'd better believe I'm going to roam around," Reskird muttered. "This is so tight it would give me the shakes, only there isn't room to shiver."

"Yeah. Me too," Bragi said. "Come on, Haaken. Let's catch that Haroun. I want to talk to him." But it took them ten minutes to get out of the barracks room. By then the youth had disappeared. So the brothers went up on the wall and looked out on the barren land and wondered why anyone would fight to defend it.

Haaken, unwittingly prophetic, observed, "What I'd fight for is to get out."

"There he is, down there," Bragi said, spotting Haroun. "Let's go."

But they missed him again. And thus they began their first commission as soldiers of the Guild.

Chapter Ten

Salt Lake Encounter

El Murid had been up late discussing the coastal war. His aching limbs left him in no mood to be wakened prematurely. "What is it?" he snapped at the insistent slave. "It had better be important, or . . . Well, out with it!"

The man gulped. The Disciple's temper had grown ever fiercer since Wadi el Kuf. "Lord . . ." He burst right into it, talking almost too fast to follow. "Lord, Mowaffak Hali insists on seeing you. He's just returned from patrol. He won't be put off."

El Murid grumbled and scowled. "Hali? Hali?" He could not associate a face with the name.

"Mowaffak Hali, Lord. The elder Hali. The Invincible." The slave eyed him oddly, as if bemused because he could not recall a man as important as this visitor.

"All right. Show him in. And if it's another petty squabble over precedence between the regulars and the Invincibles, I'll crucify you both." He beckoned a second slave. "Clothing."

He was dressing when the Invincible strode in, advancing like a trail-dirty thunderhead, brow furrowed. El Murid remembered him now. One of his favorites among the Invincibles. One of his best men. One of the most determinedly faithful. And, in all likelihood, one of the high brethren of the Harish, too.

"Mowaffak, my brother. A pleasure to see you again."

Hali halted a few paces away. "My apologies, Lord. I wouldn't disturb you for anything less than a disaster."

El Murid's lips stretched in a rictus of a smile, cracking because they were dry. "Disaster? What now?"

"The rumors are true. Aboud has engaged Hawkwind again."

El Murid's stomach knotted. He fought to keep his fear off his face. They had whipped him like a cur at Wadi el Kuf. They had branded terror upon his soul. He could not be reminded without cringing. "Hawkwind?" he croaked.

"I saw them with my own eyes, Lord. I was leading the Fourth through the gap between el Aswad and the Great Erg. My scouts reported the presence of a large body of foreigners. I took the battalion forward, and engaged briefly. They drove us off like swatting away flies."

El Murid swallowed. Memories of Wadi el Kuf swarmed, helter skelter, chaotic. He simply could not think straight.

Hali interpreted his silence as a patient wait for continued illumination. "There were a thousand of them, Lord, including many lances of heavy cavalry, and a large baggage train. They have come to fight a long campaign. I kept patrols close till they entered el Aswad, but could gather little more information. Their column was screened by Aboud's best light cavalry. I trust our agents in the Eastern Fortress will provide better reports."

El Murid just could not grasp the news. Finally, he croaked, "It *was* Hawkwind? You're sure?"

"I was at Wadi el Kuf, Lord. I haven't forgotten his banners."

"Nor I, Mowaffak. Nor I." The shock began to recede. "So. Aboud is frightened enough to hire foreigners. Why, Mowaffak? Because the Scourge of God has the temerity to defend Hammad al Nakir against Throyen predations?"

"I think not, Lord. I think the King wants revenge." Hali's tone was strained. He was hinting round the edge of something.

"Aboud has a special reason for wishing us ill? Beyond a desire to perpetuate his dynasty of darkness?"

"That's the point, Lord. There can be no dynasty. With Prince Farid dead he is left no successor but Ahmed. Our friends and the Royalists alike consider Ahmed a bad joke."

"Farid is dead? When did that happen?"

"Long ago, Lord. Karim himself undertook the mission."

"Our people did it? Karim? Meaning the Scourge of God sent him?" He hadn't heard a word about this. Why did they keep the unpleasant news secret? "What else is Nassef doing? What else don't I know?"

"He is destroying the Quesani, Lord. Using the Invincibles, mainly. But perhaps he felt Farid was too important a task to entrust to anyone but his personal assassin."

El Murid turned away, both to conceal his anger at Nassef and his disgust with Hali's obvious politicking. The Invincibles loathed Nassef. They were convinced he was the bandit the Royalists claimed.

"The Scourge of God is somewhere near Throyes. Too busy to bother with this."

"This is a task for the Invincibles, Lord."

"Have we so many otherwise unemployed, Mowaffak? Much as I loathe the Wahlig, his destruction isn't first on the list of works that need accomplishing."

"Lord—"

"Your brotherhood will participate, Mowaffak. El Nadim is in the valley. Send him to me."

"As you command, Lord." Hali's tone was sour. He started to protest entrusting Nassef's henchman with so critical a task, thought better of it, bowed himself out.

Wearily, El Murid rose. A servant scooted his way, one hand extended in an unspoken offer of help. The Disciple waved the man off. He now knew he would never recover completely. Wadi el Kuf had made of him an old man before his time.

Hot anger hit him. Yousif! Hawkwind! They had stolen his youth. The years could not soften his rage. He would destroy them. The two were in one place now, eggs in one nest. He had been patient, and the Lord had given him his reward. The eagle would descend, and rend its prey.

One smashing blow. One bold stroke, and the desert would be free. This time there would be no doubt about el Aswad. War with Throyes notwithstanding.

Pain stabbed through his leg. The ankle never had healed right. He flung his arms out for balance, and that stimulated the pain in the arm that had been broken. He groaned. Why wouldn't the bones heal? Why wouldn't they stop hurting?

The servant caught him before he fell, tried to guide him to his throne. "No," he said. "Take me to my wife. Have el Nadim meet me there."

Meryem took him from his helper, led him to a large cushion and helped him lie down. "Your injuries again?"

He drew her to him, held her for a long minute. "Yes."

"You were angry again, weren't you? It only gets bad when you get angry."

"You know me too well, woman."

"What was it this time?"

"Nothing. Everything. Too much. Bickering between the Invincibles and regular soldiers. Nassef's going off on his own again. Aboud sending mercenaries to reinforce el Aswad."

"No."

"Yes. A thousand of them. Under Hawkwind."

"He's the one?"

"From Wadi el Kuf. Yes. The most brilliant tactician of our age, some say."

"Are we in danger, then?"

"Of course!" he snapped. "Can you picture Yousif having a weapon like that and not using it?" He was shaking, frightened. The root of his anger was his fear. He needed reassurance, needed help to banish the doubts. "Where are the children? I need to see the children."

He felt settled before el Nadim arrived.

The general was as nondescript a man as the desert produced. Like all Nassef's henchmen, his background was suspect. The Invincibles said he had begun as a cutpurse, and had descended into darker ways from that. He was a puzzle to the Disciple. He was not known for his genius in the field, unlike others of Nassef's intimates, and, if the grudging reports were to be believed, he was a true believer. Yet he remained a favorite of Nassef, entrusted with commands where imagination was less needed than a legate dedicated to executing his orders.

"You summoned me, Lord?"

"Sit." The Disciple contemplated his visitor. "I have a task for you."

"Lord?"

"You've heard the news? That the King has sent mercenaries to el Aswad?"

"There are rumors, Lord. They say Hawkwind is the commander."

"That's true." El Murid grimaced, stricken by sudden

pain. "A thousand mercenaries, and Hawkwind. I'm sure you appreciate the threat."

El Nadim nodded. "It's an opportune moment for the Wahlig, Lord, what with the Scourge of God away battling the accursed Throyen."

"I want to beat Yousif at his own game. To go out and meet him."

"Lord? I'm afraid—"

"I know the arguments. I've been meditating on them since the news arrived. Tell me this. How large a force could we raise if we called in our patrols, stripped Sebil el Selib of its garrison, drafted untrained recruits, armed slaves willing to fight in exchange for their freedom, and what have you?"

"Three thousand. Maybe four. Mostly unmounted. On foot they'd have little chance against Guild infantry."

"Perhaps. How many mounted veterans?"

"No more than a third, Lord. And the garrisons here are made up of old men."

"Yes. The Scourge of God persists in taking Sebil el Selib's best defenders. Go. Call in the scouts and raiders. See how many men you can arm."

"You insist on doing this, Lord?"

"Not at all. I insist on examining the possibility. We need make no decision till we see what strength we can muster. Go now."

"As you command, Lord."

Meryem joined him as el Nadim departed. "Is this wise?" she asked. "The last time you overruled your commanders—"

"I don't intend to overrule anyone. Prick them into action, perhaps. Lay suggestions before them, yes. But, if, in their wisdom, they foresee disaster, I'll yield."

"You want to embarrass Yousif and Hawkwind the way they embarrassed you, don't you?"

He was startled. The woman was psychic. She had reached down inside him and touched a secret truth he had not wholly recognized himself. "You know me too well."

Meryem smiled, enfolded him in her arms, rested her cheek against his chest. "How could it be otherwise? We grew up together."

El Murid smiled. "I wish there were some rest from my labors."

"So long as the wicked do not rest, neither may we. Spoken by the Disciple on the occasion of his return from the Movement's greatest disaster. Don't yield now."

El Nadim approached the Malachite Throne. He bowed, glanced at the Invincibles attending the Disciple. His face remained blank. "I have assembled every possible man, Lord."

"How many?"

"Thirty-eight hundred. We could raise another two thousand if we waited for the arrival of the garrisons of the nearest coastal towns, which I have ordered here. But by the time they joined us it would be too late. The Wahlig won't await the completion of our preparations. He will use his new strength soon."

El Murid glanced at Mowaffak Hali. Hali nodded. He could find no fault with el Nadim's preparations. Mowaffak was a master at finding fault.

El Nadim endured the moment without wincing, without acknowledging his awareness that his every move was closely scrutinized.

"What of my suggestions?" El Murid asked.

"Entirely workable, Lord." El Nadim could not conceal a certain surprise at his master's having seen a military potential missed by his captains.

Hali said, "The question becomes how quickly the Wahlig will move, Lord."

"What about the men? We've dug deep and taken the dregs. Will they stand up to a fight?"

El Nadim shrugged. "That can be answered only in battle. I fear the answer, though."

"Mowaffak?"

"You're demanding a lot. They have faith but no confidence. Only a quick, clear success at the outset will hold them together."

El Murid left the throne, limped to the shrine where his angel's amulet lay. He grasped it in both hands, raised it above his head. The jewel's flare filled the hall. "This time, gentlemen, the first of heaven will strike with us. There will be no Wadi el Kuf."

He saw doubt. He saw unhappiness. Neither el Nadim nor Hali wanted him along. They feared he would become more burden than help. Nor had they witnessed the drama at the el Habib oasis. For them the amulet was more symbol than reality, without proved efficacy.

"There will be no Wadi el Kuf," he declared. "And I won't be a burden. I'll neither overrule your commands nor interfere with your operations. I'll be just another soldier. Just a weapon."

"As you will, Lord," el Nadim replied, without enthusiasm.

"Shall we attempt it?" El Murid asked.

El Nadim responded, "It's face them here or face them there, Lord. There we'll have the advantage of having done the unexpected."

"Then let's stop talking and start doing."

The country was wild. Chaos had frolicked there, leaving the hills strewn with perilous tumbles of boulders. El Nadim halted at the eastern end of a white plain which was the only memory of an ancient salt lake. The road to Sebil el Selib crawled along its southern flank. The general ordered camp made.

He rode onward with the Disciple, Hali and the Disciple's bodyguards to examine the salt pan. After a time he remarked, "You were right, Lord. It's a good place to meet them."

El Murid dismounted. He squatted, wet a finger, touched it to the salt, then tasted. "As I thought. Not mined because it's bad salt. Poisons in it." Childhood memories came, haunted him momentarily. He shook them off. The salt merchant's son was another being, simply someone with whom he shared memories.

He surveyed his surroundings. The hills were not as tall as he had imagined them, and less rich with cover. And the pan looked all too favorable for western cavalry. He offered his doubts.

"Let's hope they see only what's visible, Lord," el Nadim replied. "They'll beat themselves." Hali, puzzled, refused to ask the questions puzzling him. El Nadim did not enlighten him. El Murid suspected he was being deliberately vague. When the dust settled the Invincible would be able to stake no claim on having engineered any victory.

The party continued westward. At the far end of the

lakebed el Nadim told Hali, "Choose five hundred Invincibles and hide in those rocks. After dark. Travel the reverse slope so you leave no traces. Take water rations for five days. Don't break cover till the Guild infantry closes with my line."

"And if they don't?" Hali demanded.

"Then we'll have won anyway. They have to retreat or break through. They won't have the water to wait us out. Either way we embarrass them."

El Murid fretted. He would bear the odium if this failed. If it succeeded, el Nadim would harvest the credit. That didn't seem fair. He smiled wearily. He was getting as bad as his followers.

Hali remarked, "Our scouts say they're on the march, Lord. We won't wait long."

"Very well." He checked the altitude of the sun. "Time for prayers, gentlemen."

Hawkwind and the Wahlig reached the western end of the salt pan the following afternoon. Invincible horsemen blocked the road and skirmished with Yousif's riders till the Royalists elected to make camp.

Confidence filled that camp. The Wahlig had more and better men. He exercised only the caution necessary to abort a night assault.

El Murid missed the skirmishing. El Nadim had assigned him a small force placed well west of Hali's, where the road to the lakebed wound between steep hills. The Disciple suspected the General simply wanted him out of the way, though his companions were the cream of the Invincibles.

He did not sleep that night. He could not shake the specter of Wadi el Kuf—and this, though a smaller action, could generate even more devastating repercussions. Sebil el Selib would be vulnerable till the troops arrived from the coast. It would fall to a featherweight attack. He was terrified. He had bet too much on one pass of the dice. But it was too late to stand down.

He prayed often and hard, beseeching the Lord's aid in his most desperate hour.

El Nadim roused his men before dawn. He addressed them passionately while they ate a cold breakfast, claiming the whole future of the Movement hinged on their courage. He then arrayed his infantry across the end of the pan, with horsemen stationed on the wings. The slave volunteers he posted in front of his primary line, carrying shovels as well as weapons. His army was in place when dawn broke. A morning breeze rose from behind him.

He assembled his officers. "Keep the men to the standards," he told them. "Set an example. If the Lord won't yield us the day, let's die facing our enemies."

He had expressed the same sentiments to the troops, only now he indicated a willingness to cut down any officer who forgot his courage. He told his cavalry commanders, "The breeze is rising. Begin."

Moments later horsemen began riding back and forth ahead of the infantry. The westbound wind filled with alkaline dust. Horns and drums sounded in the distance. The enemy formed ranks. El Nadim smiled. The Wahlig would challenge him. He moistened a finger, felt the breeze. Not as strong as he had hoped. The dust was not carrying as well as he desired. "Trumpets," he snapped. "Speed them up."

Bugles called. The cavalrymen urged their mounts to a trot, kicking up more salty dust. El Nadim turned. The sun was about to break over a low, distant mountain, into enemy eyes.

He examined what he could see of the Wahlig's dispositions. Guild infantry in the center. Light horse on the wings and behind. And the heavy cavalry forming for the first charge, that should be enough to shatter his line. Good again. They were doing the obvious. Exactly what he wanted.

The breeze was not rising. "Trumpets. Speed them up again. Messenger. I want the slave volunteers to start digging."

The volunteers used their shovels to hurl the fine, salty earth skyward, putting more dust into the air.

Let them breathe that, el Nadim thought. Let them become parched of throat and sore of eye. Let them want nothing so badly as they want to break away for a drink. He glanced back. The sun was up. Let them advance into the face of that, glaring off the white lakebed.

Let the men in iron come, he thought, half blinded as they charge. . . .

"They're coming, General," an aide announced.

Distant trumpets called. Dust boiled up as the chargers started forward. "Recall," el Nadim ordered. "Let them bury their infantry themselves."

His trumpets sounded. The cavalry fled to the wings. The slave volunteers retreated through the front to form a reserve.

The enemy advanced, armor gleaming through the dust, pennons fluttering boldly. "You're great, Hawkwind," el Nadim murmured. "But even you can become overconfident."

His heart hammered. It was going exactly as he wanted. But would that be enough?

The Wahlig's light horse followed the heavy cavalry, eager to fall on the scattered, terror-stricken infantry Hawkwind's charge would leave in its wake.

Both waves went to the gallop.

And when they were two thirds of the way across the lakebed they fell into el Nadim's trap, the trap suggested by a salt man's son.

It was no manmade trap. Nature herself had placed it there. Out where the old lake had been deepest a bit of water remained trapped beneath a concealing crust of salt and debris. It was seldom more than two feet deep, but that was enough.

The charging horses, already running shakily on the powdery lakebed, reached the water, broke through the crust. Their impetus was broken. Many of the warhorses fell or dumped their riders. Yousif's light horse hit from behind, worsening the confusion.

El Nadim signaled the advance. His men poured missile fire into the uproar. Selected veterans ran ahead to hamstring horses and finish dismounted riders.

El Nadim's horsemen circled the confusion and assaulted Yousif's men from their flanks.

The enemy broke. El Nadim's horsemen harried them back to their lines, killing scores, then flew back to their stations on their infantry's flanks, howling victoriously.

"Don't sing yet," the general muttered. "The worst is to come."

The historians would declare the honors even. Casualties

were about equal. But Guildsmen had been hurled back, and rendered incapable of delivering another massed charge.

El Nadim backed away from the brine. "Water for everyone," he ordered. "Horses too. Officers, get those standards aligned. I want every man in his proper position. See to the javelins. Slave volunteers out front with the shovels." The breeze was stronger. The sun had turned the lakebed into a gleaming mirror over which heat waves shimmered. He doubted the enemy could see him.

"Come on, Yousif," el Nadim muttered. "Don't stall."

The Wahlig decided to attack before the dust and heat completely debilitated his men. The Guild infantry began its advance.

"Now we find out." El Nadim moved up to the edge of the brine. When the enemy came in range, he ordered javelins thrown. The Guildsmen took the missiles on their shields, suffering little harm. But the javelins dropped into the water, where they floated haft up and tangled feet. The Guild line grew increasingly ragged.

The slave volunteers used slings to hurl stones over their comrades' heads, further sapping enemy morale.

"Now, Hali," el Nadim murmured. "Now is your time."

And in the distance white boiled out of the rocks and swept down on the enemy's camp and mounts and reserves. The Invincibles were outnumbered, but surprise was with them. They drove off most of the horses and slaughtered hundreds of unprepared warriors before Yousif forced them back into the shelter of the rocks.

El Nadim was pleased. Execution had been perfect, and the rear attack threat remained.

But now the Guildsmen were slogging up out of the brine. His own men were half ready to flee. He galloped across the rear of the line, shouting, "Hold them! Thirst is our ally."

The lines met. His men reeled back a step, then steadied up. Only a handful lost their courage. He chevied most back into the line with strokes from the flat of his blade.

The Guildsmen were as tough as ever. Without the heat, the sun in their eyes, the bitter dust, without their thirst, it would have been no contest.

The Guildsmen who had waded the deepest water appeared less than perfectly efficient. They had lost the cohesion of their shield wall, could not get it together again. El Nadim galloped back to his slave volunteers, ordered half to add their weight to that part of the line.

Javelins and stones rained on that sector. El Nadim's troops pushed forward by sheer body weight. The Guild line bowed. El Nadim signaled his cavalry.

The majority went to challenge the Wahlig's men, still busy skirmishing with Hali's Invincibles. A handful crossed behind the Guild line to harass Hawkwind's reserves and his least steady company.

Slowly, slowly, a fracture developed in the mercenary line. El Nadim bellowed with joy, gathered the rest of his reserves and plunged into the fray.

El Murid tried to follow the battle from a remote perch. He could tell little through the dust and heat shimmer. Nevertheless, it felt right. He gathered his officers and told them. They began placing their men.

The Guildsmen fought as well as ever they had, as magnificently in defeat as in victory. El Nadim could not rout them. But he drove them into their camp, then broke off to rest his men and water his mounts.

The victors laughed and congratulated one another, battered though they were. They had beaten Hawkwind! El Nadim withdrew them to their original stations and dared the enemy to try again.

Hawkwind and the Wahlig chose to withdraw. One Guild company contained Hali while the main force moved out, headed west.

In the gloaming a man approached El Murid. "They come, Lord. El Nadim did turn them back."

"The Lord is great." The Disciple could not stifle a grin. "Good. Spread the word."

The clatter of hooves and tramp of boots swelled in the darkness. A sour aura of disappointment reached the Disciple where he crouched, praying. A small unit passed below. The vanguard, he thought. He had to await the main force. . . .

The time came. For a long minute terror paralyzed him. He could not shake his recollections of that fox den. . . . Not again. Never again. Not even for the Lord. . . .

He leapt up and screamed, "There is but one God, and he is our Lord!" And, "Attend me now, O Angel of the Lord!"

His amulet blazed, illuminating the slope. He flung his arm down. Lightning hammered the canyon walls. Boulders flew around like toys at the hand of a petulant child. The earth quivered, shivered, shook. The far slope groaned in protest, then collapsed.

The roar of falling rock obliterated the cries from below.

When the rumbling stopped El Murid ordered the Invincibles down to finish the survivors.

He settled on a stone and wept, releasing all the fear that had plagued him for days.

Chapter Eleven
Lightning Strikes

"Come on, Reskird. You're dogging it."

Haroun cocked his head. That was the one called Bragi. The northern youths argued all the time. The more so since their company had cracked on the battle line. The one called Reskird was wounded. His friends ragged him mercilessly while they helped him walk.

The clang of weapons round the rearguard redoubled. The Disciple's men were keyed to a fever pitch by their success. He wished he could drop back and use his shaghûn's skills, but his father insisted he remain with his Guild charges.

This feuding between northmen was irritating. He dismounted. "Put him on my horse. Then you won't have to carry him."

The one called Haaken grumbled, "Fool probably never learned to ride. You ever been on a horse, Reskird?"

Kildragon's response was as testy. "I know one's arse when I . . ."

A brilliant light flared on the slope to the south. A man screamed words Haroun did not catch. Then the lightning came.

Boulders thundered into the column. Horses reared, screamed, bolted. Men cried out. Confusion quickly became panic.

Haroun retained his self-control. He faced the light, began mumbling a spell. . . .

A fist-sized stone struck his chest. The wind fled him. He felt bones crack. Red pain flooded him. Hands grabbed him, kept him from falling, hoisted him. He groaned once, then darkness descended.

* * *

A sliver of moon hung low in the east. Haroun saw nothing else, and that only as through a glass of murky water. . . .

"He's coming around." That was one of the northerners. He forced his vision to focus, rolled his head. The brothers squatted beside him. Haaken had his arm in a light sling. He appeared to be covered with dried blood.

Around them, now, Haroun discerned other shapes, men sitting quietly, waiting. "What happened?"

Bragi said, "Some sorcerer dumped a mountain on us."

"I know that. After that."

"We threw you on the horse and headed for the wizard just as his men charged us. We cut our way through and wound up here with the General. More men keep turning up. Your father is out looking for strays."

"How bad was it?"

The mercenary shrugged. He was floating on the edge of shock. For that matter, everyone around them seemed dulled, turned inward. It had been bad, then. A major defeat, consuming all the hopes raised by the advent of the Guildsmen.

Haroun tried to rise. Haaken made him lie still. "Broken ribs," he growled. "You'll poke a hole in your lung."

"But my father—"

"Sit on him," Bragi suggested.

Haaken said, "Your old man's gotten along without you so far."

Still Haroun tried to rise. Pain bolted across his chest. Lying still was the only way to beat it.

"That's better," Bragi said.

"You cut your way out? Through the Invincibles?" He vaguely recalled a clash of arms and flashes of men in white.

"They're not so hot when they're not on their horses," Haaken said. "Go to sleep. Getting excited won't do you no good."

Despite himself, Haroun followed that advice. His body insisted.

Yousif was standing over him when next he wakened. His father's left arm was heavily bandaged. His clothing was tattered and bloody. Fuad was there too, apparently unharmed, but Haroun had no eyes for his uncle. Wearily, his father was interrogating the Guildsmen through Megelin Radetic.

His father looked so old! So tired. So filled with despair.

Haroun croaked, "Megelin," overjoyed that fate had not seen fit to slay the old man. His death would have made the disaster complete.

His father knelt and gripped his shoulder, as demonstrative a gesture as the man could manage. Then duty called him elsewhere. Megelin stayed, seated cross-legged, talking softly. Haroun understood only a third of what he heard. The old scholar seemed to be talking about economic forces in one of the western kingdoms and deliberately ignoring present straits. Sleep closed in again.

When next he wakened the sun had risen. He was lying on a rolling litter. He could see no one who was not injured. His mercenary saviors had vanished.

Megelin appeared, drawn by some signal from the bearers. "Where is everybody, Megelin?"

Radetic replied, "Those who are able are trying to stall the pursuit."

"They're close?"

"Very. They smell blood. They want to finish it."

But Sir Tury Hawkwind in defeat proved more magnificent than Sir Tury Hawkwind achieving victory. The defeated column reached el Aswad safely.

Physicians set and bound Haroun's ribs. He was up and around almost immediately, against medical advice, blindly trying to encompass the enormity of the disaster.

Two thirds of the force had been lost. Most had been slain in the landslide and following attack. "But that's history," his father told him. "Now the enemy is at the gate and we don't have enough soldiers to man the walls."

It was true. El Nadim had pressed the chase right to the gate and though he did not have the manpower to undertake a proper siege, he had begun siegework. He had erected a fortified camp and begun constructing engines. His men were digging a ditch and erecting a barricade across the road. That looked like the first step toward circumvallation.

"What are they up to?" Haroun asked Megelin. "Three thousand men can't take el Aswad."

Radetic was glum. "You forget. Nothing is impossible to the True Believer."

"But how?"

"Recall the night attack."

"The lightning. A sorcerer that knocked a mountain down. But El Murid hates sorcery."

"True. Yet one sorcery is entwined in his legend. It hasn't been seen since shortly after he stumbled out of the desert."

"The amulet that he claims his angel gave him? I thought that was all made up."

"It happened. Apparently he's decided to use it again. I'd guess our walls will be his next target."

"El Murid is out there?"

"He is."

"Then Father ought to sortie. If we killed him . . ."

"Nothing would please them more than to have him try."

"But—"

"I discussed this with your father and General Hawkwind. They've decided to let el Aswad take its punishment. Let them break the wall. The amulet will be useless in close fighting."

Haroun did not like the strategy. It depended too much on the enemy doing the expected, too much on his not receiving reinforcements. But he protested no more. He had a glimmering of a scheme, and did not want to make Megelin suspicious.

"Did you ask Father about those Guildsmen?"

"I mentioned it. He'll do something when he gets time."

Haroun was pleased. Bragi and Haaken had saved his life. They deserved a reward. "Thank you."

"Have you completed those geometry exercises?" Radetic had no mercy. There was no break in the studies, even for convalescence.

"I've been busy. . . ."

"Busy malingering. Go to your quarters. Don't come out till you have solutions you're prepared to defend."

"There's the old guy," Haaken said.

Bragi turned, watched Megelin Radetic make his way along the battlements. Radetic paused to talk to each soldier. "He remind you a little of Grandfather?"

"Keep an eye on those fools out there," Haaken said. "Or Sanguinet will eat you alive."

Little had been said about the recruit company's failure in battle. No fatigues or punishments had been enforced. Rumor said Hawkwind believed the recruits had done well, considering the terrain and concentrated resistance they had faced.

The veterans were less understanding. Their General's record had been sullied. Hundreds of comrades were dead. They didn't care that the briny water had been thigh deep, nor that the recruits had borne the brunt of the fury of El Murid's army. They saw more recruits surviving than members of any other company, and they were not pleased.

Radetic reached the youths. He paused between them, leaned on a merlon. Below, el Nadim's men were hard at work. "Confident as ants, aren't they?"

"Maybe they got reasons," Haaken grumbled.

Bragi did not respond. He did not know how to take the older man. Radetic was important here, yet seldom acted it. He did ask, "How's Haroun?"

"Mending. The Wahlig sends his regards. He'll thank you personally when he has a free moment."

"Okay."

"So enthusiastic! He's a generous man. Haroun is his favorite son."

"The only thing I could get enthusiastic about is getting out of here."

Radetic made a thoughtful "Hmm?" sound.

"It's hot and dry and there's nothing out there but miles and miles of nothing."

"My patrimony for a decent tree. I feel the same sometimes." Radetic patted Bragi's shoulder. "Homesick, lad?"

Bragi blustered—then poured out his story. Radetic looked interested, and encouraged him whenever he faltered.

He *was* homesick. Much as he pretended otherwise, he was just a boy forced into a man's role. He missed his people.

Bragi related his feelings about the defeat. Radetic patted his shoulder again. "No need to feel shame there. The General was surprised you held up so well. If there's any blame due, it belongs to him and the Wahlig. They got cocky. And you soldiers paid the price. I'd better move along."

Bragi did not understand what the old scholar had done, but he did feel better. And Haaken didn't look half as glum.

Sergeant Trubacik arrived moments later. "The Lieutenant wants you, Ragnarson. Get your butt down there."

"But—"

"Go."

Bragi went. He shivered all the way, though the day was a scorcher. Now it begins, he thought. Now the repercussions set in.

Sanguinet was set up in a storeroom off the stables. It was a dark, musty room, badly lighted by a single lantern. Bragi knocked on the doorframe. "Ragnarson, sir."

"Come in. Close the door."

Bragi did as he was told, wishing he were elsewhere. He could tell himself it didn't matter what these people thought, that *he* knew he had done his best, but it did matter. It mattered very much.

Sanguinet stared for fifteen seconds. Then, "Birdsong died this morning."

"I'm sorry, sir."

"So am I. He was a good man. Not much imagination, but he could hold a squad together."

"Yes sir."

"I'm preparing the report. You were there. Tell me how it happened."

"We was slogging through that salt water. A stone knicked his elbow. He dropped his shield. Before he got it up again a javelin hit right at the edge of his breastplate. Went in under his arm and got his lung, I guess."

"You took over?"

"Yes sir. The guys were kind of used to me telling them what to do. From training."

"You had only one other casualty?"

"Kildragon, sir." Reskird had gotten excited, broken formation to get at a particular enemy, and had paid the price of indiscipline.

"Corporal Stone commanded the squad on your left. He says you held your ground."

"I tried. . . . We tried, sir. But we couldn't stand fast when everybody else was pulling back."

"No. You couldn't. All right, Ragnarson. You may have the makings. I'm entering the promotion in the record. Pay and a half from the day Birdsong was wounded."

"Sir?" He thought he had missed something.

"You're taking over. Permanent promotion. Subject to the General's approval. Go back to your men, Corporal."

For half a minute Bragi stood there, dazed, wanting to argue, to protest, or something. This was not what he had expected.

"I said you're dismissed, Ragnarson."

"Yes sir." He bumbled out, returned to his post.

"Congratulations," Trubacik said, and hobbled off.

"What was that?" Haaken asked.

Bragi tried to explain, but did not understand. He just could not see himself as deserving.

Each afternoon el Nadim drew his men up in formation, offering battle. Each afternoon the defenders of el Aswad refused his challenge. This afternoon started no differently. El Nadim advanced to within extreme bowshot. He sent a herald to demand the surrender of el Aswad. The Wahlig sent him back empty-handed.

The besiegers then customarily withdrew a few hundred yards. Once a lack of response was assured they resumed their labors.

Not this time. El Nadim did not back down. He and the Disciple came to the van. The Disciple raised a fist to the sky. His amulet waxed brighter, till he seemed only a shadow of a man caught in the heart of eye-searing fire.

The lightning struck. Ten thousand boulders from the barren countryside leapt into the air and poured down on the Eastern Fortress. The lightning struck again, lashing the satellite guarding the approach and the curtain walls connecting it with the main fortress. The defenders launched flights of arrows, none of which reached their marks. The pillar of light remained rooted. The doors of heaven remained open, pouring out the fury of a dozen storms.

A section of wall collapsed, some stones bounding away down the slope, plowing furrows through the enemy ranks.

The Invincibles sent up a mighty war cry and surged forward. They scrambled up the mounds of rubble, pelted by missiles from the battlements. The going was slow. The rubble was piled high and was treacherous underfoot.

The Wahlig formed a force inside the break, and called for Hawkwind, who was more familiar with this sort of fighting.

The Disciple and most of el Nadim's army began moving across the slope, toward the fortress's western face.

The Invincibles attained the summit of the rubble and rushed down into a storm of arrows and javelins. They crashed into the Wahlig's men. Yousif's sketchy line dissolved. A melee ensued. The Disciple's troops continued to pour in, regular soldiers following the more dedicated Invincibles. One band turned to assault the gate.

The Disciple summoned the fury of heaven again. Lightning hammered the taller, stubborner western wall of el Aswad.

The northmen were stationed on the main fortress's north wall, near its juncture with the west wall, away from the fighting. Haroun joined them. "Damn them," he said. "They were smart. They made it impossible for Father to sortie."

Neither Bragi nor Haaken responded. They were completely involved in themselves, expecting Sanguinet's order to fall in and move into the fighting. They jumped each time lightning struck, though the Disciple's point of attack was well away.

No order came.

A wide section of western rampart gave way.

In the outlying sub-fortress Hawkwind launched a counterattack. He overwhelmed the enemy there, rushed into the main fortress, attacked the enemy entering through the west wall. The fighting there was among buildings and sheds, with little room for maneuver. It was confused and savage.

Hawkwind cordoned the breeched area, then pushed forward, slowly compressing the invaders. The last were evicted before sunset. The day's combat produced roughly equal losses for each side.

The defenders began clearing rubble and erecting a secondary barrier behind the gap in the west wall. The sub-fortress they decided to abandon.

The hour was late but Bragi was still at his post. There were no reliefs. Haaken was napping. So it went all around the wall. Every other man sleeping. The night was still but for the sounds of construction work.

Haroun strolled out of the night. He said, "Tomorrow they'll be rested and we'll be exhausted. My father thinks tomorrow may be the end."

Bragi grunted. El Nadim was thinking. Just wear the defense down. Morale was at a low ebb anyway, with the Wahlig's men convinced that the struggle was hopeless.

"We need help," Haroun said. "But help isn't going to come. The tribal leaders are deserting us."

Again Bragi grunted.

"They will join el Nadim. The desert will fill with men eager for the plunder of el Aswad. Something has to be done."

"Your father is doing what he can."

"Not everything. I have talents he won't use. He's afraid I'd get hurt. I could turn it around if he'd let me."

"How?"

"I came to thank you. For what you did out there."

"No thanks needed. Anyway, you already did."

"There's a debt now. My family always pays its debts."

Bragi didn't argue. He had a low opinion of human gratitude, though. Look at his father and the Thane. No two men ever owed one another more.

Haroun ambled off, seemingly distracted. The whole encounter was puzzling. Bragi decided Haroun needed a keeper.

Haroun was back within the hour. He carried a rope and small black bag. "What are you up to?" Bragi demanded when Haroun tied the rope to a merlon.

"Going to give the Disciple some of his own back."

"Who told you to? I didn't get any orders about you going out."

"I told me." Haroun pitched the rope into the darkness. "I'll be back before anybody misses me."

"The hell. I can't let you. . . ."

Haroun was gone.

Bragi leaned forward. "You don't know what you're doing. Look at you. You don't even know how to rappel."

Haaken woke up. "What're you making all that racket for?" he grumbled. "They coming?"

"No. It's that Haroun. He just went over the wall."

"Call the sergeant of the guard. Don't stand there squawking like an old hen."

"Then he'd get in trouble."

"So? What's it to you?"

"I like him."

"He's deserting, ain't he?"

"No. He's going after El Murid."

Haaken levered himself upright, stared down into the darkness. Haroun had disappeared. "Damned fool if you ask me."

"I'm going after him."

"What? You're crazy. They could hang you for leaving your post. He's dumb enough to go down there, leave him go. No skin off our noses."

Bragi debated. He liked what he had seen of Haroun. But the youth had a romantic streak that would get him killed. "He's alone out there, Haaken. I'm going." He arranged his weapons so he could descend without them getting in his way.

Haaken sighed, began arranging his own weapons.

"What're you doing?"

"I'm going to let you go by yourself? My own brother?"

Bragi argued. Haaken snarled back. The debate became so heated their squadmates came to investigate. And in moments the whole squad was talking about accompanying Bragi.

That gave him pause. It was one thing to risk his own neck, quite another to lead the squad into an action his superiors would not approve.

What motivated the men, anyway? He wasn't sure. But, then, he didn't know why he was going himself. "It's your necks if we get found out," he said. "Stay or go. It's up to you." He grabbed Haroun's rope, swung over the edge, began descending. Halfway down the rope jerked. He spied a manshape against the stars. "Damned Haaken," he muttered. And smiled, feeling warm within.

He crouched among the boulders at the foot of the wall, trying to recall an easy approach to the Disciple's encampment, wondering if anyone up top would spot him and think he was the enemy. Haaken joined him. A third man dropped to one knee on his right. Then a fourth and fifth arrived, and more, till the whole squad gathered. "You idiots," he whispered. "All right. Keep it quiet, unless you want somebody up there to plink you." He stole forward, trying to approximate the route he suspected Haroun had taken.

The fates were kind. The watch on the wall did not spot them. That no longer a worry, Bragi became concerned about enemy pickets.

He stole within bowshot of the enemy encampment without finding Haroun. "He hornswoggled you," Haaken said. "He cut and ran."

"Not him. He's around somewhere, going to pull some stunt." He looked back, eyeing the fortress from the foe's perspective. It was a huge, forbidding outline, looming against the stars like the edge of a giant's ragged saw. Not a light shown anywhere. The construction crews had finished their work. "Spread out. We'll wait here till something happens."

The enemy camp was quiet, though fires glowed behind the stockade. An occasional sentry appeared, silhouetted by the glow.

"Bragi!" somebody hissed. "Over there."

"I see it."

Just a whisper of pale lilac light limned a boulder momentarily. A lilac bead dribbled toward the camp stockade. Defying gravity, it floated upward.

A sentry tilted forward, dropped off the wall. He struck earth with a soft crump.

"What're we into here?" Haaken demanded. "That's sorcery, Bragi. Killing sorcery. Maybe we ought to go back."

Bragi rested a steadying hand on Haaken's forearm. Another lilac glimmer appeared. Another bead danced toward the camp. Another sentry fell from the stockade, dying in utter silence.

Something scraped on stone. Staring intently slightly to one side of the sound, Bragi discerned a shadow sliding toward the wall. "That's him. He's going in." He rose.

"You're not going too?" Haaken whispered.

"No." That would be certain suicide, wouldn't it? "I was going to catch him. But it's too late, isn't it?"

Chapter Twelve

Nightworks

Haroun crouched at the foot of the stockade, uncoiled with all the spring he could exact from young muscles. His fingers found purchase on top. He hung for a moment, listening. No alarm. No footsteps hastening his way. He hoisted himself till his eyes were an inch above the edge.

There were still a few fires burning, and a few men around them. Most were preparing wholesale breakfasts. Evidently El Murid meant to start early. No sentry was nearby.

He heaved upward. Part of the wall gave way, dribbling down with what seemed to him an incredible racket. The stockade was constructed of materials no better than sticks and stones mortared together with moistened clay. The clay was now dry, becoming powdery. He scrabbled for another handhold, rolled across the top and dropped onto a rickety catwalk, slithered into a shadow. He remained as still as stone then, awaiting an alarm and forming a mental map he would not forget in the heat of action.

No one noticed the noise he'd made.

How soon would the sentries be missed? Surely not long. Ten minutes? That might be too tight. He had to locate the Disciple before he could strike.

Before he moved on he assumed the camouflage of a minor spell that would avert the unsuspecting eye, making him effectively invisible till he did something blatant.

He dropped to the ground, stole along the wall till he could move into the camp in the shelter of tent shadows. He harkened to his weakling shaghûn's senses, trying to locate the Disciple through the aura of his amulet. Only a vague sense of direction came, centerward. He needed no sorcery to guess that. He wished he'd had more time with his instructors, had been able to study with the masters, and had attained a higher level of proficiency. But there had been so many things to learn, and so little time for study. . . .

There! That way. The throb of the amulet was strongest thither.

He moved like a panther, shadow in shadow. That romantic undercurrent welled up. He imagined himself more than what he was, nominated himself a mighty avenger. Dangerous as his undertaking was, he was not afraid. Fright did not occur to him. His fearlessness was the fearlessness of folly.

The camp center was set off from the remainder by a twenty-yard width of barren earth. Beyond stood a half dozen tents guarded by twenty Invincibles. These sentries were posted too close to slip past.

He could not pick out the tent occupied by the Disciple. Time fled. Any minute the absent sentries would be missed. He had to *do* something.

He made the lilac magic, sent several of the tiny, deadly balls hunting. And kept sending them as fast as he could create them.

There was no other way. There would be an alarm, and an alert, and mad confusion. In it he might get close enough to do the deed.

An Invincible shouted. Not one of those touched by a violet pellet, of course. Those would make no sound again, ever.

Still creating and releasing the killing pellets, Haroun crept forward . . . and found himself face to face with a giant in white. A giant not misled by his feeble spell of concealment. A scimitar howled down. Haroun hurled himself aside, stumbled into a low tent, tripped, scrambled into a shadow, crouched, stared back at the Invincible. The man lost him, but only for an instant. Scimitar raised, he charged.

Haroun drew his blade.

The camp was coming to life. Men shouted questions. In the circle guarded by Invincibles—a dozen of whom lay dead—tent flaps whipped open. Officers demanded reports. Haroun spotted a man who had to be el Nadim. He tried to unleash another lilac bead. But the giant was upon him again.

He blocked a stroke so strong his whole arm went numb.

The Invincible left himself open to a counterstroke, but Haroun hadn't the strength to deliver it.

Another blow fell. Haroun rolled with it. Again he could not take advantage of an opportunity. His weapon had been forced too far out of position.

Men shouted at his opponent, who shouted back.

The third stroke was as overwhelming as its predecessors. This time Haroun kicked as his blade was driven down and away. His toe connected with the giant's knee. The man staggered. He was slow getting his guard up. Haroun struck before he did so.

He whirled and ran a short way, banging bewildered warriors out of his way. He dived into a shadow behind a tent. The tent was unoccupied. He slithered under the fabric's edge.

The uproar grew. There were cries that the Wahlig was attacking. Men rushed to the stockade. As many ran hither and thither in panic. A very few sought the interloper who had slain the Disciple's guards.

The halloo moved away. Haroun peeped outside, saw no one. He crept out and slid from shadow to shadow, toward the Disciple's tent. He knew which it was now.

Behind him flames rose. In their panic some of the enemy had scattered a fire. Some tents had caught. The blaze was spreading.

The fallen Invincibles had been replaced. Haroun cursed. There was no way, now, that he could deliver the stroke he had been anticipating all day.

He would have to use the Power. He hadn't wanted to do that. He wanted the Disciple to see death coming, wanted the man to look into his eyes and recognize the boy from Al Rhemish. Wanted him to know who as well as why.

The lilac killer would not do. It would take the nearest Invincible, not a man cowering inside a tent. It had to be something else. His arsenal of petty magicks contained little that was apt. Again he cursed the chain of circumstance that had prevented his achieving his full potential as a shaghûn.

He selected a spell that would induce the symptoms of typhoid, ran through the chants softly, visualized the El Murid he recalled from Al Rhemish. He loosed the spell.

A cry of agony answered it.

Some Invincibles rushed to their master. And some rushed toward Haroun.

"What the hell is going on?" Haaken asked.

"I don't know," Bragi replied. "But he's sure got them stirred up."

"Maybe we ought to help. Maybe if they think they're under attack he can get out in the confusion."

Bragi doubted that. He had written Haroun off. The decision he faced was whether or not to rush back to el Aswad in hopes he hadn't been missed. It had to be too late. Might as well do some good here.

Some of the enemy were fleeing the camp. Within, the fires were spreading. Horses were making panic noises.

"All right. Let's go. Harass the ones running away. You guys with the bows. Shoot a few over the wall."

Alarms awakened Megelin Radetic. Groggy, he staggered from his cubicle, his seldom used sword dragging. A night attack? He hadn't anticipated that. It wasn't to the Disciple's advantage. The man merely needed to wear the defense down with hammerings like yesterday's.

He paused, listened. Plenty of people running around yelling, but no thunder. No crash of lightning striking the fortress. Maybe it wasn't an attack.

What, then?

He reached the north court to find it aboil with men rushing out the gate. He grabbed a soldier. "What's happening?" The man pulled away. So did the next he caught. Nobody wanted to spare a moment. Radetic dragged his weary bones to the ramparts.

The Disciple's camp was ablaze. Men were scurrying everywhere. Animals were stampeding with the men. There was fighting. The defenders of el Aswad were falling on their foes in a great disorderly rush. The anthill simile occurred to him. "Trite," he murmured.

It took Megelin just seconds to guess how it had started. "Haroun! You fool!" He panicked. His own Haroun. . . . He practically threw himself off the wall in his haste to get down there.

The observer within was amused. *The boy isn't your child,* it said. *He's only on loan to you.*

Even so, his heart was ripped by fear that the boy had destroyed himself in some romantic scheme for rescuing his father's fortunes.

Bragi kept his men close together, unbroken by the human stampede. Two score bodies lay around them. The enemy was easy in this state.

A rabble from the fortress arrived, as disorganized as the foe, but with blood in their eyes. The area became a slaughter yard. Bragi urged his men toward the gateway.

Entering was easy. The enemy simply ran away or piled over the stockade. Guildsmen and the Wahlig's warriors followed Bragi's squad.

What now? Where to look? Haroun wanted the Disciple. El Murid's quarters should be near the center of camp. "This way. On the double." Haaken kept the men together while Bragi ran off to the right, skirting the fires. His squad left a trail of enemy injured. Wild-eyed horses proved a greater danger than enemy weapons.

Bragi found an aisle of encampment unthreatened by flames. He turned toward the camp's heart.

Haroun stifled a cry when the Invincibles slammed him to the earth at El Murid's feet. He spat at their chieftain. The man cuffed him.

"The Wahlig's brat, Lord."

"You're sure, Mowaffak?"

"The very one who attacked you in Al Rhemish."

"He was just a boy."

"That was a long time ago, Lord. He's learned more shaghûn tricks, it seems."

Haroun watched the Disciple's face darken. He compared it with the face he recalled. The man had aged beyond his years. He looked *old*. "You'd damn me when you use a fouler sorcery yourself?"

The Invincible hit him again. Blood filled his mouth. He bit down on the pain, spat scarlet on the man's robe. "Pig eater."

"You delude yourself. I use no sorcery." El Murid puffed up with offended dignity. "I call upon the might of the Lord, as vested in me by his angel."

"Somebody is deluding himself."

El Nadim arrived. "Lord, the camp is total chaos. The

fires can't be contained. Guild soldiers are inside the stockade. We'd best get out."

The Disciple's face darkened further. "No."

"Lord!" Mowaffak snapped. "Be reasonable. This scum panicked the men. The enemy are upon us. We can't make a fight of it. It's get out or be destroyed. Now, before the panic infects the Invincibles."

El Nadim agreed. "We can rally the survivors on the road, then return." He exchanged a look with the Invincible.

Haroun caught it. Both knew there would be no second attempt on the fortress. This night would see their strength leeched. "None of you will escape," he gurgled. "You're dead men." Big talk. But maybe they *would* be destroyed. He heard the fighting now.

Agony lanced across the Disciple's features. Bodyguards rushed to support him. The Invincible captain snarled, "Get him onto a horse. Get everybody you can mounted. Riding double if you have to." He faced Haroun. "What did you do to him?"

Haroun said nothing.

The Invincible hit him. "What did you do?"

Haroun gritted his teeth and willed the pain away.

The blows fell steadily. The Invincible became workmanlike, telling him the pain would stop only when he undid whatever he had done.

The minutes felt like hours. The pain got worse and worse. Only stubbornness kept Haroun from yielding.

An Invincible rushed up. "They're headed this way."

"How close?"

"Right behind me."

The captain dragged Haroun to his feet. "We'll take him along. Is the Lord safe?"

"They're leaving through the back way now, sir. The General and some of his men are with them."

"Help me carry him." Haroun hadn't the strength to support himself. He sagged between the men, his feet trailing in the dirt. He could not see well, now. Everything was out of focus, distorted and fire-tinted.

He was going to die. They would make him break the spell, then they would kill him. . . .

He was not afraid. Despite the pain, he felt only triumph.

* * *

"There he is!" Bragi yelled. "The white robes have him. Let's go." He charged, bloody sword overhead.

One of the Invincibles looked back. His eyes widened. He ran. The other turned, assessed the situation, released Haroun and drew a dagger. He grabbed the youth's hair, pulled his head back for a throat slash.

Bragi threw his sword. It smacked the white robe's shoulder, doing no harm, but did foil the murder attempt.

Bragi went for the Invincible's legs. Haaken roared and wound up for a two-handed swordstroke. The white robe flung Haroun into their path. Bragi smashed into the youth. Haaken leapt over. The Invincible tripped him, flung the next Guildsman down atop him, sprinted into the night. Bragi's squadmates charged after him.

Bragi untangled himself. "What a mess. Haaken?"

"Right here."

"Look at this. They really worked him over."

"He asked for it. Better see if I can make a litter."

"Asked for it? You don't have a sympathetic bone in your body."

"Not for fools."

"Not that big a fool. He broke the siege." The fighting in the camp was slackening. The Disciple's men were fleeing. Had the Wahlig been able to mount a controlled pursuit none would have escaped. In the chaos, Hali and el Nadim rallied enough men to shield El Murid's withdrawal.

"That's two I owe you," Haroun croaked. Bragi and Haaken stood over him, flexing muscles tightened from carrying the litter.

"Yeah," Bragi grumbled. "Getting to be a habit."

"Here comes the old guy," Haaken whispered.

Radetic came puffing up, features oddly adance in the firelight. He dropped to his knees beside Haroun.

"Don't let the blood worry you," Bragi said. "They just slapped him around."

Haroun tried to grin. "I almost got him, Megelin. Stuck him with a spell, anyway. He's going to hurt a lot."

Radetic shook his head. Bragi said, "Let's get rolling. Hoist him up, Haaken."

Two riders came up, stared down. "Father," Haroun croaked.

"Haroun." The Wahlig eyed Radetic. "He start this, Megelin?"

"He did."

The Wahlig sucked spittle between his teeth. "I see." He considered Bragi and Haaken. "Aren't these the lads who brought him out of the pass?"

"The same. Making a career, aren't they?"

"So it would seem. See to Haroun's injuries, then get their stories. And I'll want to talk to you once we're finished down here."

"As you will."

"Fuad. Let's go." The Wahlig and his brother rode on into the confusion.

"Can we go now?" Bragi asked.

"By all means." Megelin eyed Haroun, who could not conceal his trepidation. "It'll be all right, lad. But you did get out of hand. Just as you did at Al Rhemish."

Haroun forced a laugh. "Didn't have a choice."

"That's debatable. Nevertheless, it turned out well. Assuming we save your teeth. I hope you have it out of your system now."

"What?"

"The rebellion. The foolishness. You're young. You have a lot of years left, if you don't squander them. These lads won't always be around."

Haroun closed his eyes, shivered. He *had* been a fool, throwing himself in like he was one of El Murid's Invincibles, with never a thought to how he would get away. There were a lot of tomorrows, and through thoughtlessness he'd nearly squandered his share. He owed the northerners more than he had realized.

Megelin scowled.

"Well?" the Wahlig demanded.

Radetic looked at Hawkwind. The General's leathery countenance remained blank. His vote was "present," nothing more. Megelin considered Fuad. The Wahlig's brother was abubble with rage. He had an ally there, but he and Fuad made a pathetic marriage of purpose.

Megelin recalled an instructor who had intimidated him terribly in his youth. It had taken him a decade to conquer his unreasoning fright. And only then had he been able to analyze what the man had done. He adopted the fellow's method now.

"For more years than I care to recall I have slaved thanklessly in this armpit of the world." Excessive ferocity and bombast were the keys, accompanied by exaggerated gestures and body movement. These wakened the father-fear in one's listeners. "Time and again have you asked my advice. Time and again have you ignored it. Time and again have I prepared to return home, only to have my will thwarted. I have fought for you. I have suffered for you. I have wasted a career for you. I have endured ceaseless, senseless humiliation at the hands of your family and men. All for the sake of salvaging a rockpile in the middle of nowhere, a rockpile that protects a godforsaken wasteland, inhabited only by barbarians, from the predations of bandits whose mercies the land most assuredly deserves."

His blood was rising, responding to years of frustration. "How many hundreds, nay, how many thousands of men have lost their lives over this abomination upon a hill? I have grown old here. Old before my time. Your sons have grown up here, made ancient by endless hatred and treachery and war. And now you want to abandon the place to the Disciple. For shame!"

Radetic planted himself in front of the Wahlig, fists on hips. He almost grinned. Even Fuad was shaken by his fury. "What have we lived for? What have we died for? If we go now, have we not wasted all those years and sacrifices?"

"We fought for an ideal, Megelin." Yousif's voice was soft and tired. "And we lost. The Disciple did not overthrow us physically. We ran him off again. But the ideal lies dead beneath his heel. The tribes are deserting us. They know where the strength lies, where the future lies. With the man we couldn't kill. With the man who, in a few weeks, will command hordes eager to swarm over our broken walls to plunder our homes, defile our women and murder our children. There is nothing we can do here—unless we want to die valiantly in a lost cause, like the knights in your western romances."

Megelin could not sustain his anger in the face of the truth. He and Fuad were being stubborn out of sentiment and pride. Death could be the lone reward for harkening to either. The Wahligate was lost in all but name.

Yousif continued, "Things aren't yet hopeless up north. Aboud opened his eyes enough to see the need for the General. Maybe reports from his own men, who have *seen* the enemy, will widen the crack in the wall around his reason. He still commands the strength and faith of the kingdom—if he'd just use them."

Torment and despair muddied the Wahlig's words, pain he would never confess. The decision to flee had cost him. It may have broken him as a man.

"You'll have your will, Lord. I haven't the strength to deny it. But I fear you'll find more heartbreak in Al Rhemish. There's nothing else to say. I must pack. It would be a sin if my labors of years were destroyed by ignorant fools in white."

For an instant torment controlled the Wahlig. His face reflected the horrors of hell. But he steadied himself, like the great lord he was. "Go, then, teacher. I'm sorry I've been a disappointment."

"Not that, Wahlig. Not ever." Radetic surveyed the others. Hawkwind remained inscrutable. Fuad was a study in inner conflict, an almost trite portrait of a man compelling himself to remain silent.

"Megelin," Yousif called as Radetic neared the door. "Travel with Haroun. I have very little else left."

Radetic nodded, stamped out.

"There you go," Kildragon said. "March all the way from High Crag, forced march, killing ourselves, so we can save this dump, and what do we do? Walk away. Why do they always let the morons do the military planning?"

"Listen to the old strategist," Haaken mocked. "He don't have sense enough to hold his spot in the line, but he knows better than the General and Haroun's old man, who've only been leading armies since before he was a twinkle in his father's eye."

"Keep it down," Bragi said. "We're supposed to be sneaking out of here."

"With all this racket? You could probably hear these wagons four miles away, they're making so much noise."

The Wahlig's horsemen had ridden out at nightfall, several hours earlier, in hopes of scouring the area of enemy spies. Now the main column was under way. The Guildsmen would guard its rear. The Wahlig hoped his getaway would not be noticed till he could not be overhauled.

"Ragnarson."

Bragi faced Lieutenant Sanguinet. "Sir?"

"Too much noise from your crowd. Tell Kildragon to keep it down or I'll leave him for the jackals."

"Yes sir. I'll gag him if I have to, sir."

That should have been it. But Sanguinet remained rooted, staring. Bragi began to wilt. Once the man finally did leave, Bragi told Haaken, "He knows. He has to pretend he don't on account of if he doesn't he'll have to do something about it. Even if we did save the Wahlig's kid. We're going to be walking on eggs. He'll be looking to get us on something else. Reskird, you better pretend you never learned to run your mouth."

"What did I do? I just said what everybody is thinking."

"Everybody else has sense enough to keep it to themselves. Let's move out." Bragi left el Aswad and never looked back. A glance over his shoulder would have been a glance into his past, and he did not want to rue his decision to enlist. A fool's decision, that, but he was here now, and he was of that stubborn sort which insists on enduring the consequences of its acts.

Looking ahead, he saw nothing promising. He expected to shed his life's blood somewhere on the sand of this savage, alien, incomprehensible land.

Haroun did look back. He had no choice. The litter he rode, despite insisting he could ride a horse, faced the castle.

He wept. He had known no other home, and was certain he'd never see it again. He wept for his father and Fuad, for whom el Aswad meant even more. He wept for all the valiant ancestors who had held the Eastern Fortress, never yielding in their trust. And he wept for the future, intimations of which had begun to reach him already.

Megelin joined him, and walked beside him, sharing a silence no words could give more meaning.

Before dawn arrived the column vanished into the Great Erg, unmarked by a single unfriendly eye.

Chapter Thirteen

Angel

Stunned by unexpected shifts of fortune, El Murid retreated into his fastness in Sebil el Selib. He did but one thing before further retreating into the fastnesses of his mind: he summoned Nassef from the Throyen front. He did so in a message sufficiently strong that it would be subject to no misinterpretation. Nassef must appear or face the wrath of the Harish.

Nassef made record time, urged on more by the Disciple's tone than by what he actually said. He feared El Murid might fall apart. He was not reassured when he arrived. His brother-in-law acted as if he did not exist.

For six days the Disciple sat on the Malachite Throne and ignored everyone. He drank little and ate less while venturing deep into labyrinths of self. Both Nassef and Meryem became deeply disturbed.

Nassef. Cynical Nassef. Unbelieving Nassef. He was half the problem. He was an infidel in the service of the Lord. El Murid prayed that his God forgive him for compromising. He should have shed the man a decade ago. But there was Meryem to reckon with, and there was Nassef's unmatched skills as a general. And, finally, there was the grim chance that some of the Invincibles now felt more loyal to their commander than to their prophet. It had been a mistake to hand them over to Nassef.

But the heretics within would have to wait till he had cast down the foes of the Lord without.

But Nassef . . . He took bribes from Royalists willing to buy their lives. He sold pardons. He appropriated properties for himself and his henchmen. He was building a personal following. If only indirectly, he was suborning the Movement. Someday he might try to grab it all. Nassef was the Evil One's Disciple within the Lord's camp.

But no spiritual malaise had driven El Murid into the wasteland of his soul. No. Nor was it so much the debacle before the Eastern Fortress. That hadn't proven as bad a defeat as it had seemed at the time. The enemy had loafed at the pursuit, fearing another ambush. The cause of his inturning was the decampment of the Wahlig of el Aswad.

It had come too suddenly, and was too out of character. The man was a sticker, a fighter, not a runner. Flight made no sense after his having resisted so bitterly for so long.

Yousif's withdrawal left the Disciple without focus. His plans, for so long, had been thwarted by one man's stubbornness, that he had given up looking beyond Yousif's defeat. He did not know what to do.

Yousif was gone, but he remained foremost in El Murid's mind. Why had he gone? What did he know? Finally, the Disciple summoned Nassef and put the question.

"I don't know," Nassef replied. "I've interviewed el Nadim and Hali repeatedly. I've talked to most of the men. I've lost a week's sleep over it. And I can't tell you a thing. Aboud certainly didn't summon him. Nothing is happening at Al Rhemish." Nothing that transpired in the capital escaped Nassef. He had an agent in the Royal tent itself.

"Then he knows only what we do," El Murid mused. "What fact is he interpreting differently?"

"That foreign devil Radetic is behind it."

"Perhaps. The outland idolators must hate me. They must sense the hand of God upon me. They must feel, in His wrath, the knowledge that I shall be the instrument of their chastisement. They are the slaves of the Evil One, struggling to prolong his sway over their wicked kingdoms."

Was that a suppressed smirk on Nassef's lips?

"Papa?"

The girl was skipping. His first impulse was to swat her for insolemnity before the fanes. But it had been an age since he had given her any attention.

Nassef remarked, "The child is a savage sometimes."

"And when was laughter an abomination unto the Lord? Leave us." He let her slide into his lap. "What is it, darling?" She was nearly twelve now.

Had it been that long? Life was whistling by, and he

seemed little nearer fulfilling his destiny. That unholy Yousif. Nassef had had so many successes, but they had meant nothing as long as the Wahlig had kept the Movement bottled up in Sebil el Selib.

"Oh, nothing. I just wanted to see if you were done thinking yet." She snuggled, moving in his lap.

He was shamed by the impulse the Evil One sent fluttering across his mind. Dark-winged vampire. Not with his own daughter.

She was on the precipice: womanhood was but a moment away. Soon her breasts would begin to swell, her hips to broaden. She would be marriageable. Already his followers were scandalized because he allowed her the run of Sebil el Selib, unveiled, and often permitted her to accompany Nassef on his safer journies.

He suspected Nassef wanted her himself.

And still she had no name.

"You know I don't believe that, sweetheart. Something besides your grouchy old papa brought you here." He was acutely aware of the disapproval of the priests tending the shrines.

"Well . . ."

"I can't say yes or no till you tell me."

In a staccato burst, "Fatima promised me she'd teach me to dance if you said it was okay. Please? Oh, please, Papa, can I? Please?"

"Slow down. Slow down."

Fatima was Meryem's body servant, and a successful piece of propaganda. A reformed prostitute, she was living proof that all who came seeking were found worthy in the eyes of El Murid's Lord. Even women.

It was El Murid's most radical departure from orthodox dogma, and he was having trouble selling it still.

Women had been doubly disadvantaged since the Fall. A woman had brought the nation to its present desperate plight. Now the most rigidly fundamentalist of men allowed their wives in their presence only for purposes of procreation. Even relative liberals like Yousif of el Aswad kept their women cloistered and on the extreme fringes of their lives. The daughters of the poor were sometimes strangled at birth, or sold to slavers who trained them for resale as prostitutes.

A prostitute, socially, was as far beneath a wife as a wife was beneath a husband.

Yet even in Hammad al Nakir Nature had her way with the young. "This is serious." Little girls seldom became interested in dances unless also interested in interesting boys in girls. Then they were little girls no more. And the boys were no longer boys.

It was time to speak to Meryem about veils.

"Time, he rides a swift steed, little one." He sighed. "So soon come and gone. Everything past in the wink of an eye."

She began twisting her face into a pout, sure she was about to be refused.

"Let me think. Give me a few days, will you?"

"All right," she said brightly. His asking for a delay was, inevitably, the prelude to his giving in. She kissed him, scooted off his lap, became all skinny, windmilling arms and legs as she ran away.

Disapproving priestly stares followed her passage.

"Hadj!" El Murid called to his chief bodyguard. "We're going to make a journey. Prepare."

Far south of Sebil el Selib, south of el Aswad, stood a mountain rising slightly separate from the mother range called Jebal al Alf Dhulquarneni. It was called Jebal al Djinn, Mountain of Demons, or, sometimes, the Horned Mountain. When seen from the southwest it resembled a great horned head rising from the desert. It was there El Murid met his angel when he felt lost enough to require face to face advice. He'd never wondered why the Lord's messenger had chosen a meeting place so remote and of such evil repute.

The Disciple's faith in his angel was tried severely during a long, solitary ascent which left his body feeling tortured. Would the messenger even respond after all this time? El Murid had not come seeking him since before his ill-starred visit to Al Rhemish. But the angel had promised. On Jebal al Djinn, though, even the promises of angels seemed suspect.

The mountain was not a good place. It was cursed. No one knew why any longer, but the evil inhabiting the stones and trees remained, palpably beating upon any intruder. Each visit more than the last, El Murid wished his mentor had chosen somewhere more benevolent.

He hardened his resolve. Evil had to be defied in its very fastnesses. How else could the righteous gain the strength to resist the Darkness when it came against their own strongholds?

His doubts grew as a night and most of a day creaked past and there was no response from his heavenly interlocutor. Another evening was gathering. His campfire was sending shadows playing tag over barren rock.

The emissary arrived in a display of thunder and lightning that could be seen for leagues around. He raced his winged steed three times around the horned peaks before alighting fifty yards from the Disciple's fire. El Murid rose. He gazed at his own feet respectfully.

The angel, who persisted in assuming the shape of a small old man, limped toward him over the shattered basalt. Slung across his back was a cornucopea-shaped instrument which looked far too massive for his strength.

He swung his burden down, sat upon it. "I thought I would hear from you sooner."

El Murid's heart fluttered. The angel intimidated him as much now as when he had been a boy in the desert so long ago. "There was no need. Everything was going the way it should."

"If a little slowly, eh?"

El Murid glanced up shyly. A shrewd look had narrowed the angel's eyes. "Slowly, yes. I got in a hurry. Wadi el Kuf taught me the folly of trying to force something before its time."

"What's happened now?"

El Murid was puzzled because the angel had to ask. He told of Yousif's strange flight after the recent siege, and of an impending crisis in his own household. He begged for guidance.

"Your next move is obvious. I'm surprised you summoned me. Nassef could have told you. Gather your might and strike. Take Al Rhemish. Who will stop you if the Wahlig is gone? Seize the Shrines and your family problem will resolve itself."

"But—"

"I see. Once burned, twice cautious. Twice burned, petrified. There will be no Wadi el Kuf. No surprises from children deft with the Power. Tell Nassef that I will be watching personally. Then unleash him. He has the genius to pull it off." He sketched a plan, displaying a knowledge of desert affairs and personalities which quieted the Disciple's doubts. "Before we part, I'll give you another token."

The old man slipped off his seat and knelt. He whispered to the horn, then hoisted it and shook it. Something tumbled from its bell. "Have Nassef transmit this to his agent in the Royal Tent. The rest will follow if he strikes a week later."

El Murid accepted a small teakwood box. He stared at it, baffled.

The old man dashed to his mount and took wing. El Murid shouted after him. He had only begun to discuss his problems.

The winged horse swooped round the horned peaks. Thunder rolled. Lightning clawed the sky. Gouts of fire hurtled back and forth between the horns. Two blasts smashed together and erupted upward, forming some giant sign El Murid could not make out because it was directly overhead.

The blinding light faded slowly. And when El Murid could see once more, no sign of the angel could be found. He returned to his fire and sat muttering to himself, staring at the teakwood box.

After debating several seconds, he opened it. "Finger cymbals?" he asked the night.

The box contained an exquisite set of zils, worthy of a woman who danced before kings.

"Zils?" he muttered. What on earth? But a messenger of the Lord could not be wrong. Could he?

He searched the sky again, but the angel was gone.

Decades would pass before he encountered the emissary again.

"Zils," he muttered, and stared down the mountain at the campfires where Nassef and the Invincibles waited. His brother-in-law's face filled his mind. Something would have to be done. After Al Rhemish had been taken?

"Nassef, attend me," he called weakly when he finally stumbled into camp. It was late, but Nassef was awake, studying crude maps by fire and moonlight.

El Murid's brother-in-law joined him. With the exception of the Disciple's chief bodyguard, everyone else withdrew. "You look terrible," Nassef said.

"It's the curse. I hurt all over. The ankle. The arm. Every joint."

"Better get something to eat." Nassef glanced up the mountain, frowned. "And some sleep probably wouldn't hurt."

"Not now. I have things to tell you. I spoke with the angel."

"And?" Nassef's eyes were narrow.

"He told me what I wanted to hear. That the Al Rhemish apricot is ripe for the plucking."

"Lord—"

"More listening and less interrupting, please, Nassef. There'll be no Wadi el Kuf this time. I don't mean to try sweeping them away with sheer numbers. We'll use the tactics you developed. We'll move by night, along the trails Karim followed when you sent him to slay Farid."

If he expected a reaction from Nassef he was disappointed. Nassef merely nodded thoughtfully.

He still wondered about that incident. Aboud's hysteria had been predictable, though his turning to mercenaries had come as a surprise. Hali had provided a detailed report on the attack. Karim's force had sustained startlingly heavy casualties. The man should have brought more of his soldiers home. But, then, Karim was Nassef's creature, and the Invincibles who had accompanied him were not.

"But first, these have to be delivered to your agent in the Royal Tent."

Nassef opened the box, then peered up at the horned mountain. Just three people knew who that agent was. He and the agent were two of those. The third was not El Murid. The Disciple, he was sure, had been unaware that such an agent existed. "Zils?" he asked.

"The angel gave them to me. They must be special. Carry out his instructions. Nassef?"

"Uhm?"

"What's the situation on the coast?"

"Under control."

"Do we really dare try Al Rhemish with just the Invincibles?"

"We can *try* anything. It would be a bold stroke. Unexpected. I don't think a move that way will complicate the eastern situation. It's winding down there. I had Karim take over. He'll subdue the Throyens. They were ready to talk when I left. A few weeks of Karim's attentions and they'll accept any terms. And El-Kader has shattered the last resistance at the south end of the littoral. El Nadim will hold Sebil el Selib. With Yousif gone there will be no trouble out of el Aswad."

The Disciple sighed. "Finally. After all those years. Why did Yousif run, Nassef?"

That was the critical question. "I wish I knew. It keeps me wondering what he has up his sleeve. Yes. We'll try for Al Rhemish. It's worth a try even if it doesn't work. It'll be a spoiling raid if nothing else. Yousif will be more dangerous there than he was at el Aswad, where his resources were limited."

El Murid still carried Yousif's taunting note. He studied it for the hundredth time, fixed though every word was in his memory.

"My dear Micah," he read aloud, "Circumstances compel me to be away from my home temporarily. I beg to leave it in your curatorship, knowing you will attend it carefully in my absence. Do feel free to enjoy its luxuries during your stay. May you anticipate all your tomorrows with as much eagerness as I anticipate mine.

"Your Obedient Servant, Yousif Allaf Sayed, Wahlig of el Aswad."

"Still a mystery to me," Nassef said.

"He's mocking us, Nassef. He's telling us he knows a secret."

"Or Radetic wants us to think he does."

"Radetic?"

"The foreigner must have composed that. Yousif isn't that subtle. It smells like a sneaky bluff."

"Maybe."

"Let's not play his game. Forget the message. In Al Rhemish he can whisper the words of the Evil One directly into the King's ear. He can gather the Royalist strength against us."

"Yes. Of course. We must do as the angel says, and strike hard, now, at the very nest of the vipers."

"Whatever his reasons, Lord, I think Yousif made a mistake. Without him to block the road I don't think the Royalists can stop us. As long as we don't meet them head-on, in a test of strength. They retain the advantages they had at Wadi el Kuf."

"Gather the rest of the Invincibles. This year in Al Rhemish for Disharhun."

"It will be a delight, Lord. I'll begin now. Give my love to Meryem and the children."

El Murid sat silently and alone till long after Nassef's departure. The critical hour was at hand. He had to wrest the most from it. His angel had suggested that the resolution of many troubles lay in the taking of Al Rhemish. And he had begun to get a glimmering of what could be done.

"Hadj."

"My Lord?"

"Find Mowaffak Hali. Bring him to me."

"Yes, my Lord."

"My Lord Disciple?" Hali asked as he approached. "You wanted me?"

"I have news for you, Mowaffak. And a task."

"At your command, Lord."

"I know. Thank you. Especially for your patience while it was necessary that the Scourge of God direct the blades of the Invincibles."

"We tried to understand the need, Lord."

"You saw the light on the mountain?"

"I did, Lord. You spoke with the angel?"

"Yes. He told me it's time the Invincibles liberated the Most Holy Mrazkim Shrines."

"Ah. Then the Kingdom of Peace is at hand."

"Almost. Mowaffak, it seems to me that worldly elements crept into the Invincibles during my brother's tenure. Perhaps this is our opportunity to expunge those. The fighting at Al Rhemish will be bitter. Many Invincibles will perish. If those who are the most trustworthy are elsewhere, on a secret mission . . ."

He said no more. Mowaffak understood. He wore one of the cruelest smiles the Disciple had ever seen.

"I see. What would that mission be, Lord?"

"Use your imagination. Choose your men and inform me of the nature of the task I've assigned you. And we'll celebrate Disharhun in Al Rhemish."

Hali kept smiling. "It shall be as you command, Lord."

"Peace be with you, Mowaffak."

"And with you, Lord." Hali departed. He walked taller than El Murid had seen in some time.

After a time, the Disciple called softly, "Hadj."

"Lord?"

"Find the physician. I need him."

"Lord?"

"The mountain was too much for me. The pain . . . I need him."

The physician appeared almost immediately. He had been sleeping, and had clothed himself hastily and sloppily. "My Lord?" He did not look happy.

"Esmat, I'm in pain. Terrible pain. My ankle. My arm. My joints. Give me something."

"My Lord, it's that curse. You need to have the curse removed. A philter wouldn't be wise. I've given you too many opiates lately. You're running a risk of addiction."

"Don't argue with me, Esmat. I can't cope with my responsibilities if I'm continuously preoccupied with pain."

Esmat relented. He was not a strong man.

El Murid leaned back and let himself drift in the warm, womblike security of the narcotic.

Someday he would have to find a physician who could outwit his injuries and the curse of the Wahlig's brat. The pain bouts came every day now, and Esmat's dosages had more and more difficulty banishing them.

The desert was vast and lonely, just as it had been during the advance on Sebil el Selib so long ago, and as it had been during the desperate flight from Wadi el Kuf. It seemed to have lost its usual natural indifference, to have become actively hostile. But El Murid refused to be daunted. He enjoyed the passage, seeing whole new vistas, wild new beauties.

It was a matter of years no more. Just days remained. Hours and days, and the Kingdom of Peace would become a reality. In hours and days he could turn his mind to his true mission, the resurrection of the Empire, the reunification of the lands of yore in the Faith.

The days and hours of the infidel were numbered. Those sons of the Evil One were doomed. The Dark One's long ascendancy was about to end.

Rising excitement made a new man of him. He became more outgoing. He bustled here and there, chattering, fuss-ing, joking with the Invincibles. Meryem complained that he was destroying his sublime image.

He began to recognize landmarks seen years ago.

The bowl-shaped valley was nearby. And not a soul had challenged them. The angel had been right. And Nassef had been as competent as ever, slipping them past Royalist pickets as if they were an army of ghosts.

He laughed delightedly when he glimpsed the spires of the Shrines from the lip of the valley, standing like towers of silver in the moonlight.

The hour had come. The Kingdom was at hand. "Thank you, Yousif," he whispered. "You outfoxed yourself this time."

Chapter Fourteen

Stolen Dreams

To Haroun it seemed Al Rhemish hadn't changed at all. The dust, the filth, the vermin, the noise were all exactly as he recalled them. The heat was as savage as ever, reflecting in off the walls of the valley. Hawkers cried their wares through the press of tents. Women screeched at children and other women. Men made sullen by oppressive temperatures exploded violently when tempers collided. If there was any change at all, it was that there were fewer people than during his previous visit. That would change as Disharhun approached, he knew. And the tension would heighten as the capital became more crowded.

There was a malaise in the air now, a continuous low grade aggravation which went beyond what one would expect. No one put it into words, but the appearance of the Wahlig of el Aswad, with his household and troops, had initiated a process yet to run its course: stirring guilt and shame amongst those who had done nothing to aid or support Yousif's long fight in the south. His presence reminded them, and they resented it. A pale shadow of fear, too, haunted the capital. The reality of the threat posed by El Murid could no longer be denied except by a willful closing of the eyes.

"And that's what they're doing," Radetic told Haroun. "Blinding themselves. It's the nature of Man to hope something will go away if it's ignored."

"Some of them act like it's our fault. We did everything we could. What more do they want?"

"That, too, is human nature. Man is a born villain, narrow, shortsighted and ungrateful."

Haroun cocked an eye at his teacher, smiled sarcastically. "I've never heard you so sour, Megelin."

"I've learned some bitter lessons out here. And I fear they'll apply equally to the so-called civilized people back home."

"What's going on over there?" There was a stir around his father's tent. He spied men bearing the shields of the Royal household.

"Let's find out."

They encountered Fuad near the tent. He looked puzzled.

"What is it?" Haroun asked.

"Ahmed. He's asked your father and Ali to be his guests tonight. With the King."

Radetic chuckled. "Surprised?"

"After the way they've ignored us since the first few nights, yes."

A chill trickled down Haroun's spine. His gaze swept the surrounding hills. Nightfall was not far off. Shadows were gathering. He had a sense of foreboding.

"Tell Yousif to keep his views to himself," Radetic suggested. "They're not socially acceptable right now. Aboud is old and slow and needs time to adjust to the loss of the southern desert."

"He'd get used to it faster if that idiot Ahmed would get out of the way."

"Maybe. Haroun, what's the matter?"

"I don't know. Something strange. Like this isn't any ordinary night coming on."

"Allegorical thought, no doubt. Beware your dreams tonight. Fuad, do tell the Wahlig not to get exercised. If he wants to make headway with Aboud he has to become acceptable company first."

"I'll tell him." Fuad departed wearing one of his most fearsome scowls.

"Come, Haroun. You can help with the papers."

Haroun's shoulders tightened. Radetic had no end of papers and notes, all totally disorganized. He could spend years getting them sorted—by which time another mountain would have collected.

He glanced at the hills again. They seemed unfriendly, almost cold.

* * *

Lalla was the pearl of Aboud's harem. Though she was a scant eighteen, and without benefit of marriage, she was the most powerful woman in Al Rhemish. The capital was drenched in a flood of songs praising her grace and beauty. Aboud was mad for her, a slave to her whim. There were rumors that he would make her a wife.

She had been a gift, years ago, from a minor Wahlig on the lost coast of the Sea of Kotsüm. She had not caught Aboud's attention till recently.

Aboud was an infatuated, silly and proud child. He wasted few opportunities to flaunt delights only he should have known in their entirety, taunting his court with his favorite toy. Night after night he summoned her from his seraglio and had her dance before the assembled nobles.

Yousif gazed on her lithe form. He appreciated Lalla as much as did any man, but at that moment his thoughts were far away and fraught with guilt. His heart would not accept the conclusion of his reason. He could not shake despair over having abandoned his trust and ancestral home.

He and his son Ali were guests of Crown Prince Ahmed. Ahmed was the only member of the court not yet disgusted with his attempts to initiate a major campaign against the Disciple.

Yousif was restless. There was a wrongness afoot in Al Rhemish, though it was nothing he found concrete. The feeling had been growing all week, and tonight it was strong enough to make his skin crawl.

There was a wrongness, too, about Ahmed. Especially when he looked at Lalla. His lust lay naked in his eyes, but there was more. He seemed agitated, and could not restrain a wicked, greedy smile. Yousif feared that smile foreshadowed grief.

Lalla spun close, shaking her lithe, smooth young hips inches from his eyes. His malaise lessened. When Lalla danced, even his cares soon faded. Her beauty had a narcotic quality.

How Ahmed stared! As though he had sampled those delights and become so addicted that he would kill to make them his own. Madness backlighted his gaze.

Nervousness had given Yousif a strange sensitivity to the undercurrents flowing around him. A paranoid sensitivity, he chided himself. Ahmed was not alone in staring. The faces of a dozen wild sons of the waste told him they would kill to possess the dancer.

He began to grow uneasy again. Even Lalla's melodious zils could not still his troubled heart completely. It had been a bad day. News had come from the south, at last, and it was not good.

El Murid had climbed the Horned Mountain. Something ominous had occurred there. A fire in the sky had been seen for a hundred miles. El Murid had come down decisive and determined. He had summoned the tribes to his banner, to help extirpate the Royalists evil. And rumor said thousands were responding, inspired by the awesome display over the evil mountain.

There was also word that the Scourge of God had left his forces in the littoral. He had gathered the Invincibles and was on the move. The fox was loose in the henyard, and no one in Al Rhemish apparently cared.

A magical wall erected on foundations of willful blindness isolated the bowl valley containing Al Rhemish. Reality could not penetrate that rampart of wishful thinking. The Royalist overlords had retreated from the world and immersed themselves in their pleasures. Even the hardest, the most practical, the most pragmatic among them were becoming as dissolute as the Crown Prince.

Yousif was bewildered. He had known most of these men for decades. There were dark forces at work here—how else to explain what was happening? They seemed to have resigned themselves, were seizing what pleasure they could before the end.

But all was not lost. Any fool could see that. Here in the north there were enough loyal warriors to crush El Murid twice over.

Yousif cast a covert glance at his host. The Crown Prince was a sour note, a distinct off-pitch element in the festivities. Why had Ahmed insisted his remote southern cousins be his guests tonight? Why was he so nakedly excited and lustful?

Aboud could be pardoned his dissipations. He hadn't many years left, and was terrified of the Dark Lady. He was trying to recapture the ghost of his youth. But Ahmed, Ahmed had no excuse.

Yousif had polled the more hardheaded Royalist nobility.

His brother wahligs agreed that Ahmed was a disaster in the making. He had assumed a dangerous influence over his father since Farid's death. His suggestions had resulted in several minor defeats by guerrillas operating near Al Rhemish. But those same hardheads would do nothing when Yousif suggested they take the initiative. . . .

Kingdom and Crown were decomposing while yet alive. The stench of corruption filled the land. And no one would lift a hand to halt the process. The pity of it all was that Aboud was so much stronger than El Murid. A determined, decisive leader could destroy the Disciple easily.

His anger stirred his adrenaline. He swore. "He can be put down!"

His neighbors looked at him askance. They did that a lot. He'd earned a reputation as a singleminded boor of a country cousin already.

"Really, Yousif," Aboud admonished softly. "Not while Lalla is dancing."

Yousif's glance flicked from the King to his heir. Ahmed wore a wicked smile. A moment later he slipped quietly away.

Yousif wondered no more than a moment. Ringing zils and shimmering veils and flashes of satiny skin at last captured his undivided attention. Lalla was dancing just for him.

"Would you quit that?" Reskird snapped. "You're driving me crazy."

"Quit what?" Bragi asked, halting.

"Pacing. Back and forth, back and forth. Think you were ready to have a kid."

Haaken grunted agreement. "What's the matter?"

Bragi hadn't been conscious of his pacing. "I don't know. Nervous energy. This place gives me the creeps."

The mercenaries had pitched camp on the western wall of the bowl, separate from the rest of Al Rhemish, but not separate enough to suit the men. There were strong tensions between native and outsider. The Guildsmen mainly stayed to themselves and radiated contempt for the barbarism of Al Rhemish and its people.

Reskird said, "I heard we won't be here much longer. That they're going to pay us off and let us go."

"Can't be too soon for me," Haaken said.

Bragi sat down, but didn't stay seated long. In moments he was circling the fire again.

"There you go again," Reskird snarled.

"You're making *me* nervous," Haaken said. "Go for a walk or something."

Bragi paused. "Yeah. Maybe I will. Maybe I can find Haroun, see how he's doing. Haven't seen him since we got here."

"Good idea. Look out you don't have to save his ass again." Reskird and Haaken laughed.

Bragi scanned the star-limned hills, uncertain what he was seeking. The air had an odd feel, as though a storm were in the offing. "Yeah. That's what I'll do."

"Don't take too long," Haaken admonished. "We've got midnight guard."

Bragi hitched his pants and walked away, his pace brisk. He was out of camp in minutes, passing among the tents of pilgrims here for Disharhun. By the time he reached the permanent part of town his nervousness had dwindled. He became preoccupied with the problem of locating Haroun among people whose language he did not speak. He had no idea where the Wahlig had pitched camp.

His wanderings took him to the wall enclosing the Most Holy Mrazkim Shrines. He forgot his quest and became a simple sightseer. He hadn't been into town before. Even by night the alien architecture was bemusing.

Haroun could not sleep. Nor was he alone. All Al Rhemish was restless. Fuad had been sharpening his sword since sundown. Megelin paced constantly. Haroun was tired of the old man's nattering. Radetic's customary verbal precision was absent. He rambled through vast, unrelated territories. Nervous energy was building up, and could not discharge itself in any special direction.

The first startled cries gave purpose, provided relief at last. They burst from their tents into the moonlight. The compound was a-crawl with white-robed Invincibles.

"Where the hell did they come from?" Fuad demanded. "Altaf! Beloul! To me!"

"Megelin, what's happening?"

"El Murid is here, Haroun. Back for Disharhun, it would seem."

In minutes the fighting was general, and chaotic. Royalists and Invincibles fought where they found one another, the majority on both sides acting with no goal greater than surviving the attack of the foe.

"The King is dead!"

Ten thousand throats took up that demoralizing cry. Some Royalist partisans shed their arms and fled. The rot Yousif had sensed now betrayed how deeply it had gnawed the fiber of Royalist courage.

"Ahmed betrayed his father!"

That declaration of filial treachery was more demoralizing than news of the King's demise. How could a man fight when the heir of his sovereign was one of the enemy?

"Father is it, then," Haroun told Radetic.

"Absolutely." Megelin seemed bemused. "But he's . . ."

"I'll find him," Fuad growled. "He'll need me. He's got nobody but Ali to guard his back." He hit the nearest Invincibles like a windmill of razor steel.

"Fuad!" Radetic shouted. "Come back here! You can't do anything."

Fuad could hear nothing.

Haroun started after him. Radetic seized his arm. "Don't you be a fool too."

"Megelin—"

"No. That's stupid. Think. You're just heartbeats from the throne. After your father and Ali, who else? Nobody. Not Ahmed. Never Ahmed. Ahmed is a dead man no matter who wins. Nassef will want him living less than we do."

Haroun tried to break away. Radetic's grip held. "Guards," he called. "Stay with us." Several of the Wahlig's men obeyed. They had overheard Radetic. "There has to be a pretender, Haroun. Otherwise the Royalist cause is dead. After you, Nassef has next claim."

White robes kept pouring into Al Rhemish. Confusion and panic ran before them. Twice Megelin and the guards beat off attacks. Radetic kept gathering Royalists.

A company of Invincibles appeared, hunting Yousif's family. They were determined. Radetic fought like a demon, revealing tricks of the sword seldom seen outside Rebsamen practice halls. His stubbornness inspired the men he had assembled. Haroun fought beside him, trying to win a minute's respite so he could employ his shaghûn's skills. The Invincibles gave him no chance. His companions began to falter.

Haroun tried to dig into his kit anyway. A swordtip buzzed past his ear. He fumbled the kit, lost it.

The Invincibles couldn't be stopped. He was going to die. . . .

An unholy bellow slammed the belly of the night. Swinging his sword with both hands, Bragi Ragnarson hit the Invincibles from behind. In seconds half a dozen went down. Some scrambled away from his insanity. The northerner attacked those who remained, pounding through their sabers with his heavy sword.

They broke too. Haroun laughed hysterically. "Three times," he gasped to Megelin. "Three times!" He staggered toward Bragi. The northerner waved his sword and called the Invincibles cowards, daring them to come back. Haroun threw his arms around the big man. "I don't believe it," he gasped. "Not again."

Bragi stood there panting, watching the white robes. "I found you, eh? I've been hunting since sundown."

"Just in time. Just in time."

Bragi shuddered. "I didn't think that could happen to me. My father could go crazy when he wanted, but . . . what's going on? How did they get here? I better get back to camp." He was confused. His voice was plaintive.

Radetic said, "You can't get there from here, lad." There was heavy fighting on the slope below the mercenary encampment. "Stay here. Gamel. Find a Royal standard. Let's give our people a rallying point."

Radetic did his utmost, parlaying the Royal name, but the collapse continued. Al Rhemish was doomed. Even with the mercenaries making vigorous sallies from their encampment, the inertia of the rout could not be turned.

Haroun almost whined as he asked, "Megelin, how could Al Rhemish be overrun so easily? There are too many loyal men here."

"Most of whom ran for it right away," Radetic replied.

A group of youngsters came in led by a wounded officer.

"Nobles' sons, sire," he said. "Take care. . . ." And he collapsed.

Haroun stared down, bewildered. "Sire?" he whispered. "He called me sire."

"The word is spreading," Megelin said. "Look. The mercenaries are pulling out. Time we did too. You men. Round up whatever animals and provisions you can."

"Megelin—"

"No room to argue anymore, Haroun." Radetic told Bragi, "Watch him. Don't let him do anything silly." He spoke Trolledyngjan.

"I have to get back to my outfit," Ragnarson protested.

"Too late, son. Way too late." Radetic resumed arguing with Haroun.

Haroun gradually accepted Megelin's truth. Al Rhemish was lost—and with it his entire family. He had no one but Megelin and this strange northern youth. Angry, with hatred knotting his guts, he allowed Radetic to lead him into the night.

Ahmed waited among the dead, holding a limp, frightened Lalla. His personal guards surrounded him, duty-bound despite loathing him for his patricide and treason. A dozen Invincibles watched them, indifferent to the carnage.

Ahmed's heart ripped at him like some cruel monster trying to tear its way out of his chest. "I did it for you, Lalla. I did it for you."

The girl did not respond.

The Invincibles snapped to attention. A darkly clad, hard-eyed man strode in. The hem of his djaballah dragged through a pool of blood. He grunted disgustedly.

There was blood everywhere, on the walls, the floors, the furnishings, the bodies. The bodies were piled deep. More wore white than the bright colors favored by Royalists. Aboud would explode when he saw . . . Ahmed giggled. For a moment he had forgotten who had died first.

The newcomer asked a question Ahmed didn't catch. He had no attention to spare. Lalla was crying.

A hand closed on his shoulder. Pain lanced through his body. "Stop!" he whined.

"Get up." The newcomer squeezed harder. Ahmed's guards watched, indecisive.

"You can't do this. It's death to lay hands on the King." He reached for Lalla.

"Don't be a damned fool. You aren't King of anything. And you'll never be."

"Who are you?" Though frightened, Ahmed retained the Quesani arrogance.

"The Scourge of God. The man with whom you've been corresponding."

"Then you know I'm King. You agreed to help me take the throne."

Nassef smiled thinly. "So I did. But I didn't say I'd let you keep it." To the Invincibles he said, "Lock this fool up till we can deal with him."

Ahmed was stunned. "You promised. . . . Lalla . . ." He had betrayed his family and murdered his father so he could become King and possess Lalla. It had been her idea initially. . . .

"I did promise you the woman, didn't I? Lock her in with him."

"My Lord!" Lalla protested. "No! I did everything you told me."

"Take them," Nassef said. He turned to a man who had followed him inside. "Get this cleaned up before the Disciple gets here."

"No!" Ahmed shrieked. He stabbed the nearest Invincible, whirled, slashed at another. His bodyguards jumped in enthusiastically.

Ahmed faked a rush at Nassef. The Scourge of God stumbled, avoiding the expected blow. Ahmed swerved toward the exit. His guards followed. "After them!" Nassef bellowed. "Kill them. Kill them all." He faced Lalla. "Get her zils. Can't have her playing tricks on us too." He smiled cruelly. "Save her for me."

Haroun paused halfway up the eastern slope of the bowl, looked back. A third of Al Rhemish was aflame. Fighting persisted, but would not last long. On the far slope the mercenary camp was ablaze. Hawkwind had abandoned it to the Invincibles. "I'm sorry," he told Bragi. "You can catch up with them later, I guess."

"Yeah. I just wish my brother knew I'm all right."

Radetic said, "Let's don't waste time, Haroun. They'll be after us soon."

"Listen!" Bragi said. "Somebody's coming."

Hooves pounded toward them. Swords leapt out of scabbards.

"Hold it!" Haroun ordered. "They're not Invincibles."

Someone snarled, "It's Ahmed." Someone else cried, "Kill him!" Men surrounded the Crown Prince. Curses flew.

"Back off," Radetic snapped. "You don't know anything against him. The rumors could have been planted. Bring him here, Haroun. Let him tell his story." Privately, Radetic believed the worst.

Ahmed scarcely had time to admit his guilt. The party topped the ridge and came face to face with the enemy.

"It's El Murid!" Haroun cried. "Come on!"

The Disciple's bodyguards and household far outnumbered them, but the guards were scattered. The main party were dismounted, either seated or sleeping.

"Maybe there is a God after all," Radetic mused as he spurred his mount. One bloody stroke could turn the war around. Without El Murid there would be no Movement.

With Bragi beside him, Haroun slashed through the Invincible pickets. He chopped down at unprotected noncombatant shoulders and heads. Women screamed. People scattered. Royalist war cries filled the night.

The Invincible bodyguards threw themselves at the Royalists with an insane fury. They valued their prophet more than their lives.

"Where are you, Little Devil?" Haroun shouted. "Come out and die, you coward."

Ahmed urged his mount up beside Haroun, opposite Bragi. He fought with an abandon no one would have believed possible an hour earlier.

A boy scampered across the rocks ahead of Haroun. He spurred his mount. Another horse hurtled in from one side, turning his attack. For an instant he looked into the eyes of a girl. He saw fire and iron, caught a glimpse of a soul that could be intimidated by nothing. And something more . . . then she was gone, dragging the boy toward safety. Haroun shifted his attention to a woman chasing the pair.

He was startled. He knew her. She was the Disciple's

wife. Veilless again. He slashed. His blade found flesh. She cried out. Then he was past, wheeling, searching. The Disciple himself had to be somewhere nearby.

Something slammed into him. He felt no pain then, but knew he had been wounded. Bragi hacked at the Invincible responsible while Ahmed engaged another two. A fourth closed in. Haroun forgot the Disciple, fought for his life.

Five minutes passed. They seemed eternal. He heard Megelin shout in a voice filled with pain, rallying the Royalists, ordering a withdrawal. He wanted to overrule Radetic, to stand and fight. This chance dared not be wasted. . . . But he understood why Megelin wanted to go. Outnumbered, the Royalists were now getting the worst of it. Half were down. Most of the rest were wounded.

"Haroun!" Megelin cried. "Come on! It's over!"

Bragi brushed a sword aside, grabbed Haroun's reins. Haroun wobbled in his saddle. His wound was deeper than he suspected.

Though gravely injured, Radetic directed the withdrawal. "Capture some horses!" he snapped. "Some camels. Anything. We've got wounded with nothing to ride."

The Invincibles might have taken them then had they not been more interested in the welfare of their prophet and his family.

"Let's go. Let's go," Radetic grumbled. "You men. Help those two get onto their animals."

Haroun looked back once. The battleground was littered with dead and dying. The majority were followers of the Disciple. "Did we get him?" he croaked at Bragi. "Do you think we got him?"

"No," the northerner said. "We didn't."

"Damn! Damn damn damn!"

Bragi snorted wearily. "If he doesn't have a god on his side, he has a devil. Ride. They'll be after us as soon as they get themselves sorted out."

Chapter Fifteen

King Without a Throne

Twenty-one horses, twenty-three men and eight camels made up the caravan. They straggled across a bleached-bone desert beneath a savage noonday sun. Only the most gravely wounded rode. Those afoot cursed and coerced the faltering beasts along the rocky, dusty, wind-whipped bottom of a dry wadi. Humiliation, despair and the anticipation of death were their marching companions. Ahmed's treachery was an agony each man bore like a brand, but no man wore it more painfully than did Ahmed himself.

For each man only the will to resist, to survive long enough to avenge, remained. The kingdom had been lost, but its blood, its Crown, lived on and would be preserved against tomorrow.

These things didn't occur as discrete thoughts. The men were too weary. Determination was baked into their bones. Consciously they were preoccupied with the heat, with thirst, with exhaustion. In the short run only one thing mattered: taking another step.

The wadi dissolved into a badland of tent-sized boulders. "This is the place," Ahmed croaked.

"I forbid it," Haroun replied. "I'm King now. You deferred to me. I forbid it."

Ahmed gestured. Men took positions among the rocks. "God go with you, sire."

"Damn it."

"Haroun." Radetic's voice was half whisper, half groan. "Let the man die the death he chooses."

"He's right," Bragi said. He began to collect the remnants of water carried by those who would stay in ambush.

Haroun agonized. These men hardly knew him. It was not meet that he should leave them to die. "Ahmed—"

"Go, sire. Their dust draws close. We die for the Blood. By choice. Just go."

Bragi finished gathering the water. "Haroun, will you come on? Do I have to drag you?"

"All right. All right." He started walking.

There were six of them now, all but Megelin walking. Radetic rode, his guts slowly leaking onto his animal's back. Haroun led his horse. Bragi tried to keep the animals and three youngsters together.

I'm a king, Haroun told himself. A king. How can that be?

Ali was dead. Yousif was dead. Fuad was dead, as were his sons. Ahmed had chosen to die in atonement. Now there was only Haroun bin Yousif. After him, the Scourge of God.

He would not permit Nassef to take the kingdom.

It wasn't much of a kingdom, he reflected. And one he could claim only at the cost of fortunes in blood and tears. If he tried . . . He glanced back. There was no sign of the ambush. He sent Ahmed a grudging, silent salute.

In the final extremity, in the hour of crisis, Ahmed had shown more character than anyone expected. He had the *mafti al hazid* of old, the high death-pride that had made Ilkazar's legions stand fast even in the face of certain destruction.

The dust raised by the pursuit was close. Nassef himself was on the trail. No one else would press so hard.

Haroun saw Bragi stumble as he forced a recalcitrant camel into line. The youngsters were about done in. There was no hope left. Not if he tried to save the whole party.

"All or none," he told himself. "All or none." He thought he and Bragi could make it if they abandoned the others.

Carrion birds planed the air, patiently awaiting the death their presence guaranteed. Nassef needed but chase them to track his prey.

Haroun swung his gaze to the ground ahead. "Step, step," he muttered again and again. Slowly, he coaxed Radetic's mount in the shadows at the bottom of another wadi. How far to the mountains? he wondered. Too far. Already his flesh strove to betray his will, to surrender to the inevitable.

A smile cracked his lips. They had gone after the Disciple like mad dogs, hadn't they? Almost got him, too. Almost got his wife. Almost captured the pearl of his seraglio, the daughter who would finally receive a name this Disharhun.

Her wide-eyed, wild look, struck over awe and determination, all overridden by hard determination to save her brother, haunted him still.

His smile widened. Meryem must have been hurt worse than he had thought. Nassef's pursuit was implacable and tireless, the relentless hunt of a man obsessed with a personal debt. He must be killing his men trying to catch up.

Haroun's wound, on the outside of his left arm, was shallow but painful. He was proud of it, carried it as a badge of courage.

Radetic groaned. Haroun glanced up at the old man. Poor Megelin. So pale, so shaky. He had come so far, in the pursuit of knowledge, and his heart had betrayed him. He should have gone home when his contract expired. But he had lost his affection to a family, and a place, and was about to pay the ultimate price for that indiscretion. Haroun bin Yousif had been forced to become a man and warrior within a matter of hours. Now he faced becoming a leader, a king. While lost in an unfamiliar desert, punished by heat and thirst, aided by one bewildered foreigner, with El Murid's jackals yapping at his heels.

He *would* survive! He *would* avenge his father and brothers, his uncle, and even his mother. And Megelin. Megelin most of all. Beloved Megelin, who had been more father than Yousif. . . .

He paid little attention to his surroundings. He clung to the meandering wadi as long as its tendency was northward, toward the Kapenrung Mountains and the border of Hammad al Nakir. Bragi and the youngsters stumbled along behind, satified to follow his lead. Grudgingly, the wadi walls provided protection from the sun and wind.

Haroun's thoughts drifted to El Murid's daughter. What *was* it that he had seen in her face? Someday . . .

The fall of Al Rhemish would leave one vaguely palatable taste in the Royalist mouth. The Invincibles had been badly mauled. The Disciple would be unable to press his advantage quickly. The scattered loyalists might have time to regroup and counterattack. Ahmed's sacrifice would steel thousands of wavering hearts. It was the sort of gesture Hammad al Nakir loved.

Haroun tried to banish the heat and misery by dwelling on the larger picture. He considered the faithful. Some would scatter according to plans long ago formulated by his father and Radetic. If necessary they could regroup outside Hammad al Nakir. The gold in the banks at Hellin Daimiel would finance their war of liberation.

If he accepted the challenge of fate, if he became their king, could he gather and wield them? Without Megelin? The old man would not last much longer. . . .

Rationality deserted him when Megelin fell. The old foreigner meant everything to him. Yousif had given him life. Megelin had nurtured and loved him, and had sculpted him into the man he would become.

He tried to lift Megelin and found that the old man's heart had stopped. "Megelin. Not now. Don't give up now. We're almost there. Megelin! Don't die!" But even the command of a king cannot stay the Dark Lady.

Radetic's death was the final straw's weight. He could withhold his grief no longer. "Damn you!" he shouted toward the south. "Nassef! Micah al Rhami! You will die a thousand deaths for this. I will take a vengeance so cruel it will be remembered for a thousand years." He ranted on, madly. One remote, cool part of him told him he was making a fool of himself, but he couldn't stop.

His companions didn't care. They simply sat on rocks and waited for the vitriol to burn away. Bragi did try to comfort him momentarily, ineptly, recalling his own agony at his father's death.

Haroun's recovery began with a fit of self-loathing when he cursed Bragi for showing solicitude. The northerner withdrew, sat on a rock and ignored him. That hurt Haroun, exposing him to yet another level of pain. Was he insane, offending the only friend he had?

In a still moment he heard distant sounds of fighting. Men were selling their lives. He must not belittle their sacrifices. He had to go on and, if it came to that, had to let the desert claim him before he yielded to the Scourge of God.

Eyes still moist, he kissed his teacher's cooling cheeks. "I mourn, Megelin. This wasteland is no resting place for a don of the Rebsamen." Vulture shadows ghosted along the wadi walls. "But I have to leave you. You understand, don't you? You were always a student of necessity." He rose. "Bragi! Let's go. They'll be through the ambush in a few minutes." The sounds of fighting were diminishing already.

He pushed on, into the night, knowing darkness would not stop Nassef. Only the Dark Lady herself would stay the Scourge of God. The three youngsters grew progressively weaker. Horses halted and refused to go on. The camels grew increasingly balky. Bragi became fractitious. He did not know how to handle the animals.

Haroun slaughtered the weakest horse, caught its hot blood, passed it around. Their water was gone. He prayed to no certain god for strength, for guidance, for a miracle. His future kingdom became confined to that narrow and perhaps endless passage of the desert.

Deep in the night, under a silver, uncaring moon, the wadi faded. If he paused to listen Haroun could hear men and animals in the distance. Nassef was gaining again.

Moments after he departed the wadi he halted, confused. Before him stood a strange old tower. He recognized the type. Ilkazar's emperors had erected hundreds to house local garrisons. Their ruins could be found wherever the Imperial legions had passed. He was baffled because he hadn't expected to encounter evidence of human habitation in the waste.

Bragi came up beside him. "What's that?"

A sad keening came from the tower.

Haroun shook his head. He glanced back. The boys had collapsed.

The keening came again.

"That's no animal," Bragi said.

"The wind?"

"Maybe it's a ghost."

Haroun reached out with his shaghûn's senses. Incompletely trained, attenuated by hunger and exhaustion, they told him nothing. "I don't get anything."

"Look!" A wan light illuminated a face behind an archer's embrasure.

"That's no ghost."

"Maybe we can get water."

"Could be a bandit hideout. Or a demon's lair. Or a sorcerer hiding from El Murid." But if the magical or supernatural lurked there, his shaghûn's senses should have warned him.

He listened. The sounds of horses and men hung just on the edge of hearing. "I'm going to investigate."

"Nassef is too close."

"I might find something. Water, at least."

"Yeah. Water."

"Let's go." It was hard to get moving again. His joints ached, his muscles begged for respite. His wound sent wires of pain crawling toward his shoulder. He was afraid it would fester. Somehow, he had to elude Nassef long enough to cleanse and cauterize it.

Bragi cuffed horses, camels and boys and got them moving again. Battered sword in hand, Haroun approached the tower step by leaden-footed step. Once around the tower he stalked, seeking an entrance.

"Find anything?" Bragi asked.

"No."

"What are you going to do?"

"Look again. You stay here."

"What about Nassef?"

"I won't be long." He went around the tower again. And this time he found a black cavity at its base, facing south. He was perplexed. The opening hadn't been there before, yet he could sense nothing magical. Was he so weak his shaghûn's senses had fled him completely?

The keening resumed. It stirred images of a whole people grieving. It wakened a surge of emotion, of empathy.

Haroun gasped.

In the doorway stood a child, or imp, or cherub, naked, hands on hips, grinning impudently. It demanded, "Candidate, what do you fear?"

Though conventional images formed in immediate response, Haroun suspected the imp meant something deeper, was trying to evoke the nightshapes that lurked in the deeps of souls. Snakes, spiders, El Murid and the Scourge of God could be handled with boot heels and blades. The devils of the soul were more formidable.

Startled and puzzled, he could think of no appropriate reply.

He glanced at his companions. They had fallen asleep where they had stopped. Even the animals had surrendered to exhaustion. He listened. The pursuit seemed no closer.

The imp grinned again, shrugged, stepped backward, vanished. Haroun was baffled. That was sorcery, yet his shaghûn's senses hadn't detected a thing. He started to follow the imp. . . .

Things exploded from the doorway. The first was a blinking, puzzled lion which, pausing to assess its situation, died under Haroun's blade. Then came vampire bats that ripped and tore and let his blood a dozen times before he finished the last. Then came snakes and scorpions and spiders.

He never considered flight. He defeated each wave by summoning reserves of energy, anger and courage he didn't know he possessed.

Then came the nebulous thing, the real enemy, the dark shifting form on which he painted his own faces of horror. It flung parts of itself to the sides, to strike from behind. With it came scents and whispers of evil that tore at already tortured nerves.

He stepped back, raised his torn left arm to shield himself. With a cackling, wicked roar the thing doubled in size. Haroun swung wildly. His blade encountered nothing, yet elicited a screech of pain.

Weariness threatened to drag him down. Pain became unbearable. He knew he was doomed. Yet he persisted. The screech convinced him his sole hope was attack. He stumbled forward, sword cleaving Night in wild strokes.

Darkness took him into its gentle arms. For a moment he thought he saw a beautiful, weeping woman approaching, and knew he had glimpsed the face of Death. There was one instant of trepidation and reluctance as he remembered the Scourge of God close behind him, then nothing.

He wakened to warmth and daylight and a sense of well-being. A bent old man stood over him, examining his injuries. Imp-Child watched from a doorway.

He was inside the tower. Its interior was no ruin. He tried to rise.

The old man restrained him. "Let me finish." Haroun found his accent difficult. Sad tones crowded his reassuring smile.

"What time is it? How long have I been here?"

"Three days. You needed the rest."

Haroun surged up. The old man pressed down on his chest with all the weight of the world.

"My people—"

"All safe and well. Resting and healing at the foot of the tower. Your enemies won't find them. Child!"

Imp-Child brought a copper mirror with a surface clouded by age. "Stare into your own eyes," the old man said. He did something strange with his fingers.

At first Haroun was too shaken by changes in his appearance to see anything else. Youth had fled him. The brown of his skin had deepened. His thin, long face had become an emaciated death's head. His hawkish nose had become more shadowed and pronounced. His eyes looked haunted. Anger and pain had etched deep furrows across his forehead.

Then he began to discern the hunters deep in the pools of his eyes. The Scourge of God and two score Invincibles followed a trail implacably.

There was something wrong. Their eyes blazed with madness. They were within a mile of the tower, but never glanced its way.

"They're following their own trail around the stronghold," the old man said. He giggled crazily.

Haroun glanced at him and surprised a malice which instantly transformed into sorrow. "Four hundred winters of despair," his savior said in a voice gone sepulchral. "And finally you've come. I hope it's you. Pray, be the One. This charge has grown tedious. I long for the embrace of the Dark Woman."

Haroun felt he was an audience of one. There was something subtly unconvincing about this old man. "Where am I?" he demanded.

"The place has no name. A watchtower. It had a number once, but I've forgotten it."

"Who are you?" The old man seemed not to hear. "Why are you helping me? *If* you're helping."

"Because you are of the Blood. Because you are the Candidate."

Haroun frowned. "Candidate? For what?"

"For the Invisible Crown."

Each answer left Haroun more baffled. "Why are you hiding out here? This is the least explored part of Hammad al Nakir." The inquisitiveness and skepticism he had acquired from Radetic kept him from accepting the old man's answers. "You'd better tell me a story, old man. A good one.

This is all crap and wasted time. I should be heading for the border."

The old man looked surprised and disappointed. "I am the son of Ethrian of Ilkazar, the wise man who predicted the Fall. He was unable to avert that disaster. During the destruction of the Imperial City, hoping to revivify the Empire one day, he smuggled myself and the symbols of Imperial power through the besiegers' lines. He sent me here under a compulsion to await the coming of a suitable Imperial heir. Someone Fate would bring here. Someone of the Blood. I am to test him, and, if he is worthy, to invest him with the Imperial power. My father meant to join me, but he was killed. I've been trapped here for four centuries. Never before has a candidate come."

The story dovetailed with known history and old legend. But when, his head swimming with visions of armies rallying to his Imperial standard, Haroun asked specific questions and received only evasions in reply, his credulity faded. "Get serious, old-timer. You're dodging like a hare chased by a fennec. Give me straight answers or go away."

The old man reddened. He cursed, and stalked out of the room.

Imp-Child giggled, winked at Haroun, followed.

Haroun stared at the bronze mirror, watching Nassef follow an endless trail. He wanted to go down, collect Bragi and move on. Instead, he fell asleep.

The old man returned that night. "Come with me," he said. Puzzled, Haroun followed him to the tower's parapet, which was spectral in the moonlight. He watched distant manshapes doggedly pursue a circular trail.

A milky globe rested atop a tripod standing at the parapet's center. It glowed softly. "Look into this," the old man said.

Haroun looked. And saw the past. He watched his father, brother, uncle and King Aboud die brave deaths. Aboud fought like the lion he had been as a young man. He watched his mother and sisters die. He watched the confrontation between Ahmed and Nassef. He could not turn away, though each second was an eternity of torture. Something compelled him to study Nassef in action.

The scene changed. He recognized the desert near the ruins of Ilkazar. A horde of horsemen milled nearby.

"Those are Royalists," the old man said. "They began gathering when news spread from Al Rhemish." Flick. A change of time. "Earlier today. These are El Murid's men, commanded by Karim and el-Kader, who on their own initiative followed Nassef and the Disciple."

The enemy spied the Royalist host. They charged. The Royalists scattered like chaff before the wind. In minutes there remained no foundation upon which the Royalist cause could be rebuilt. Haroun sighed. The arrangements his father and Megelin had made, for camps beyond the border, would have to serve to rally the cause.

Haroun divined a bleak future. Exile. Warfare. The constant threat of the Harish kill dagger.

The old man crooned over the globe and showed him what it might be like. Endless flight and fear. Frequent despair. He shuddered at the prospects.

Then the old man said, "But that need not be." Flick, flick, flick. "Here. Here. Here. We can reach back. A moment of blindness. A strayed swordstroke. A captain's horse stumbling at an inopportune moment. Little things can shift the course of history."

"You can do that?"

"If you wish." The battle before the ruins reappeared. "Here. An order misinterpreted."

"That's too easy," Haroun muttered, though he was not sure why. "But tempting." Was it something Megelin had taught him? "What's the price?" There would be a price. Nothing was free. The more desirable it became, the crueler the cost. It would be more bitter than the price he had paid already.

A childhood memory surfaced. At four he had broken a glass mirror belonging to his mother. His father had had it imported from Hellin Daimiel. He had spent a fortune acquiring it. Haroun's whispered plea to the unseen, then, had been, "Please, make it didn't happen."

In a way, that was what magic was all about. Putting off payments by taking the apparently free route, the characterless route, the easy way. But there were traps and ambushes along that track, cunningly hidden and all unpleasant.

Ahmed had tried the easy way. Ahmed was dead and dishonored. Generations would curse his name.

The old man did not answer his question. Haroun stared

him in the eye. "No. The past is done and dead. Let it lie." But it hurt to say that.

The old man smiled. Haroun thought the smile guileful, as though the man had gotten the answer he wanted.

"Nor will I change the present," Haroun said. "I'll make my own future, for good or ill."

"Excellent. Then on to the tests."

"Tests?"

"Of course. I told you the Candidate must be tested. For courage, for wisdom, for . . . You'll understand in time. My father was determined that there be no more kings like the Golmune Emperors. Come with me."

Haroun wondered what the old man's real stake was. His story became increasingly unconvincing. He seemed, deliberately, to be fostering the fragile, probably futile dream of a Royalist return. And certainly was pushing the fantasy of a resurrected Empire. *That* insanity could be left to El Murid.

Several levels down, Imp-Child lighted candles and stoked up a fire. The old man settled himself on a worn chalcedony throne. Haroun faced him across a dusty table. Atop the table lay three purple pillows. On those rested a bronze sword, a robe of ermine and, to the eye, nothing. But something heavy had crushed the third pillow deeply. The sword was green with verdigris. The ermine had been the home of generations of moths.

"We begin," the old man said. "Take up the sword."

Puzzled, Haroun grasped the worn hilt.

"This is the sword Ashkerion, forged by Fallentin the Smith, which bought the victory celebrated at Sebil el Selib. The man who bears this blade needs fear no enemy. It defends against all attack. It's always victorious."

Though Haroun had heard of the sword Ashkerion, there was no proof it had existed. He recalled that Fallentin was said to have cast the blade into the sea after securing the throne. He had feared it, for it had developed a will of its own. He thought it might deliver itself into the hands of an enemy.

Haroun let go. "No. Ashkerion had a treacherous reputation. And a man could grow too dependent on a weapon like that. He could grow too arrogant in his power." He envisioned Megelin nodding. Megelin would say something like that.

"Pretty speech," Imp-Child grumbled.

The old man was startled. "You reject the sword? But you have to take it."

"No."

"Take the robe, then. Take up the robe and the authority it represents."

Haroun remained unconvinced that this man had waited four hundred years to crown a new emperor. He suspected motives unrelated to those proclaimed. He could not fathom what they might be, though.

Would it hurt to humor the fellow? That might lead him nearer the truth.

He slung the ratty ermine across his shoulders.

Imp-Child squealed delightedly. "It didn't turn to dust! He *is* the One."

The old man was less exuberant. "The Crown, then," he said. "The Invisible Crown that will fit none but the One. The Crown so heavy only a man determined to fulfill its obligations can lift it. Take it up, Haroun."

Haroun lingered over the third pillow, intimidated by the old man's statement. Finally, he reacted. His fingers touched something his eyes denied. He tried lifting it. It yielded only slightly, slipping sideways. Its weight was astonishing.

"You have reservations," the old man said. "The Crown can tell if you're not wholly committed to people and empire."

"No," Haroun said. "I don't trust you."

Which was true. But the old man was right, too. Haroun faced a tough decision. Was he prepared to pay the dreadful price demanded of a king in exile? He had been too busy staying alive to face that question.

"A king *must* be responsible," the old man said. "He *is* his people and kingdom. Kings are made to put the burden upon."

Not the best argument to sway a wavering youth, surely.

Haroun surrendered. Not to that old man's dream, but to his own. To a dream his father and Megelin Radetic had shaped.

He acknowledged himself King in Hammad al Nakir.

It meant guerrilla camps, grim deeds and murder done to little apparent purpose, but always with a hope that he would be moving toward peace, unity and restoration.

The vision both depressed and excited him.

He lifted the crown again. This time it rose as lightly as a wisp of cotton.

"It fits!" Imp-Child squealed, and danced a wild jig.

Haroun snugged the crown upon his head. It bore down so hard he staggered. It suddenly became as light as a silver circlet, then as tenuous as a forgotten obligation.

He had a feeling it would permit no forgetting. He had sold his freedom for a dream.

The old man said, "All men who have an interest in the affairs of Hammad al Nakir, be they friend or foe, now know that a King has been crowned for Ilkazar."

"The King Without a Throne," Imp-Child intoned. "The Lord in Shadow."

Haroun *felt* the knowledge of himself leak into a hundred minds. He felt the rage swell in El Murid and his captains, felt the elation blossom in Royalist commanders riding hard with despair running at their stirrups. Nowhere did he sense a rejection of his right.

The moment faded. The contact died.

"You refused Ashkerion," the old man said. "Beware, then. Turn your back on no man. Choose your successor wisely, and before you yourself depart this pale. Otherwise the Crown will go down with you, and be forgotten again. And I will be recalled from the darkness, to await another Candidate."

Haroun glanced at the old bronze sword. He reached—then drew back. As if sensing final rejection, the blade disappeared. Eyes wide, Haroun turned to the old man.

The alleged son of Ethrian the Wise had vanished too. Only dusty bones sat on the chalcedony throne.

Imp-Child considered him gravely. "Thank you. For the old man's freedom. For mine. Take your people away now. Your pursuers won't see you go."

There was a flash and a pop. When Haroun's senses cleared he found himself alone with bones and dust and three empty pillows.

A hint of dawn rosed the sills of the windows. For a moment he wondered if his visit hadn't been a hallucination.

But no. It had been real. He had healed. He wore a ragged ermine mantle, which he removed. And he felt driven to reclaim the usurped throne he'd never seen.

It was a need he would do anything to fulfill.

He went down dusty stairs and out a doorway which disappeared behind him. Looking north, he saw the dawn-tinted, snow-capped peaks of the Kapenrung Mountains. One day. Maybe two. He surveyed his companions. Bragi, the boys and all the animals were in a deep sleep beside a pool of water. They all looked healthier than when last he had seen them.

On a distant ridgeline a band of horsemen paused to study the land ahead, then stumbled forward along a trail which had no end.

"Wake up, Bragi. Time to get moving."

The old man stepped from behind the chalcedony throne. He carried a huge cornucopia. He stuffed its bell with pillows, bones and such. He muttered to himself while he worked.

"The stage is set. The struggle will last a generation."

He whipped around the throne, dragged a squawking Imp-Child from hiding. "Crafty little wretch. Thought I'd forget you, eh?" He booted the imp into the horn's bell. It tried to scramble out. He grunted as he strained to overcome it. "In, damn it! In!" The cherub squealed piteously and popped out of sight.

The old man leaned against the windowsill and watched the fugitives straggle away. He chuckled malevolently. "Now for Nassef," he said, and crooked a finger at the riders in the hills.

"What happened?" Bragi asked. "It seemed like I dreamed for days."

"I'm not sure," Haroun replied. He told what he could recall. "But I don't know if it was real. I already feel tired again."

They paused atop a ridgeline and looked back. There was no sign of a watchtower.

Haroun shrugged. "Real or not, we have to go on." He seemed to feel a heavy weight atop his head. He glared at the mountains before them, started forward, grimly determined.